FOUL

A DI Ambrose mystery

by P J Quinn

Stairwell Books //

Published by Stairwell Books
70 Barbara Drive
Norwalk
CT 06851 USA

ISBN: 978-0-9833482-0-7

Printed and bound in the USA by ECPrinting.com
Layout design Alan Gillott
Edited by Alan Gillott

Stairwell Books is based in Connecticut, USA and York, England.
For further details contact rose@stairwellbooks.com.

www.stairwellbooks.co.uk

About the authors

Pauline Kirk is the author of two novels*: Waters of Time,* Century Hutchinson 1988; Ulverscroft 1991, and *The Keepers*, Virago (Little, Brown), 1996 and 1997. Ten collections of her poetry have been published, including *Walking to Snailbeach: Selected and New poems*, and the most recent, *Dancing through wood and Time*, in which some of her poems are set to music by the York composer, Martin Scheuregger. She is a member of the Pennine Poets group, and editor of Fighting Cock Press. Her poems, short stories and articles have appeared in many anthologies and journals, and been broadcast on radio.

Jo Summers has written numerous articles for the legal press and national newspapers. She has just completed *Islamic Wills, Trusts and Estates: Planning for this World and the Next* with Mufti Talha Ahmad Azami and Shahzad Siddiqui (Euromoney Books) and is writing *The UK Tax Handbook for Offshore Trustees* (due to be published in September 2011). Future projects include a UK tax textbook for the University of Connecticut, USA.

With thanks to

Frances Pearce, Martyn Gowar, Nicky Pallis, Marian Smith and Corinne Souza for proofreading, comments and encouragement

To Paul and Pete for putting up with us

Act 1

'Foul Play'
A DI Ambrose mystery
Prologue

"**Operator.**"

[*Male voice, agitated*] "**We need the police.....or an ambulance**...[*muffled, speaking to someone else*] well, which do I ask for?.......[*louder again*] **yes, ambulance please**."

"**What number are you calling from, sir?**"

[*muffled again*] "She wants the phone number....how am I meant to know?"

[*Sound of telephone being taken forcibly*]

[*Lady's voice, slight Germanic accent but firm and clear*] "**Operator, ambulance please. There's an injured lady and a lot of blood. They had better come quickly - I do not know if she will live.**"

"**Your name?**"

"**Olga Greenbaum, of the Chalk Heath Players. We're at the Theatre. Phone number 2189. Can you please put me through to the ambulance service? They can inform the police. There's been an accident, except** [slight pause] **well, I'm not sure it was an accident.**"

CHAPTER ONE
20th November 1958 7.11pm

Ambrose shivered as he walked towards the Theatre. An eerie fog swirled around him. He caught its sooty taste in the back of his throat. He could no longer see his motorcar, still only feet away.

He ducked as he entered the Theatre. At six foot four he often had trouble getting into buildings. Still, his height and solid build gave him a huge advantage with suspects. He could be quite frightening without getting physical. He couldn't remember ever using force to get a confession. He wasn't sure his colleagues could all say the same.

As he stood looking round the foyer a memory surfaced. He was at the theatre with his grandparents, his tenth birthday treat. It was hard to believe he'd come back for a murder investigation.

"Over here, sir," a voice called.

Ambrose turned towards the red headed speaker. He nodded a greeting and felt his mood lift. Despite their differences, Ambrose knew DS Winters was a superb sergeant, with just the right mixture of curiosity and tact. He was also highly ambitious for his age. Winters wasn't quite 40 but looked a good deal younger.

"Evening," Ambrose replied, "I take it the public have gone home?"

The Theatre was in semi-darkness; just a few dim lights to guide them. Ambrose peered at the adverts on the foyer wall. He recognised the face of a well-known radio crooner. This is where you end up when you're no longer popular, he thought. The local brass band was another one to miss, he was sure. Then he spotted a poster for Gilbert & Sullivan's "The Pirates of Penzance". It was last year's production by the Chalk Heath Players. That was the name the woman had mentioned to the operator. So, this wasn't their first performance.

"Luckily for us, sir," Winters interrupted his thoughts, "they were just rehearsing tonight. Their next show doesn't start for another two weeks. Plus they were only doing one scene."

"So how many people do we have to interview?" Ambrose continued to look around him, seeing easily over Winters' head.

"Well sir," the younger man replied, "only the lead people were here at the time. About a dozen more turned up half an hour ago. They take all the other parts, the servants, butlers and so on. I guess the 'skivvies' need less practice than the rest! Anyway, we took their details and sent them home. We can see them later if you want but the good news is we only have twelve people to interview now."

"Has the body been removed yet?"

"Well, the lady's been taken to hospital but she's not dead," Winters replied. "So I'm not sure she counts as a 'body' yet."

"So why on earth was I called in?" Ambrose was surprised. Since his promotion to Detective Inspector, he only dealt with murder cases.

"Well, the doctors don't hold much hope the victim will survive. She took a nasty blow to the back of the head then broke her nose when she fell. Blood everywhere I'm afraid."

"I'm not squeamish, Sergeant," Ambrose replied. "We saw plenty of blood and death right here in Britain you know. We didn't all have to go to the front line."

Winters shuffled uncomfortably. He wanted to say that the War was a long time ago, but thought better of it.

Instantly Ambrose regretted his comment. He usually avoided any reference to his feelings or home life. He knew he shouldn't have argued with his son: it always put him in a bad mood.

"Have the next of kin been informed?" he asked briskly.

Winters shook his head. "I'm afraid we don't know who they are," he said. "Miss Monroe lived alone and had no family - not that the people here know about. Miss Greenbaum says there was a niece who came to shows two or three years back, but she hasn't been recently."

Ambrose frowned. "There must be someone," he insisted. "Employers"–

"We've found out where Miss Monroe works," Winters cut in quickly. He didn't want the DI thinking he'd missed an obvious lead. "She's something important in the courts. No one will be there now. I'll send a PC first thing in the morning. We'll check her papers at home too. If she's got a passport, next of kin should be shown."

3

Once again, Ambrose frowned, this time more in concern than criticism. It was awful to think of a woman being brutally attacked with no one close to worry about her.

"Rotten, isn't it?" Winters commented, as if knowing his boss's thoughts. "Perhaps there was a family quarrel, or she lost everyone in the bombing. We'll find out what we can, sir, as soon as people are up and about."

"What was used to bash her head in?" Ambrose queried.

"Ah well, there you have it sir," Winters shrugged. "We don't know yet. I have people doing a thorough search back stage to find anything with blood or hairs on it. We have lots of possibilities – the whole place is littered with metal scaffolding, props and the like but so far we haven't found the weapon."

"I don't suppose anyone was found standing over the victim covered in her blood?" Ambrose looked hopeful.

"'Fraid not, sir," Winters replied. "Since there's no clear suspect, I assumed you'd want to do the first round of interviews here, as usual. I spoke to everyone and *suggested* they might want to be questioned here rather than under caution at the station. They all agreed. Or if any of them did want to object, they kept quiet."

"Good news, indeed," Ambrose replied. He was glad he'd worked with Winters before so he didn't have to explain what he wanted. It made things so much easier. He wondered whether he ought to call Mary to tell her he'd be back later. Then he thought again. Even interviewing a dozen people properly would take hours. Besides, Mary was used to being a policeman's wife. He wouldn't need to tell her not to wait up.

"Still at least we know one thing already," Ambrose turned.

"What's that sir?"

"We can presume this time the butler didn't do it."

Winters groaned.

CHAPTER TWO

Ambrose and Winters walked together into the darkened auditorium, with just the floor lights and the glow of the emergency exit signs to guide them. The curtain was raised on the stage but the only glow came from two small lights near a baby-grand piano at the front.

"When I arrived the stage was lit," Winters explained, "but the technical chap said they can't afford to keep the lights on. Apparently they have to pay for the electricity used during rehearsals. Seems a bit mean given they're already paying to hire the stage. The total cost is £5 per rehearsal, which he says they have to meet from their own funds."

"Who's the 'technical-chap'?" Ambrose asked.

"A guy called Douglas Moody. Aptly named if you ask me. Let's put it this way, he isn't the most cheerful of souls. Oh and he looks a lot like a larger version of your son, sir."

Ambrose turned in surprise, unwelcome images flooding into his head. "You don't mean he's a 'teddy boy' do you?"

Winters grinned. "I'm afraid so, sir. He's got the lot: knee-length jacket, black drainpipe trousers, bootlace tie and ridiculously bright yellow socks. Oh and you should see his hair!"

"I can't wait," Ambrose grimaced. He knew most of his friends were having problems with their adolescent boys but he dearly hoped his son would grow out of it soon. It seemed only last year that Joseph was still in shorts and enjoying Scout camps. What he would give, Ambrose mused, to go back to those times. Now it was non-stop rock and roll and weekly trips to the Odeon to see James Dean or Marlon Brando.

Ambrose was certain he'd never rebelled as a teenager. Come to think of it, Ambrose didn't think he'd ever rebelled at all. Unless you included that time in 1944 but that was different. At least then he'd been a rebel with a cause.

"You'd better watch out, you've got this ahead of you," Ambrose warned.

"I hope not sir," Winters said earnestly. "I've sent my eldest to the RC school and the other three will follow him when they're older."

5

'You think sending your children to a religious school will protect them from temptation?" Ambrose enquired. "Well I hope it works, for your sake. Believe me, it's no fun watching your child turn into someone you don't particularly like. For me, interviewing Mr Moody could be too much like sitting at home arguing with my son." Ambrose laughed suddenly.

"Well you'd better prepare yourself," Winters smiled. "Mr Moody's got the whole outfit. I forgot to tell you about the large amount of keys jangling in his pockets and the silly shoes."

"Brothel creepers," Ambrose couldn't help himself; the words just slipped out.

"Sorry sir?" Winters looked slightly shocked.

"I am reliably informed, by my son, that the shoes are known as 'brothel creepers' or 'sneakers'," Ambrose explained, "on account of their quiet soles. I just hope to God my son doesn't actually know what a brothel is," he added.

"Shouldn't think he does, sir. There's only one knocking shop that I know of in Chalk Heath and we have that staked out most nights," Winters was matter of fact. "But if we do spot your son anywhere near the place, I'll personally make sure you're the first to know."

Ambrose glared. He could never quite tell whether Winters was pulling his leg. "So what's Moody's role here?" he changed the subject.

"Mr Moody is in charge of the props, the lighting, the microphones and anything else non-theatrical if you see what I mean. As he's the only one, it seems, who can change a light bulb he pretty much rules the roost back stage. I thought we might wish to speak to him first."

Ambrose turned back to look at the stage. He was surprised to see the orchestra would be sitting directly in front of the stage and on the same level as the audience. He was sure he remembered the musicians being sunk down. After all, wasn't that why they called it an 'orchestra pit'? It looked more like someone had removed the first few rows of seats and put the orchestra there instead. The only divider was a small black screen about waist high. Perhaps the orchestra needed to see the stage for this production, he mused.

"People sitting near the front won't have a good view of the stage," Ambrose commented. "They'd have to look over the heads of the orchestra players, and anyone sitting behind the pianist would have a crick in their neck after five minutes."

"Well it could be worse, sir," Winters replied cheekily. "Imagine how it would be if everyone in the band were your height. There'd be no point selling tickets for the first five rows."

Ignoring the jibe, Ambrose drew closer to the stage. As he did so, he realised the black screen was actually a curtain. Presumably the band members could get to and from their seats through the curtain. They certainly wouldn't be able to do that, however, without being seen. Once in place, they'd have to stay put until the interval or the end of the show.

"Can you show me back stage, please, to where the lady was found? What did you say her name was?"

"You'll love this, sir, she's called Marguerite Monroe."

"What was she, some faded starlet who used to be in music hall?" Seeing Winters shrug, Ambrose added, "never mind, I suppose we'll have to ask the others. Where are they, by the way?"

"I put them in the men's dressing room. There are just two dressing rooms, which I understand is way below average judging by the grumblings on that score. They were using one of for the women and the other for the men."

"Don't the stars have their own dressing room?" Ambrose asked in surprise.

"Not these days they don't, sir. The theatre was damaged heavily in the Blitz. One side was completely destroyed and it's just been patched up. The owners can't afford to rebuild it, so nowadays the cast have to make do with what's left. Everything else has gone," Winters gestured vaguely to the right hand side of the theatre.

He continued. "The two stars of the show get a little screened off section in the corner of each room. That was Miss Monroe (she was definitely a Miss apparently) and Archie Framilode who plays the lead male. They do have good names these people, don't they?" Winters looked up at Ambrose and smiled. "Mr Framilode is also the director and I think he snaffles the best parts just to make sure he has his own dressing area. I heard some of the others casting doubt on his acting ability. It seems an attempted murder isn't enough to stop petty jealousies rearing their ugly heads."

"Perhaps these petty jealousies are the cause of us being here," Ambrose sighed. It looked like they had a long night ahead of them.

CHAPTER THREE

Ambrose was staring at the stage. He could just make out what appeared to be trees, painted on a wooden screen. "Do we know what show they're rehearsing for?" he asked.

"Yes, I asked Mr Moody. He told me it's called *Wedding Belle*. They've adapted *High Society,* only they've had to change the name for legal reasons. Do you remember that film? It came out a couple of years back – the one with Grace Kelly and Bing Crosby. Did you see it?" Winters glanced at Ambrose, who looked blank.

"I went with the wife," Winters continued. "She loved it. Kept humming the songs for weeks afterwards. Anyway, it's about this rich heiress who's about to get married, but then her ex-husband turns up and she falls for him again. Of course, that's the abridged version. Apparently the stage show lasts over two and a half hours, with interval. Miss Monroe was playing the rich heiress and Mr Framilode was her former husband."

"That's exactly the same plot as *The Philadelphia Story,*" Ambrose replied. "I didn't know they'd made another version." His eyes glazed as he remembered. "I saw *The Philadelphia Story* three times when it first came out. It was 1940 I think. I used to have a bit of a thing for Katharine Hepburn. Still, I'll admit Grace Kelly is rather good looking too."

Snapping himself to the present, he turned to Winters. "Can we go back stage?"

"This way, sir."

They moved to the left of the auditorium, towards a door with a green Emergency Exit sign. "This leads back into the foyer, sir. When there's a performance, people with seats at the front can enter here and it's the quickest route to the bar in the interval," Winters explained. "There's a fire exit on the other side too, otherwise the theatre would be a death trap! I checked though and they're both firmly locked."

They passed the door and carried on to the front of the auditorium, so that the orchestra 'pit' was on their right.

"I spoke to the pianist, a Mr hang-on-a-minute-I'll-check-my-notes sir," Winters was flipping through his note book. He drew breath then carried on. "Mr Michael Black is the pianist and he was here in the orchestra pit the whole time, so he says. He volunteered that information when I took his name. He was with his mother, believe it or not. Mrs Brenda Black was roped in for the last few rehearsals, to help turn the pages on his music and to remind people who've forgotten their lines."

"The prompt," Ambrose interjected.

"The what, sir?"

"She was acting as the prompt, the person who sits on the sidelines with a script and whispers the next line if the actor has forgotten it."

"Oh, right, thanks, sir. I forgot you're keen on the theatre and books and so on. Yes Mrs Brenda Black was acting as the prompt. It's a real family occasion, sir, as there's a Kathy Black too. I haven't yet managed to find out what relationship she is to the others. I thought you'd take a dim view of me starting the interviews without you."

Ambrose nodded curtly.

Winters led the way up a flight of steps to the left of the stage. "This door leads to the back stage area," he explained.

They passed through small double doors that could barely be seen when they were closed. Ambrose noted that they opened outwards, presumably to allow the actors easy exit if they needed to get into the auditorium. He remembered seeing a musical with his grandparents where the singers came amongst the audience. He presumed most theatres would have similar access. Come to think of it, he couldn't immediately see a handle on the outside. Maybe they didn't want the audience getting back stage without permission. A rather handsome fair-haired PC was holding the doors open from the other side. Ambrose recognised young PC Sutton and smiled at him.

As they went through the doors, Ambrose was immediately surprised. He'd entered a brightly lit corridor. For some reason, he'd thought the subdued lighting in the auditorium would continue here too. He'd always imagined behind the scenes to be a hive of whispered, shadowy activity. It looked more like a factory with overhead fluorescent strip lighting. It dawned on him that the backstage crew would need to see exactly what they were doing; otherwise mistakes could be made.

"Damn!" he exclaimed.

10

"Sir?"

"I'd hoped there would be loads of shadows. You know, places where our would-be-assassin could hide, waiting for his victim. It looks like she'd have been able to see him coming a mile away with whatever weapon he'd got in his hand. Or hers," he added as an afterthought. "After all, women commit murder too, sadly."

Winters raised an eyebrow. "I doubt a woman would have had enough strength to cave Miss Monroe's head in," he pointed out. "Not unless your female assassin was built like a Russian shot-putter," he grinned.

"Well, we'll have to look out for muscular women amongst the cast," Ambrose replied evenly. "Besides, it's best to keep an open mind until we find the weapon. Can you show me where Miss Monroe was found?"

They moved down the corridor, further back stage. Ambrose noted a door on his left marked 'Green Room'. Further ahead, on the same side, he could see two doors marked "Storage". He didn't need to ask.

"The Green Room is where the actors sit to be close to the stage before they come on. I've no idea why they call it that, though, as it certainly isn't green. I asked about the storage rooms too. The first one is used for bar supplies and the second for props," Winters explained. "We're going through them both but haven't found anything with blood on it so far."

"Is the theatre successful, do you know?" Ambrose asked suddenly.

"I doubt it sir. I don't suppose the Chalk Heath Players smash box office records. However, I checked and the theatre has a good safety record. They had their annual fire inspection recently and there's no record of any accidents. At least not until now and this one looks deliberate."

Finding a door marked "Stage" on his right Ambrose opened it. He could see nothing but a heavy grey curtain, a few feet in front of him and stretching away from him in both directions. Curious, he entered and discovered a gap in the curtain just to his right. He peered through. He was faced, about two feet away, by another curtain made of darker material. Glancing left he saw a gap in that curtain and walked towards it.

11

Ambrose popped his head through and found himself near the back of the stage, looking out at the darkened auditorium. He guessed this double curtain system was to stop the light shining onto the stage from the corridor. He'd always wanted to stand on stage but it seemed small and oddly disappointing. He returned the way he had come in. The door made no sound as he shut it, he noted.

They continued down the corridor for about six feet then turned right. They were facing a narrow corridor, which Winters explained ran along the back of the stage. To their left was a series of screens. As he touched one, it felt light and flimsy in Ambrose's large hand. This one was painted like the inside of a house. The one behind looked like a garden scene. Glancing up he saw similar screens hanging above the stage. He wondered if Mr Moody was also in charge of lowering the screens. He also wondered if anyone had checked them for signs of blood.

Winters seemed to read his mind. "We've checked the screens, sir," he said. "No sign of blood I'm afraid, although most of them smell strongly of paint and turps." He wrinkled his nose slightly as he spoke, forcing his freckles closer together.

Winters and Ambrose carried on walking. At the end of the corridor they stopped. They were faced with a larger corridor, stretching from their left to right. They were standing at a T-junction.

"Left heads down towards the dressing rooms," Winters explained. "We need to turn right towards the stage."

Ambrose saw that the wall opposite was made of large grey breezeblocks. It looked like all the bricks this side had been replaced. So this was where the theatre was bombed, he thought. There were no storage rooms this side and no Green Room. The breezeblocks seemed to stretch for miles in both directions. Ambrose shuddered at the relentless grey. It reminded him of something he'd worked hard to forget.

"This wall is pretty oppressive, don't you think?" he mused out loud.

Winters shrugged. "I guess no one spends long standing here, sir. And at least it keeps the roof up. If you'll just follow me."

Before they could move, however, a rather portly man rushed down the corridor towards them.

"You'll want to speak to me first," he announced, breathless.

"And why might that be?" Winters asked calmly.

"Because I'm the Director and lead, of course. And because I *am* the Chalk Heath Players. If there's anything you need to know about the company, I'll be happy to oblige."

"That's very kind, Mr Framilode," Winters replied.

"Archie, my dear boy. Everyone here calls me Archie."

"There will be a great deal we'll want to know, I'm sure," Winters agreed, very politely. "But not yet, we have quite a bit to deal with first." He fixed Archie Framilode with a firm stare.

"Oh -" Archie said, looking quite hurt. "Of course, if you wish..."

He lingered, clearly unused to being dismissed. "Well, then ... But if I can be of help, don't hesitate to call me. There are bound to be things here you find puzzling. The theatre is a very special world you know."

"Indeed," Winters said coolly. "Thank you again for your kind offer." He glanced at the WPC who had belatedly caught up with Archie. "Please escort our good director back to the dressing room. We'll let him know when we need to speak with him." He didn't need to add 'and this time keep him there', his voice said it all.

"Nicely done," Ambrose said watching while WPC Meadows escorted Archie down the corridor. "That one will need keeping in his place, or he'll run us as well as the play. Now, perhaps you can show me where the attack took place?"

"Certainly, sir, this way."

CHAPTER FOUR

Ambrose turned right after Winters. They were walking along the corridor next to the stage. This corridor was more dimly lit. It was hard to see to the end. "Is there an exit to the auditorium this side?" Ambrose asked.

"Not since the bombing, sir. They had to shore up the building. At least it means our culprit couldn't have escaped this way." Winters replied. "It doesn't look like he went past the stage either, or he'd have been seen by the pianist and his mother. He could have gone out the back though. I'll show you that when we go to the dressing rooms."

Ambrose surveyed the corridor. He couldn't see any sign of blood. On a hunch, he looked to his right. He found, as he'd expected, a door marked "Stage" and opened it (again silent he noted). He was faced by another grey curtain and after a quick glance he confirmed the existence of the darker curtain behind it. He spotted the gap in the second curtain to his left. This was much closer to the front of the stage than on the other side. Perhaps they could choose where to have the gap, he mused, depending on where they needed access to the stage. He turned to go back into the corridor, slightly perplexed.

Winters gestured for him to stay where he was. "Actually, sir, as they say in the panto, it's behind you!" he smiled.

Curious, Ambrose moved back towards the grey curtain. This time instead of turning left to the stage, he glanced right. Then he understood.

"We're here, sir."

"Funnily enough" Ambrose replied, "I'd worked that out for myself."

Even in the dim lighting, Ambrose could see clearly. He was looking down at the unmistakable stain of blood on wooden floorboards. It was indeed a very large stain. Miss Monroe would be lucky to survive a wound like that, he thought, although he recalled Winters saying most of the blood was from her nose. Still, he'd seen people survive worse and die from lesser injuries so you never could tell. He wondered if Miss Monroe was a fighter.

"One of the other actors found her first, but apparently a number of the cast heard a strange noise, possibly when she fell to the floor. No reports of blood curdling screams though," Winters noted.

Ambrose appeared not to have heard. He was standing, staring at the blood on the floor, his hands clasped behind his back. "Was Miss Monroe on her way onto or off the stage when she was attacked?" he queried.

"Funny you should say that, sir, but Mr Framilode asked me the same question. According to him, she shouldn't have been this side at all. He didn't go into detail, but said something about her ignoring the stage directions. Apparently that was most uncharacteristic."

Ambrose felt a sense of satisfaction. The dim lighting between the curtains certainly gave more scope for someone to sneak up on the victim. They might even have been able to hide safely in the curtains until she arrived.

"Well," Ambrose said finally, "I guess we'd better start interviewing the cast and crew. Should we start with Mr Moody, the 'king of back stage'?"

"Certainly. This way, sir," Winters replied as they returned to the corridor through the stage door.

They passed, to their left, the screens Ambrose had examined earlier. Just beyond, they saw a red brick wall, clearly original, running parallel to the new grey breezeblocks on their right. Half way along the bricks was an old doorway, now filled in with yet more grey.

Ambrose paused in front of the ancient exit. "Where did this lead to?" he asked.

"This used to be the access to the orchestra pit and under stage area," Winters replied. "The theatre took a hit from a doodlebug. Not the full blast luckily: that caught the shops next door where there's still a big hole. You'll see it in the morning, sir. It's not safe to go below the stage now, so it's been filled with rubble and bricked off. I've checked: there's absolutely no way anyone can get in or out."

"Well that explains why the orchestra are in front of the stage," Ambrose noted, "and why this side of the theatre is so make-shift." He tried to ignore the monumental greyness of the wall as they carried on down the corridor. At the end they saw, to their right, a set of large doors.

"This is the loading bay, sir, although they call it the 'scene dock' for some reason," Winters explained. "They probably use silly words just to confuse the rest of us. Anyway, Mr Moody says occasionally touring productions come here and this is where their kit is brought in. They weren't using these doors tonight so I'm pretty sure no one could have got through here. There's no handle outside, so they definitely couldn't have let themselves in – deliveries report to the receptionist and she opens up for them. She's the only one besides the stage manager with a key."

"Neither the receptionist nor the stage manager were here tonight?"

"No. I called on the stage manager earlier. He was safely at home with his wife watching their new telly. He said he had his key with him all evening. A couple of neighbours swore he'd never left the house, too. They're a nosy lot round there," Winters smiled. "The receptionist was at home as well. PC Sutton checked on her. She was playing whist all evening, with her husband and his mother."

"Are you certain these are actually locked?" Ambrose asked, stretching a hand to the lever.

Winters stepped forwards quickly. "Oh yes, sir. I borrowed the stage manager's key earlier, and got shouted at by half the neighbourhood. It's almost impossible to shut the doors once they're opened. You have to go round and give them a good kick, and even then it's a case of banging them half a dozen times before they fit back." Winters grimaced. "There's no way anyone in the theatre could have gone out through here, without everyone in the vicinity knowing."

They turned so the locked doors were behind them. Ambrose was surprised to be faced with yet another corridor. This one must run parallel to the stage, he thought. On the right he noticed two rooms. "The first one was used as a dressing room by the men, sir, and the second was for the women," Winters explained.

Walking quickly past them, Ambrose came to the end of the corridor. To his right was another door. "This is the cast's exit to the outside toilet and the streets, sir. It's the only way our chap could have escaped, if he was able to get past everyone else without being seen - unless of course he's still here. This is kept open whenever there's anyone in the theatre. After all, the cast have to be allowed to go to the lavatory! And you'll be pleased to hear this door opens and closes easily without having to wake the neighbours," Winters noted.

"In front of you, sir, is the technician's room, which is Mr Moody's domain," he continued. "It's right next to the second store room we saw earlier. If you turn left, you go back into the corridor that comes from the auditorium, past the Green Room. It's all pretty symmetrical really but I've asked a WPC to draw us a plan in case it helps. I'm not quite sure where everyone was at the time Miss Monroe was clobbered, but that's clearly one line of questioning, sir. Just out the back you'll find (if our chaps haven't taken them away yet) some cigarette butts. If those are from this evening, it looks like at least one person, possibly two, was having a smoke outside."

"What makes you say that?" Ambrose queried.

"Well, sir, some of the butts have red lipstick on and some don't. I figured we're talking more than one person, one being a woman."

"One wearing red lipstick," Ambrose corrected, "but even the men will be wearing stage make up for the actual production. We'll have to check whether this was the dress rehearsal."

Ambrose stopped, then turned suddenly to Winters. "And why on earth would they have been smoking outside?"

Winters grinned. "Apparently they're not allowed to inside. Seems the theatre's worried about it being a fire hazard. I'm told the rule's very strictly enforced."

Ambrose shrugged in surprise. They turned back towards the dressing rooms.

"The first dressing room is slightly larger so that's where everyone is waiting, for now," Winters added. "I thought you'd want to do the interviews in the smaller room."

"Splendid," Ambrose replied.

They walked into the ladies' dressing room, to the screened off section that Miss Monroe had been using. "We've been through every inch of it, sir, and made an inventory of everything," Winters said. "It's all been fingerprinted and photographed so if you're happy to use this room for the interviews, I'll bring Mr Moody in."

Ambrose blew fingerprint dust off a chair and sat down. Just one glance around showed him that the chance of any meaningful fingerprints here was low. It didn't seem to have been cleaned for a very long time. Every surface was covered with smudges. Besides, any of the cast could have had a reason to come in here, so their fingerprints even in this part of the room wouldn't mean anything definite. On the other hand, holding interviews where the injured lady had been dressing might have a psychological effect.

DS Winters had arranged the chairs already, Ambrose noted. He would face each person they interviewed and Winters would be behind the suspect. He knew from previous experience that this was Winters' favourite technique. Ambrose got the eye contact and Winters was very good at asking unnerving questions from the rear. Ambrose had seen suspects having to twist round in their chairs so often they must have felt sick.

Ambrose wished they had a stenographer to take notes of the interviews, but it was far too late to call one now. He knew Winters could write extremely quickly but sometimes it wasn't entirely legible. Still, hopefully they'd only need to do formal interviews at the station tomorrow, under caution, when they'd heard what everyone had to say for themselves.

Ambrose smiled to himself. He was hoping that the guilty party might just confess straight away. He knew he was being optimistic, but he certainly wasn't expecting problems with this amateur dramatics group. It wasn't as if they were seasoned criminals, he thought.

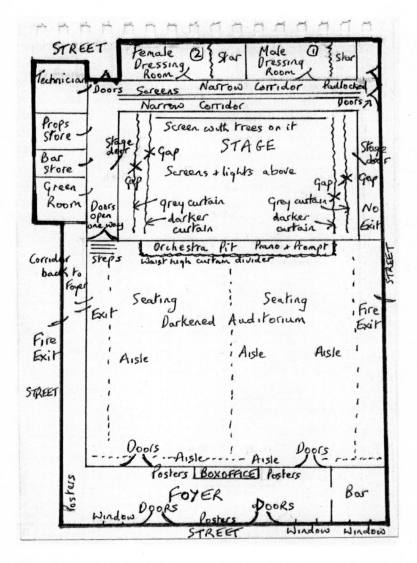

WPC Meadows's hand-drawn map of the theatre and back stage area.

CHAPTER FIVE

Douglas Moody was shown in and ushered to the seat in front of Ambrose. There was an unmistakable metallic clinking sound as Douglas swept his long jacket behind him and sat down. He flicked something off his trousers and smoothed his lapels.

Winters quickly recorded in his notebook that Mr Moody was about 5'9", slightly built, unhealthily pale with brown eyes. His long black hair was greased and swept back, leaving a large quiff at the front. Even that seemed solid; it didn't move an inch as Moody sat down.

"This is just an informal interview, Mr Moody," Ambrose explained. "Just for our records, can you please confirm your date of birth and occupation?"

"I don't see how my age has anything to do with it," Douglas replied. He looked at Ambrose then decided to comply. "28th August 1933. I'm an electrician."

"And for the record, where do you live?" Winters chipped in.

"With my mother." Douglas paused as if expecting comment. When none came he added, "59 Chapel Place."

"Mr Moody, can you please tell us your position in the Chalk Heath Players?" Winters continued from behind.

Douglas addressed himself to Ambrose. "I don't have a position. I just do the technical stuff." He shrugged slightly.

"And that includes?" Ambrose prompted.

"Anything that needs a bit of practical ability. This lot can't wire a plug without a manual."

"And where were you at the time of the attack on Miss Monroe?" Winters continued.

"In the Technician's room. Can't see as I can be of much use to you." Douglas twisted round to look at Winters.

"You may have seen or heard something unusual," Ambrose suggested.

"Nah. I don't see or hear anything in there. It's like a ruddy cupboard." Douglas turned back to look at Ambrose.

"Surely you can see the stage?" Ambrose was surprised.

"No I can't," Douglas replied, sulkily. "I was fixing a broken spot light. My services weren't required on the stage apparently."

"Weren't you needed to do the stage lighting?" Winters persisted.

"I was doing the lighting for the first half hour or so," Douglas explained to Ambrose. "But then they decided they didn't need me, so I went to fix the light."

"And did you see anything unusual happening on stage tonight when you were there?" Winters carried on.

"No. Just the usual messing about trying to get cues right."

Ambrose changed tack. "Were you required on stage yourself at all?" he asked.

"No. There weren't going to be any scene changes - just the one set. I was doing the lighting at first, but then Archie decided he didn't need it. Guess it was too tricky for them all to stand in the right place," Douglas sneered, patting his quiff as he spoke. He started getting a pack of cigarettes out of his pocket. A glare from Ambrose made him put them away immediately.

"You're not allowed to smoke in here," Winters pointed out. He continued, "So you were free tonight, then, after you left the stage?"

"Free to work ruddy hard," Douglas retorted. "I had to get the lighting sorted. I found the reason that light didn't work: electrical fault. Whoever used the stage last time didn't know what they were doing, that's for certain. They'd used the wrong fuse and burnt out half the cables. It took me ages to fix. I had to rewire the whole thing." He finished with an exaggerated sigh, as if he took the broken light as a personal insult.

"And you didn't leave your room at all?" Winters asked.

Douglas suddenly stood, jangling as he did so. "Nope," he replied. "And Heather can back me up on that." He clearly thought the interview was over.

"Who is Heather?" Ambrose motioned Douglas to sit down again.

"Heather Broomhead," Douglas answered, reseating himself with a glare and another jangle. "She was in here by the door, working on the costumes. She'd have seen if I'd gone in and out."

"We will check, of course," Ambrose glanced at Winters to see if he'd made a note.

"Can you explain your relationship to the rest of the company, please?" Winters took over the questioning. "Are you employed by them?"

"I ain't doing it for free," Douglas pointedly ignored Winters and addressed his reply to Ambrose. "That old fart Framilode doesn't pay much, but it's better than working at the Ironmongers on Saturdays."

"I'd like you to give a bit more detail about your duties," Winters continued. "What do you have to do for this show in particular? I believe it's called '*Wedding Belle*'."

"I've already told you," Douglas turned to glare at him.

"Answer the question, Mr Moody," Ambrose intervened.

"Huh," Douglas lent backwards. As he spoke, he stretched out his legs so his feet were almost under Ambrose's chair.

"Well I see to the lighting rig, work out what spots to use and the angles. That doesn't happen of its own accord, even if the precious actors think it does. Then there are the sound effects. You've got to make sure they come in at the right time. There's the sets to change too, and the props to put on stage. In a proper company you'd have different people doing that, but this lot can't afford it." Douglas pulled his legs in and rocked his chair back.

"And the screens at the back? Are they your responsibility too?" Ambrose queried.

"Who else do you think sees to them? Not hopeless Archie, for sure," Douglas retorted.

"What about the stage?" Winters asked the back of Douglas' head. "Do you have to make it move at all?"

Douglas didn't turn. It was as if he hadn't heard the question. Then he shrugged his shoulders and answered. "No. A bit of it at the front used to - for pantomimes and things, but it's not working properly. This is a pretty cheap theatre. There's not much fancy stuff here, most of it's broken. It's not needed anyway for this ruddy show."

"One last question, Mr Moody," Winters continued. "Have you any idea why someone might attack Miss Monroe?"

There was an even longer pause this time before the answer. "None at all. I don't know what goes on in productions – I just do the lighting and sets."

"Did she have any enemies?" Ambrose persisted.

"Like I said," Douglas replied, spitting on a handkerchief and using it to wipe one shoe. "I don't know anything about the cast. She seemed a decent sort to me. Bit past it of course - couldn't get the high notes any more. But she knew about acting, and how the theatre works. Not like some of the new ones."

"Thank you, Mr Moody. That will be all, but please remain in the other room," Ambrose terminated the interview. "We may need to speak to you again tonight."

Douglas stared at Ambrose, sighed loudly before marching towards the door, jangling.

Winters waited for Douglas Moody to leave the room, then turned to Ambrose. "As I said, sir, he's hardly the most cheerful of chaps is he? And that hair is something else isn't it? I know it's not fashionable, but give me a short back and sides any day!"

Ambrose grimaced. "If my son turns out like that, I'll disown him. It's a shame he can't take your lead. Joining the army would do him a power of good."

Winters smiled. "I think you need to give your kid some credit, sir" he replied. "I'd like to think he doesn't swear quite so often as Mr Moody and I bet he doesn't pong as much."

"True," Ambrose conceded. "My wife wouldn't let him in the house if he did!"

"I'll wager that our Mr Moody isn't a total lay about, though," Winters suggested.

"What makes you say that?" Ambrose was surprised.

"Well, I fancy the man can be quite handy with his fists when he wants to be. Did you spot his muscles under that ridiculous jacket? And I wouldn't mind an excuse to check his pockets. That might not have been just a bunch of keys we heard but these teddy boys often carry knuckle-dusters you know."

"Is that a fact?" Ambrose raised an eyebrow. He couldn't believe his son would carry a weapon every time he went out.

"Do you buy the 'I know nothing' routine, sir?" Winters queried.

"Far too early to tell," Ambrose replied. "We'll obviously have to speak to Heather Broomhead to see if she can confirm his story. I fancy leaving her a little while though. If there are any discrepancies, I find they have more time to appear if you leave people waiting. We'll also have an opportunity to observe Mr Moody while we do the other interviews."

"Should I put Mrs Broomhead last then sir?"

"Yes, good idea. We'll be able to see if anyone else saw Douglas Moody or Heather Broomhead that way."

"Right, sir, anything else?" Winters looked up from his notebook.

"Yes, do you have any spare eau de cologne for Mr Moody?"

Laughing, Winters went to fetch Archie Framilode. As director, it was true he should be able to shed more light on the rehearsal than anyone else.

CHAPTER SIX

Even if they hadn't already met, Winters would have been able to guess which of the men was Archie Framilode just by sight. He matched every stereotype Winters could think of for a local solicitor. Archie was plump, but trying to deny it. His trousers were just a little too tight, forcing his belly over the top of the belt. The shirt looked like the buttons might spontaneously pop off if he breathed in too deeply. His suit jacket would never meet at the middle. His hair was receding and his glasses were quite fashionable but with extremely thick glass. They gave him the air of a myopic mole. Yet Archie was quite clearly used to being obeyed.

Despite Mr Framilode's pompous air, however, Winters felt that deep down the solicitor was a decent guy. Winters was polite as he led him to the interview area. Ambrose ushered him to the 'hot seat'.

"Am I under caution?" Archie asked, his voice quivering slightly.

"Not at all," Ambrose assured him. "This is just an informal interview, so we can eliminate you from our enquiries."

"I bet that's what you always say," Archie sighed as he sat down.

Winters had already established that Archie was born on 14 May 1901.

"I'm afraid I live alone since my dear wife died last year," Archie explained. "My address is 'The Hedges', Avenue Lane, Chalk Heath. That's the North side, near the Parish Church."

Winters smiled into his notebook as he jotted the details down. Archie might just as well have said 'I live in the smart end of town you know'. There was no way Winters would ever be able to afford to buy a house near the Parish Church, no matter how much his wife might nag him to move up in the world. He still couldn't quite believe he'd been able to purchase a house at all. He was certainly the only one in the Winters clan who could afford it, as he was constantly reminded by his envious siblings.

"Mr Framilode, can you please tell us your role in the Chalk Heath Players?" Ambrose smiled encouragingly.

"Certainly. I'm the director and the lead male. Last year I played the Sergeant Major in *Pirates* and the year before I was Nanki-Poo in

The Mikado. That's only right and fitting, you know, since I set up the Players in the first place. Well, Marguerite and I set it up and we run it together but I'm the only one to put money in. I pay for the rehearsals, printing the programmes etc. That's why it's only fair that I own everything - the sets, props and so on. Marguerite adds the theatrical knowledge, that's her side of the bargain."

"Why is that?" Winters asked.

"I earn a lot more than she does," Archie replied. "My practice is pretty lucrative and although I've just taken on Alex, I'm still doing well. Have you met Alex Baker-Smythe yet?" Archie turned to Ambrose, who shook his head.

"Alex is my new recruit. He joined my firm about five months ago. I've high hopes for him, I can tell you. Alex reminds me of me, at his age. He's very good looking and a bit of a ladies' man. I'm coming to the point when I want to take things a bit easier and Alex is such a hard worker. He used to be in the City, at one of the very biggest firms, you know," Archie added proudly.

"Indeed," Ambrose replied and sighed inwardly. This was going to be a long interview.

Smiling expansively, Archie settled back into his chair. "He was quite a catch for me," he confided. "I've no doubt it's a huge drop in salary for him. I'm just lucky he's made the decision that he doesn't want to work in the city anymore, for the sake of his health. His doctor told him to move here you know. I've even been thinking of passing my firm over to him, not immediately but perhaps in a few years. Alex is a great lawyer and I'm sure he'll also be a key Player in next to no time. When I found out he was interested in the theatre, I knew he was the right man to hire! Did I tell you he even helped write the play, from the film?"

Ambrose wanted to move things along. "Thank you for that background," he said. "Tell me about Marguerite. Did you notice anything different about her tonight?"

"She was a bit on edge this evening," Archie admitted. "She really had a go at Heather – she's our costume lady, have you met her yet? I don't know what it was all about but Heather had done something wrong and Marguerite was furious. We all heard her shouting but I think it was just nerves. Marguerite always gets nervous before a

26

show, although come to think about it she normally only gets nervous a few days before the opening night.

"Perhaps it's because *Wedding Belle* is more ambitious than some of our previous shows, particularly with *High Society* - the film it's based on - being so recent. Of course, adapting something is a lot of work, and we did it all ourselves. Besides, Marguerite always feels more comfortable with Gilbert & Sullivan. I had a real battle to persuade her to agree to something more original this year. She wanted to do *HMS Pinafore* but we did that one five years ago, so I thought it would be better trying something different. I hoped if we offered something modern and popular, we might get a better audience. I still think that was the right decision to make. Don't you agree?"

"Quite right, I'm sure," Ambrose replied. "Can you tell me about the scene you were rehearsing this evening?"

"It's one of the more difficult scenes," Archie replied. "That's why we were having a separate rehearsal. Actually it was Marguerite herself who suggested it. But she was quite correct. We did need to spend time on this bit. I wanted everyone to get their entries & exits just right, before we added the rest of the Players, the ones with the supporting roles. Gosh, that reminds me, they were meant to turn up about an hour ago and they don't know what's happened."

"That's all right sir," Winters commented. "I met them all and explained they weren't needed for tonight. I think they all went home."

"They'll have gone to the Queen's Arms more likely," Archie humphed.

"Quite," Ambrose replied. "Was this evening a dress rehearsal?"

"No, it wasn't the Dress. We were just rehearsing one scene. It's the scene after the party. Do you need me to give you the libretto? I think I told you that Alex helped me write it?"

"The what?" Winters looked up from his notes.

"Sorry, theatre jargon," Archie apologised. "I use it all the time. Do let me know if you need me to explain anything. The libretto is the script for the play. Do you know anything about *Wedding Belle*? It's just like *High Society* but we've changed all the names. There's a big party to celebrate the forthcoming marriage between Teresa Laud (that's Marguerite's role) and her fiancé Geoffrey. He's played by Frank Thomas. Would you like a list of who plays which role?"

"That would be most helpful, thank you," Ambrose nodded.

"I'll get that to you. I did it last week for the programme. Anyway, Frank is only on the stage for a few minutes at the beginning. He has a blazing row with Marguerite's character, because she's drunk, and he storms off. He's not needed for the rest of the scene."

"Where does he go when he's left the stage?" Winters enquired.

"Well, the Green Room might have been a bit crowded, so he may have gone to the dressing room," Archie turned and explained. "I was front of house so I could see the stage but most of the actors would have been in the Green Room. Frank would only have been in the way. You'd have to ask him where he went."

"Then what happens?" Ambrose continued the questioning.

Archie turned back. "Mark, the journalist, has come on stage. He's played by Alex. Well the scene goes like this. After Geoffrey (Frank) has stormed out, Mark sings to Teresa (Marguerite). He's drunk too of course but it's still a great song and Alex does it so well. Michael, our Musical Director, arranged all the songs. Anyway, then Mark kisses Teresa. I bet at that moment, all the women wish they had Marguerite's role. Teresa has to run off with Mark running after her. But neither of them goes far."

"Why is that?" Winters asked.

"Well, Mark has to come straight back on, as if he's still running after Teresa. Marguerite isn't seen again but has to stay close enough to the stage to be heard when she does her next line. She has to call to Mark to come and find her. Basically they're running around in a forest behind the house. We skipped the scene changes and the staff to keep it simple. We were going to add those in when we'd all got our bits right but sadly we never finished the rehearsal. Gosh, I feel awful. I haven't asked about Marguerite. Is she going to be all right, do you know?" Archie looked at Ambrose, alarmed.

"It's too early to tell, Mr Framilode," Ambrose replied. "She has a big dent in the back of her head, I'm afraid."

"Poor Marguerite," said Archie. "I can't imagine how that happened. I don't suppose there's any chance it was an accident? No, I didn't think so. I just can't believe why anyone would want to injure

Marguerite. Oh dear Lord, you don't think they actually wanted to *kill* her do you?"

"We're keeping an open mind at this stage," Ambrose replied.

"Quite right, of course you are. It's so ironic though.'

"What is, sir?" Winters looked up with interest.

"Well, Marguerite being hit on the back of the head, just after she had her new haircut. I have to admit, I didn't like it. In fact I thought it was pretty ghastly, but then I've no idea what is fashionable these days and I'm not one to boast on the hair stakes, am I?" Archie ran his hand over his balding head. "Still I suppose her hair is the last of Marguerite's worries right now."

"Can you tell me more about this evening's rehearsal please?" Ambrose carried on. "My sergeant mentions you were wondering why Miss Monroe was found where she was."

"Sorry? Oh yes, I was confused about that," Archie replied. "Marguerite only has to wait off stage briefly for her next line, calling to Mark. Although she calls him Connaught just to be confusing. He's known as Mark Connaught. Teresa calls him by his surname. I realise that's a little odd given he's just kissed her but that's what they did in the film so we're sticking with it."

"So what is meant to happen next?" Ambrose persisted.

"Marguerite comes off Stage Right and usually just stays in the wings there, until her next line. Then she's not needed again until the end of that scene, so normally she goes to the Green Room. We have to be careful though. It's almost impossible to hear dialogue clearly in the Green Room and the dressing rooms are just too far away. Sometimes we have to stand in the wings waiting for our next entry, to make sure we don't miss it. That's why we put the curtains up. Marguerite really wouldn't have wanted to go far, in case she missed her line. I can't imagine why she was round the other side; it just doesn't make any sense to me. Still, it wouldn't really have mattered where she was when she did her next line, so maybe she thought she'd try a different position for effect. She should have consulted me first though. After all, as the director I'm meant to make that kind of decision." Archie looked put out.

"I understand you've known Miss Monroe for some time?" Winters asked. "How did you first meet?"

"Through my work. I did something for her a long time ago: nothing important. We just got chatting and found we had a mutual interest in the Theatre and it went from there really. You know that Marguerite used to be in the West End before she became a secretary? I think sometimes she's really regretted leaving the stage, even though she was glad to have a more steady income. It's a hard life, being an actor you know."

"Can you tell us a bit more about the work you did for Miss Monroe, sir?" Winters persisted.

"Er, well, I can't really remember to be honest," Archie looked at his feet. "It was a long time ago. I don't see how it's relevant."

"It's not important, sir, just a bit of background," Ambrose interjected. "Can you think of anything else we might need to know?"

Archie frowned, as if he were thinking hard. "Not right now. If anything else comes to me, I'll let you know."

Ambrose rose. "Well, that's been very helpful sir. If I could trouble you for the cast list, that would be really useful."

"Yes of course. I'll get it for you right now. Would you like me to stay on hand in case you have any other queries?"

"Yes that would be most kind," Ambrose smiled. Archie sprang up and fairly bounded for the door.

They watched as Archie left and walked back to the men's dressing room, accompanied by a uniformed PC. Ambrose turned to Winters.

"Any thoughts?" he asked.

"Too early to tell," Winters replied, "but if you ask me there's definitely something he's not telling us about how he met Miss Monroe. I get the impression he remembers every bit of work he's ever done for every one of his clients. I don't buy his sudden memory loss."

"Neither do I," Ambrose replied. "It's interesting though that he claimed not to remember. Most solicitors I know would have said they couldn't breach client confidentiality. I wonder why he didn't mention that to us."

"What happens if Miss Monroe does die? Would the client confidentiality then fall away?" Winters mused.

"Now that's a thought," Ambrose replied. "So by 'forgetting' he's effectively saying he won't tell us, even if she does die. I wonder what secret can be so important."

"I know we don't see it very often these days, sir, but perhaps he's just being honourable?" Winters suggested. "If he's given his word to Miss Monroe, he may feel bound by that even if she's no longer around."

"I get the impression you quite like our director," Ambrose noted.

"I think that underneath that slightly pompous exterior, there's a pretty decent guy struggling to get out!" Winters smiled.

CHAPTER SEVEN

DS Winters ushered Alex Baker-Smythe into the interview room, noting that Alex was blond, about 5' 9", slight and clean-shaven. He wore a subtle and probably very expensive eau de cologne, possibly foreign. Winters conceded that Alex might indeed be considered handsome.

Ambrose welcomed Alex as he sat down.

"Can I please have your date of birth and occupation for my records," Winters opened the questioning.

"Certainly," Alex turned to look at Winters. "I was born on 21 October 1929. I am a qualified Solicitor. Do I take it this is a voluntary interview, given I've not been cautioned?"

"That's correct," Ambrose replied.

"And your address, please, sir?" Winters interjected from behind.

"I'm lodging at 21A Tatton Grove," Alex replied. Then suddenly he exclaimed, "just a moment, I'll get neck ache if you're sitting at odd angles like that." He stood up and moved his chair, so he could see both Winters and Ambrose at the same time. "That's better." He sat down again. "It felt like I was watching lawn tennis," he smiled.

Ambrose laughed. "Can you tell me what happened this evening?"

"Yes, of course," Alex replied. "If I'm repeating what others have already told you, just let me know. I don't want to waste your time."

"We'd rather hear everything you have to tell us," Ambrose assured him. "We can decide later what's important."

"Right, of course. By the way, how is Marguerite? Is there any news?" Alex looked concerned.

"She's still in hospital and it's too early to say I'm afraid," Winters explained. He looked up and found Alex's clear blue eyes looking back at him, full of concern.

"I do hope she isn't badly hurt," Alex replied.

"We all do, sir. If you can tell us what happened that will help," Ambrose lent forward slightly.

"Of course although I'm not sure I'll be much help. It was all pretty much as per usual, I mean there was nothing obviously wrong. I went on stage just after Frank and Marguerite. I have to wait until they've started their argument before I wander on and make it all a lot worse. Frank left the stage as usual and I did my song to Marguerite. We pretended to kiss and she ran off the stage. I ran after her."

"Did you see Miss Monroe when you left the stage?" Ambrose asked.

"No, I didn't. I did think that was a bit odd," Alex reflected, 'but I thought, well, perhaps she had a call of nature or something. I mean, it wouldn't have been the end of the world if she'd missed her next line; that's what the prompt is there for, although I'm afraid Mrs Black isn't too good at it. It's all a bit new for her, I fear," he smiled. "Marguerite doesn't actually come on stage again for ages, so she could have wanted a bit of a break. We'd been rehearsing for an hour already and I was getting a little tired so I guess Marguerite was too. It was actually the third time I'd had to sing my song. It's hard staying in tune and putting all the emotion in when you've done it all twice already!"

"I'm sure it is," Ambrose replied. "Now, I'm told you found Miss Monroe. What made you go looking for her?"

"Well we heard the noise. I mean Olga and I were on stage and just when Marguerite is meant to call, there was this really odd sound."

"Can you describe the noise?" asked Ambrose.

"There were two noises I think. First there was the sound of something falling. It was like dropping a sack of potatoes on the floor. I actually felt the vibration through my feet. Then there was this odd clanging noise. I thought at first it was a bell, but it didn't sound quite right. It was definitely metallic, I think."

"So you and Olga decided to investigate?" Ambrose continued.

"To be honest, I think I'd have carried on but Olga was certain there was something wrong. I don't know how she knew, but she was clearly right."

"Did you run off stage in front of Olga?" Winters looked up from his notes.

"No it was the other way round. Olga looked at me, said something like *"That does not sound right"* and she turned and ran off stage. I was behind her going through the curtains. I don't know what made me look left but I did. That was when I saw Marguerite on the floor."

"I'm sorry if this upsets you," Ambrose said kindly, "but we need to know what you saw."

"Poor Marguerite," Alex closed his eyes as he tried to remember the details. "She was just lying there, on her front. There was blood everywhere. Look, I got some of it on my sleeve when I went to see if she was alive. I checked the pulse on her wrist."

"Do you remember which wrist you checked?" Ambrose examined the bloodied sleeve.

"Oh, dear. No I'm afraid I don't. It was the nearest one to me, that's all I remember."

"Did she have a watch on that hand?" asked Winters.

"That's a good point," Alex exclaimed. "No she didn't. I'm certain there was no watch when I felt the pulse. So, it must have been her right hand - I'm sure she wears her watch on her left."

"Thank you," Ambrose smiled. "Can you describe her position on the floor?"

"Well she was facing towards me, not away. I took it that she was planning to go off stage after she'd done her line. I don't know why she wasn't on the normal side though. It's all very strange," Alex said with a frown.

"Does anything else stand out as being strange?" Ambrose raised his eyebrows.

"I can't think of anything. Olga had run off stage into the corridor. I think she'd thought the noise had come from there. When she came back through, she was with BJ. He always waits that side before his entrance. As soon as Olga saw me checking Marguerite's pulse, she shouted to stop the rehearsal. Up until then, I'm not sure how many people would have known there was anything wrong. I mean the first noise I heard wasn't that loud. The bell-type noise was louder, but most people would probably have ignored that. It certainly wouldn't be the first time someone's dropped something off stage when we've been rehearsing. I'm afraid Mr Moody does it quite frequently. It drives poor Archie mad!"

"Tell me how you get on with Mr Framilode." Ambrose rubbed the base of his neck. He definitely had a headache coming on.

"What do you mean? I just work with him; we don't see each other socially. We work together pretty well really. I had been a bit nervous moving from a really large firm to one where there's just the two of us. It would be pretty dreadful if we didn't get on but fortunately I think Archie sees me as a bit of a chip off the old block. He keeps telling me how I remind him of himself at my age, if you see what I mean."

Ambrose started rolling his head from side to side, in an attempt to relax his neck. "How did you find the job with Mr Framilode?" he asked.

"I saw an advertisement in the *Law Society Gazette*," Alex replied. "Normally I don't have time to read the *Gazette* but I was getting really fed up at work and the City air was bad for my chest. It was so lucky that the first time I'd read the *Gazette* in absolutely ages, I saw Archie's vacancy.

"Coming out here was the best thing for me," Alex continued. "I haven't coughed anything like so much since I moved, and it's been great getting involved with the Players. I used to do quite a bit of acting and writing when I was at Oxford, but once you go into the Law, there isn't much chance to be creative. I've thoroughly enjoyed working with him and Michael on this show." Smiling ruefully, Alex shook his head. "I'm afraid sometimes Archie and I found ourselves talking about the play, when we should have been doing client work." The smile became a boyish grin. "You'd better not tell any one!"

"Did you know straight away that Mr Framilode was thinking of passing his firm to you?" Winters queried.

"No, absolutely not! His advertisement just asked for a junior lawyer. My doctor told me to leave the City and I fancied trying my hand at a bit of everything. Before, all I did was loan agreements and I was getting really bored. Plus I didn't like the politics of large city firms, where you're just one of dozens of junior lawyers." Alex grimaced.

"When did Mr Framilode first mention he was thinking of passing his practice to you?" Winters persisted.

"Do you think this is relevant? Well, of course you do as otherwise you wouldn't have asked. Please excuse me. He mentioned it first in the office one day about a month or two back, but I thought it was a joke. He made rather light of it. But then he mentioned it again, more seriously this time, after a rehearsal. We haven't gone into any details though and I don't think Archie's planning on retiring for a few years yet. He's not even sixty."

"Thank you Mr Baker-Smythe," Ambrose said. "Is there anything else you can tell us that you think would help?"

"No, I can't think of anything I'm afraid. I really wish I could help you. I feel so dreadful for poor Marguerite."

"Do you know Miss Monroe professionally?" Winters asked. "We understand she's a legal secretary?"

"Good Lord, don't let Marguerite hear you say that! She's a clerk at the Law Courts." Seeing Winters' lack of comprehension, Alex explained. "She's responsible for administration at one of the courts. She fixes the court list, makes sure the judges have the right documents and so on. She's extremely efficient but I'm afraid she can be quite, well, *frightening* at first," Alex smiled ruefully.

"Why do you say that?" Ambrose prompted.

"When I first joined Archie, he sent me to court to do a really simple hearing. It should have been all done within ten minutes." Alex frowned.

"Normally the clerk puts cases like that at the top of the list, reserving the longer and more complex cases until later. Unfortunately, Marguerite took an instant dislike to me." Alex shrugged then carried on. "I don't know if it was just because she didn't know me, or perhaps she thought I needed to be taken down a peg or two. Either way, she put me bottom of the list but forbade me from leaving the building. I had to wait over five hours for my hearing, without anything to eat or drink."

Ambrose was surprised. "What did Archie say when you got back to the office?"

"He was furious with Marguerite. He telephoned her straight away. She claimed she didn't know that I was Archie's new assistant," Alex looked embarrassed.

"But you think otherwise?" Winters guessed.

"It was just a feeling, but I was sure she knew exactly who I was. I thought perhaps she was doing it to get back at Archie for some reason," Alex shook his head slightly. "Of course it made things very awkward the first time I arrived for a rehearsal with the Players.

Marguerite looked most uncomfortable. She never did apologise though," Alex added, almost as an afterthought.

Ambrose placed a fatherly hand on Alex's shoulder. He was surprised to see Alex jump slightly. "You have been extremely helpful," Ambrose reassured him, "but would you mind waiting in the next room a bit longer? We may need your assistance again this evening."

Alex nodded his acquiescence as Winters ushered him to the door.

When Alex had gone, Ambrose scratched his head.

"Something troubling you, sir?" Winters asked.

"I don't get why Marguerite went off the stage one side, ran all the way down that corridor behind the stage, to go back on stage the other side, only to be facing back the way she came when she was hit. It makes no sense whatsoever."

"Now you put it that way, sir, it certainly is a puzzle," Winters agreed.

The door to the dressing room opened suddenly. This door isn't silent, Ambrose thought to himself, noting the slight rasp the hinges made. Archie Framilode was walking in. He hadn't knocked. Ambrose smiled to himself: it was clear Archie still thought he was in charge.

"I apologise for interrupting," Archie said. "I've got the document you wanted."

"Oh excellent, thank you," Ambrose replied. He took the paper from Archie.

"I do hope this helps you," Archie said, as he left the room. He looked pleased to be of assistance.

Winters peered over Ambrose's shoulder. The document was the list of the Players and which parts they each had.

CAST OF PLAYERS

Teresa Laud	**Marguerite Monroe**
CJ Dudley Howard	**Archie Framilode**
Diana Laud	**Kathy Black**
Geoffrey Keldridge	**Frank Thomas**
Mother Laud	**Sara Worsley**
Seb Laud	**Larry Lyndon**
Uncle Wally	**BJ Godfrey**
Lisa Imrie	**Olga Greenbaum**
Mark Connaught	**Alex Baker-Smythe**

"That looks pretty straightforward," Ambrose noted.

Winters nodded, suppressing a sigh. Seeing the list brought home to him just how many people they still had to interview. He was glad his wife's sister was staying with them. Fran would give him hell, otherwise, for working another night, especially with the baby being so ill. The fog definitely wouldn't be helping little Caitlin's chest. He had learnt to dread November - and cases that looked simple at first sight.

CHAPTER EIGHT

"Who do we have next?" Ambrose tried not to yawn. It was going to be a long night. He wished he'd been able to eat something earlier. He realised it was his fault for interrupting teatime to remonstrate with his son.

"Miss Olga Greenbaum," Winters replied, putting the chairs back into his favourite positions.

"Another wonderful name," Ambrose commented. "There must be an agency somewhere renting names to theatrical types."

"In Miss Greenbaum's case I think it's genuine. I gather she's German. She's been in England for about ten years. According to gossip, Miss Greenbaum fled here with her mother just after the War. She still has a bit of an accent. She loses it when she's on stage apparently."

"Must be a good actress," Ambrose commented. "Who told you her background?"

"A rather talkative and extremely ample lady called Mrs Worsley," Winters said, smiling. "You'll have the pleasure, if that's the right word, of interviewing her later. If you can get a word in that is. Mrs Worsley seems a little scared of our German immigrant. Described her as 'formidable'. Apparently Miss Greenbaum works in one of the posh ladies' boutiques in Chalk Heath. You know, the sort you can't afford for your wife to walk past, in case she decides she likes something in the window. I'll show Miss Greenbaum in."

Olga Greenbaum entered. She looked pointedly at the three chairs, then remained standing.

"Do sit down Miss Greenbaum," Ambrose invited, indicating the vacant chair between him and DS Winters.

"I think we will all get neck ache sitting like that," Olga said. "If you don't mind, I'll pull my chair to the side – like this." She took the chair firmly and angled it so that she could see both of them at once. She sat knees together, back upright.

"That's better!" she exclaimed. "Now, I understand you need my details. I was born on the 5th of February 1921 and I am Sales

Manageress at the Chalk Heath Boutique," Olga announced. "I live in a small flat above the shop, with my mother."

Winters noted the details and then added "Physical appearance: about 5'7", green eyes, red hair (probably enhanced) and immaculate." Olga was in a light blue dress, nipped in at the waist with a large white belt. She wore ankle socks and slip on flat shoes. Her hair was held in place by an Alice band. She was by no means unattractive.

"Thank you for coming in so promptly, Miss Greenbaum," Ambrose began. "I believe you play Lisa Imrie, the female journalist."

"Yes that is correct." The faint Germanic accent was quite appealing. Winters found himself warming to Olga.

"And you were with Mr Baker-Smythe when he found Miss Monroe?" Ambrose continued.

Olga nodded. "Yes," she replied clearly.

Winters looked up from his notepad, "And you subsequently spoke to the emergency services?" he asked.

"Yes."

"Would you mind describing the events leading up to this call?" Ambrose asked. This woman was likely to be a good witness, he reflected. "Go right back please, to ten minutes or so before you learnt that Miss Monroe had been attacked."

"Certainly. I had been in the Green Room waiting for my cue. I am always careful to be ready and waiting, so I left earlier than was strictly necessary."

"Excuse me interrupting, Miss Greenbaum," Winters said, "but who else was in the Green Room with you?"

"Kathy and Sara. I passed Larry in the corridor. He was going to the Green Room also."

"And after you left the Green Room," Winters continued, "you went where?"

"I waited in the wing for my cue, and then ran on stage, ready to bump into Mark - that is, into Alex," Olga replied confidently.

"Did you see anyone else?" Winters persisted.

Olga paused for a second, frowning slightly, then said, "BJ was standing just outside the stage entrance. Sorry I should explain. We all call him BJ, but his full name is Brian J Godfrey. He plays Uncle

40

Wally. He was due to come on stage after me, but he likes to be ready early too."

Ambrose took over the questioning. "You saw no one else?"

Once again Olga paused for a second, as if to ensure she recalled every detail. "Alex," she said, "as we were both on stage. I saw Michael and his mother at the piano in front of the stage. And Archie too, of course. As Director, he was watching the scene from the front, ready to come on later."

Ambrose tried to get a clear picture in his mind. "Only you and Mr Baker-Smythe were on the stage at this point?" he asked.

"Yes. Teresa has run off: I run on, and bump into Mark who is running back into the garden looking for her. It is very like one of the farces by Georges Feydeau. You have heard of him?" Olga was surprised to see Ambrose nod. Winters was astonished. He didn't even know how to spell the name.

Olga continued. "People are running on and off stage all the time, from different directions. That is why we were rehearsing just that one scene so many times. Always someone would be late coming or going, and the action must be quick to have effect. Besides, Archie wanted things exactly right. He is a good director, but he does tend to complicate things."

"In what way?" Winters asked.

"He likes to have the light cues sorted from the start - and any music or prop cues as well. We had to be in the right place for the spots, and get our entrances and lines right. Some of us were not ready for that yet," Olga replied carefully. "You understand? The scene is at night, but whoever is speaking must be in the light. Several times people got their line right, but were just beyond their spot. We were all getting tired, and a little cross, I am afraid. We were very glad when Michael suggested we try again without the lights. It's not like Michael to take an interest in such things. Perhaps his mother is a good influence on him."

"When did you first become aware that Miss Monroe had been attacked?" Ambrose asked. "Did you see or hear anything out of the ordinary?"

Once again Olga paused. There was a slight tremor in her voice when she continued. "There was an odd thud, as if something heavy had fallen off stage," she said. "I felt it through the boards. The only

41

noise was a metallic clang, a bit like a metal door slamming. It did not sound right. So I ran towards the sound, but when I got offstage I could see nothing odd. I was afraid Archie would be cross at another interruption, so I turned to get back on stage as quickly as I could."

"Was Mr Baker-Smythe with you then?" Winters asked.

"Yes, he followed me. He had moved more to the left than me, and saw what I did not. Poor Marguerite! It was terrible! When I saw Alex leaning over her, I was sure she was dead."

"And then?" Ambrose prompted.

"I think I may have screamed - only a little scream but enough for everything to stop. People came running to see what was wrong. I said we must ring for an ambulance at once."

Pausing, Olga looked into the distance, as if seeing it all again. "That was when Archie made the call from the box office," she went on, "but he got very nervous. I had to take over. I had followed him because I knew he would make a mess of such a call. Don't misunderstand me, please. I am very fond of Archie, and I respect him as a director and as an actor, but he does get flustered."

Ambrose nodded "One last question," he said. "Are there any tensions in the company?"

"No more or less than in any other."

Winters was intrigued. "How do you mean?" he asked.

"There will always be disappointments, perhaps a little jealousy," Olga replied, "when one gets a part the other wants. I am sure Kathy would love to be the lead, but no one else can look the part of the younger sister. Sara must hate always being the mother figure, especially when she is so much younger than Marguerite.

"The changing rooms are poor and people can get on each other's nerves if they take up too much room. The owners keep saying the theatre will be rebuilt next year, but it never happens. There is no money. All the same, they should at least build another toilet. In this day and age there should not be just one toilet for everyone – and definitely not *outside*." Olga's expression conveyed her distaste.

"And as I say Archie wants everything right," she continued, "when sometimes it would be easier to cut a corner. But such things are only minor. Most of the time we get on very well, all of us, and we are proud of what we do. The Chalk Heath Players are known as one of the best amateur groups in the area. This dreadful thing that has happened ... it must be someone from outside. It cannot be one of us."

"That's what we will try to find out, Miss Greenbaum," Ambrose assured her.

"I hate to raise this," Winters was slightly diffident. "Do people sometimes see *you* as an outsider?"

Olga stared at Winters for what felt, for him, to be a very long time. She sighed.

"Yes of course you are right. I was not born in England. I was not even born in Ireland," she replied. Winters wondered how on earth she knew he was of Irish descent. He'd been born right here in Chalk Heath, and he worked very hard to make sure he never spoke with his mother's Irish accent.

"I was born in Vienna," Olga continued sadly. "When Hitler came to power he decided that Austria should be part of Germany so he invaded in 1937. It was called *'Anschluss'*. I think he was trying to recreate the old Habsburg Empire." She hesitated then added. "There may be some here who wonder if I am a Nazi. I can assure you nothing is further from the truth. The Nazis killed my father for opposing the 'union' of Austria and Germany. It was very dangerous but he stood up for what he thought was right. My mother escaped and took me to Switzerland."

Olga paused, then carried on, her voice trembling slightly. "My family lost everything in the War. My parents were both professors, now I work in a ladies' clothes shop to pay my rent and support my mother. But I would like to think that the Players have gone beyond prejudice and now accept me. There have been no difficulties even if there may be idle tittle tattle in some quarters," she finished firmly. It was clear she knew exactly who was gossiping behind her back.

There was an awkward silence.

"Thank you for being so clear," Ambrose rose to see Olga to the door. "I am afraid we need you to remain in the next room for now," he added.

"Your thoughts?" he asked after Olga had left the room.

"Not sure," Winters replied, sharpening his pencil. "I would imagine some of the others are a bit afraid of Miss Greenbaum. Mr Baker

43

Smythe might be, for example," he paused. "I wonder what she looks like, though, when she lets her hair down."

"Literally or metaphorically?"

"Both," Winters replied. "I imagine there may be hidden depths behind that rather prim exterior."

"I hope that isn't wishful thinking on your part," Ambrose commented. He didn't wait for a reply. "She seemed like a good witness, though," he observed. "Likely to notice things – and remember them. Can you read back what she said about the noise?"

Winters examined his notes, screwing up his nose slightly as he read out loud. *'The only noise was a sort of metallic clang, a bit like a metal door slamming. It did not sound right*," he quoted carefully. "Do you think it could have been the outer door?" he asked. "The one back stage that was unlocked?"

"Yes – that was what I was wondering," Ambrose replied. "When we saw it, it was pinned back on a latch, but someone might have done that just before we came. Could it have slammed as an intruder ran out?"

"I'll check," Winters replied.

"No - send WPC Meadows. I need you here. She can also tell us what sort of noise it makes. It's got to sound metallic. Both Mr Baker-Smythe and Miss Greenbaum used that word."

Winters paused. "Are you sure it's sensible to send someone so, well *junior*, to check? This is important."

"I am aware how important it is," Ambrose replied sharply. "I am also aware you would not have questioned my decision if I'd decided to send a male officer. At some point you need to accept that women are just as intelligent as men, and in some cases probably more intelligent," Ambrose sat down briskly.

With a shrug and a scowl, Winters left the room to relay the message to WPC Meadows.

"And" Ambrose said quietly to the vacant room, "there's much more to a woman than how many children she can have."

CHAPTER NINE

"OK. Who's next?" Ambrose asked when Winters returned.

"Mr Brian John Godfrey, sir, known as 'BJ' to the rest of the cast. He was quite mortified when I asked him for his full name. I don't think 'Brian' is the image he wants to portray. Bit of a ladies' man I suspect."

"What makes you say that?"

"He was definitely ogling Kathy Black's legs just now and she's wearing *trousers*!"

"Dreadful!" Ambrose replied, laughing.

Ambrose began the interview. "Good evening, Mr Godfrey," he said, indicating the vacant chair. By now Winters had given up his favourite ploy; he'd left the third chair where Olga had so resolutely moved it.

BJ smiled as he sat down. "Call me BJ," he replied affably. "Everyone does." He handed over a folded piece of paper. Ambrose opened it and read: "Name: Brian John Godfrey, Date of Birth: 21 September 1916, Occupation Accountant."

Taking the note, Winters looked surprised. "Very efficient," he commented, glancing back at BJ. Winters would never have guessed BJ's profession. As if hearing his thoughts, BJ grinned.

"I know I don't look like an Accountant, but we're not all stuffed shirts. Oh and just in case you're inclined to think I attacked Marguerite, I'm sorry to disappoint you. I was in the pay corps in the War. Never had to fire a shot I'm pleased to say. Don't think I'd have the guts to injure another human being. Well, I might have broken a few hearts in my time but that's all I'm guilty of!"

Ambrose and Winters exchanged glances, but neither replied.

"And your address please?" Winters carried on, noting that BJ was about 5'11", slender, with dark hair that was starting to grey at the temples. Then he added in his notes, "very blue eyes, distinguished."

"101 Duncan Road," BJ replied amiably. "And before you ask, I live alone. Single. Never did marry. Not interested in the little wife and offspring bit if you must know."

Winters raised his eyes and examined BJ. He wondered if BJ was likely to be picked up in one of the police raids of the local brothel. Or whether BJ was more likely to prey on other men's wives.

"Can you remind us which part you play?" Winters asked out loud, keeping his thoughts to himself.

"I'm Teresa's Uncle Wally, my dear boy - the absent-minded one. I even forget the party I'm giving for my niece. Then I pretend to be her father. Great fun."

His tone annoyed Winters but he kept his manner neutral and continued: "And where were you when Miss Monroe was found?"

"I didn't know she'd been lost! Oh, I see what you mean. Waiting back stage, my dear boy. Mind if I smoke, by the way?"

An ominous note entered Winters' voice. "Mr Godfrey, I would prefer it if you didn't refer to me as 'your dear boy'," he said coldly. "And we're reliably informed you're not allowed to smoke in the theatre."

"Sorry, dear boy," BJ replied cheerfully. "There I go again. Habit, I'm afraid. And I do object to this tiresome smoking ban. It's not as if the whole place will burst into flames the instant I light up!"

Ambrose intervened: "Mr Godfrey," he said firmly. "I don't think you're taking this as seriously as you should."

"Oh, but I do take it seriously. Poor Miss Monroe has been clobbered on the head. That's not a nice thing to do, even if she did murder the top notes and looked *nothing* like Grace Kelly. But all this, it's like a trashy detective novel. Isn't it a tad ......*theatrical*? And it's so late. I'm beginning to wish we hadn't agreed to stay."

Ambrose swallowed his irritation and replied, "We're very grateful that you did. If you answer our questions directly it will speed things up. Where were you five minutes before the attack on Miss Monroe was discovered?"

"Standing in the corridor, outside the stage door."

"And why were you there?" Winters asked. His fingers were beginning to ache and he stretched them out before gripping the pencil again.

"I was waiting to come on stage," BJ replied, "after Olga and Alex had finished their scene."

Ambrose glanced at the map WPC Meadows had drawn: "Was that the side Miss Monroe was found?" he asked.

"Yes, but don't you go making anything out of it. I never saw her. As I said, I was outside the stage door."

"Did anyone see you there?" Winters pressed.

"Don't know, dear lad, possibly not. Sadly our extremely beautiful young understudy, Julie, wasn't there tonight. Normally she watches everything from the wings, so she'd have been able to vouch for me. In fact, if she'd been here tonight she might have seen everything. Such a shame, all round really, that she wasn't there." BJ sighed dramatically.

"So I think I'm *sans alibi* as they say. No, wait a moment. Olga passed me - on her way on stage. And of course I saw Larry before that. We walked together from the dressing room and I left him toddling his way slowly to the Green Room. Bless him, he might just have got there by the time it was his turn to go on stage "

Ambrose sighed. The man was irrepressible, but there was no point in forcing him onto the defensive – not at this stage. Ambrose decided to change tack. Sometimes surprise was a good way of regaining control of an interview.

"Which side of Mr Lyndon did you walk?" he asked.

"Which side? Goodness, how can that be of any importance? Oh well, let me see. Yes, I placed him safely on my right hand side so I was looking away from the breezeblocks the whole way. The wall really is rather ghastly don't you think? It's so sad the owners didn't replace that side of the theatre when it was bombed. There used to be rooms there, you know. Now all we have are endless grey blocks made of clinker and soot. I really didn't want to look at that the whole way and Larry does walk rather slowly these days."

Winters closed his eyes for a second, visualizing the corridor round the back of the theatre. "Did you see anyone else near the dressing rooms?" he asked.

"I'm afraid not, my dear boy. Oh hang on a minute, perhaps I did. Yes, I saw Heather going into the ladies' dressing room but even you can't pretend there's anything sinister in that."

"And when Miss Monroe was found, where were you then?" Winters persisted.

"Still waiting to come through the stage door."

"Did you see or hear anything?" Ambrose asked. He leant back on the hard chair, trying to make himself more comfortable.

"A whacking great thud followed by a clang - or it might have been the other way round. Then Olga came bursting out to see if I had tripped over my feet."

Ambrose's patience was wearing very thin. "You don't sound very concerned about Miss Monroe's injuries," he commented.

"Frankly, I find it hard to believe it wasn't some dreadful accident. Marguerite is a bit clumsy. She must have collided with one of the props. I'm sure there'll be a perfectly sensible explanation."

Ambrose got up to stretch his back: "Mr Godfrey," he said very firmly. "I'm afraid it's clear that someone did attack Miss Monroe."

Winters decided it was time he took over the questioning again. "Have you any idea who might want to harm her?" he asked.

"All of us at times - when she was doing her prima donna act. But none of us would have actually done so. Other than Sara perhaps."

"Why do you say that?" Winters asked, looking up sharply.

"She's never got on well with Marguerite," BJ admitted. "And Sara was a little catty about Marguerite in the programme notes for our last production. They were very funny, of course, but I doubt Marguerite saw the joke. I'm sure it's because Sara's hugely jealous of Marguerite always having the leading role. Mind you, she's hugely everything, poor girl!

"Sara claims to have a glandular problem," he continued, 'but she's merely a closet eater. Do you know, I saw her in the Green Room one day, on her own and stuffing her face with a chocolate éclair? She put it in her cardigan as soon as she saw me. I dread to think what her pockets are like. I wonder what else is in there. A cream cake, perhaps? Or maybe a large meringue!" He laughed loudly, throwing his head back as he did so.

"I gather you dislike Mrs Worsley," Winters remarked.

"I don't dislike the woman. I just can't take her seriously. You wouldn't if you saw her and Larry trying to dance together. He has difficulty getting his arms round her waist, and tries so hard to be gentlemanly about it."

Ambrose finally snapped. Returning to the chairs, he stood beside BJ, taking full advantage of his height: "Mr Godfrey," he said. "I don't think you understand. You appear to be a likely suspect. You were near the victim at the time she sustained her injuries, and from what you say, no one saw you between Miss Greenbaum going on stage and the attack being discovered. You could have hit Miss Monroe over the head, and immediately stepped back outside the stage door."

BJ stared back at him. "Inspector," he replied, coolly. "Consider what you are saying more carefully. I wouldn't have had time to come through the door, onto the stage, move down between the curtains, clobber Marguerite and then go back out. And I would have had to do it without anyone hearing the stage door open or close. Besides, what did I use as a weapon and where did I put it? I gather there wasn't anything near where you found poor Marguerite. In any case, what motive would I have had?"

"We were hoping you would tell us," Winters replied, equally cool. "Oh and for the record, the stage door doesn't make any noise when you open it."

"Why would I, or anyone else in the company, want to harm one of our leading members?" BJ retorted. "There may have been petty jealousies amongst us, but we've always been a tight-knit, friendly company - all of us wanting to put on a good show. We couldn't do it without Marguerite. We hardly know each other outside the context of the Players, so it's very unlikely any of us would have an external reason for harming her. I certainly don't, as I'm sure you'll admit after a proper investigation."

Ambrose could see the logic but he was not going to let BJ think he had won the argument. "We shall see," he said quietly. "Please don't go far, Mr Godfrey. We may need to talk to you again."

"Make me sweat while I wait, is that the idea? Well, it won't make me reveal anything unexpected, because I don't know anything ... Except ... Damn you! You're making me suspicious of everything."

"Suspicious of what, BJ?" Winters asked.

BJ's expression was no longer faintly amused. For the first time, he looked serious. "It is remotely possible," he conceded. "I don't know... Marguerite could have been blackmailing someone. She once mentioned that she 'had something' on one of us, but she didn't go into details. We were all demob happy after the last night of a show, and I thought she was joking. But now... You've made me wonder. Maybe - just maybe - someone wanted to shut her up."

"Who?" Ambrose asked.

"I've no idea, but you've made me uneasy. Nothing's ever going to be the same in the company after this."

Ambrose moved away. "I suspect you're right, Mr Godfrey," he agreed. "Nothing is ever the same after an attack like this. One final thing: am I right that you and Miss Greenbaum are, shall we say, *intimate*?"

"Good god! How on earth did you work that out?" BJ blurted in surprise. "Well I shall certainly take care when I'm near you again. No one in the Players has any idea. Yes, you're right, in a way. Olga and I have an understanding. It's a rather loose arrangement, but it works fine for both of us. Neither of us wants a little cottage and children but we have fun together in our own way. Now unless you've got anything else to amaze me with, I'll sit and stew quietly in the other dressing room as you ordered!"

"How *did* you know that, sir?" Winters asked after BJ had closed the door behind him.

"Well, you said that none of the others knew BJ's full name, but Olga had already told us he's called Brian. And I was wondering why she would run off stage when she heard the strange noises," Ambrose replied.

"She seems so unflappable," he carried on. "I thought Olga must have had a special reason to be concerned about Mr Godfrey. She knew he was standing by the stage door waiting to come on. As soon as she found out he was ok, she came back on stage to carry on the rehearsal. I'd say she had no idea that someone had attacked Marguerite."

"Hmm, that's very interesting, sir," Winters replied. "Adultery amongst the cast, eh? I suppose you Methodists aren't too bothered by that type of behaviour." Winters was only half-joking. He was aware he was treading on dangerous ground mentioning religion but he felt he knew Ambrose well enough by now. They should be able to discuss such issues without causing offence.

Ambrose frowned slightly. "I thought your new pope was trying to improve relations with other religions. Or does that not include us 'heathens'?" he laughed quietly.

"Well I guess I'm lucky you don't think the Pope is the anti-Christ!" Winters replied. Then suddenly he added, "Does that mean you go to the same church as Pauline Meadows?"

"It's called the Chapel," Ambrose confirmed. "But before you say anything else, that isn't why I asked her to help us. She's highly intelligent and extremely capable. I gather she's shown up quite a few of her colleagues when they've missed something. In fact, if I believe station gossip, you'll know all about that!"

Winters didn't have time to reply. They were interrupted by a knock on the door.

CHAPTER TEN

WPC Meadows approached cautiously. "Sorry to interrupt you, sir," she said directly to Ambrose, "But you asked about the back door." She hesitated, feeling that she was most definitely intruding.

"Yes, that's right," Ambrose nodded, gesturing to the brunette to enter. "And what was the result?"

WPC Meadows approached the chairs and directed her answer at Ambrose. He couldn't help but notice she kept her hazel eyes steadfastly away from where Winters was sitting. She looked smart in her dark blue uniform, the skirt reaching just below her knees.

"It's kept clipped back most of the time the theatre's open, to give ventilation. It shouldn't be possible for anyone to sneak in that way as the outer gate is locked, but the odd local lad has climbed over in the past. I'm told they've had some thefts back stage. It does make a noise when it's slammed, but it's not particularly 'metallic' and it's not very loud. It's more like a soft 'thud'. I asked PC Sutton to stand on stage when I slammed the door. He said he didn't hear a thing."

"Thank you," Ambrose replied. "That was very helpful," he added as WPC Meadows retreated hurriedly.

Ambrose turned back to Winters.

"It doesn't sound like it was that door," Winters commented, business-like. "Mr Moody was right next to it and he didn't mention hearing it slam."

"True, although an attacker could still have got in that way," Ambrose mused.

"Surely they would have been seen, though? One or other of the cast would have spotted a stranger, even if Mr Moody didn't. I suppose it's possible it wasn't a stranger," Winters added.

"That's possible. But would there have been time to hit Miss Monroe and then run to the back door afterwards? Even if it did make a metallic sound, that seems to have been heard at virtually the same time as the thud."

"Unless it took Miss Monroe a moment or two to fall?" Winters suggested.

"Not after a blow to the head like that," Ambrose replied.

"No, I didn't think so either," Winters agreed. "But if it wasn't the back door slamming, which door was it?"

Ambrose took out the map WPC Meadows had prepared and scrutinised it carefully. Finally he shook his head. "Was it a door at all I wonder?" he asked.

"And if it wasn't, what was it?" Winters asked in return.

"Perhaps our next witness will give us some idea. Mrs Black seems another capable sort. Bring her in please."

Brenda seated herself facing the two detectives. She was about 5'4", slight, with silver-grey hair and brown eyes. Neatly dressed in a white blouse and long dark green skirt, she wore a light green shawl, probably hand knitted, on her shoulders. Her hands showed signs of arthritis, but otherwise she moved and sat easily. 'I hope I'm that good at her age," Ambrose found himself thinking.

Brenda was happy to give her details for Winters' notes.

"I was born on the 14th of April in 1886. I am now retired. I used to be a concert pianist and music teacher. I live at 78 Chatworth Avenue, alone since Michael married. My dear husband died in the battle of the Somme." She fixed Ambrose and Winters with a hard stare. "I have lived through two world wars so there's nothing you can do to intimidate me," she finished triumphantly.

"Mrs Black, we have no intention of trying to intimidate you," Ambrose assured her. "We just need to ask you a few questions so we can get a better idea of what happened this evening." He smiled when Brenda looked more relaxed. "You are Michael Black's mother - is that correct?" Ambrose continued. "And you are acting as temporary prompt?"

"Yes. That's right. The lady who usually does it was taken ill a few weeks ago. Michael suggested I help out until she's better. I turn the pages for him too, when he's accompanying the singers. It makes it easier for him he says."

"Your son is the musical director I gather - not just the pianist." Winters commented.

"Yes. And a very good one," was the instant reply. "He wrote all the music for the play, did you know that? And he's ever so patient with the singers."

"Oh? Forgive me for saying this," Winters asked with an air of innocence, "but I have heard that he had difficulty leading the professional musicians during the last show."

"Then you heard wrong! Michael gives very clear direction. It's not his fault if the musicians only turned up for the last rehearsals, and then chattered so much they couldn't hear him. They'd probably spent the whole interval in the bar too. Professional musicians shouldn't need telling how to play, anyway. Michael has enough to do leading this lot. Some of the singers can't hold a note, or keep pitch..."

"No criticism of your son was meant, Mrs Black," Winters said quickly. "I was merely repeating what I had heard suggested."

"I'd like to know who said that!" Brenda started to rise, then thought better of it. "So would Kathy I'm sure! For all her deficiencies, she'd be furious if someone criticised Michael in front of her."

"Kathy is your daughter-in-law?" Ambrose decided to defuse the situation.

"That's right," Brenda smiled slightly. "Michael and Kathy married nearly a year ago. She was my star pupil, you know. He must have known Kathy since she was eleven," Brenda noted, then added hurriedly, "of course they only started courting after her eighteenth birthday. And don't you believe that nasty woman. He did *not* marry her just to get away from me. He loves her dearly. Anyone can see that."

"What nasty woman?" Ambrose asked, perplexed.

Mrs Black pursed her lips. "It was just something Sara said." She sniffed loudly. "Of course, I suppose I might have misunderstood what she meant," she added. Her expression suggested she did not believe so for one moment.

"Besides," Brenda added. "There's nothing wrong with the difference in their ages. Mr Godfrey clearly doesn't have any problem courting young Julie when he thinks no one is looking!"

Ambrose cast a meaningful glance at Winters. He was wondering how Olga would react to BJ going after a much younger woman. His colleague, in turn, was wondering if BJ was having any success.

"You must be very pleased that Michael's married. Is it too early for grandchildren?" Winters enquired pleasantly, trying to ease the situation and failing.

"I have no idea," came the curt reply. There was clearly an issue here.

Ambrose intervened again. "I'd like to talk about the events leading up to the attack."

"Of course: not that I can tell you much," Brenda turned her eyes to Ambrose.

"You may have seen or heard something of use. Tell us what you were doing just before Mr Baker-Smythe found Miss Monroe," he asked.

"Standing next to the piano, turning Michael's music for him. I was also trying to watch the script, and give the actors their cues if they missed them. It's not easy doing two jobs at once."

"I'm sure it isn't," Winters smiled. "So you were in the orchestra 'pit' the whole time?"

"Yes, all rehearsal in fact," came the reply. "And so was Michael."

"Did you see or hear anything strange?" Winters continued.

"No. But then I wouldn't - not above the piano."

"Did you see who left the stage just before the attack was discovered?" Ambrose looked closely at Brenda. She returned his gaze, unflinching.

"Of course. I have to watch what everyone's doing so I can prompt them if necessary."

With a slight sigh, Ambrose tried again. "Could you run through who did what this evening? It would be very helpful."

Brenda replied. "It's all very complicated. I'm really not convinced it should be this difficult but Alex insisted. It should go: Geoffrey (that's Mr Thomas), then Teresa (Miss Monroe), then Mark (Mr Baker-Smythe). After a few minutes, they all go off stage left, but not at the same time. A scene change and a song from the staff should follow that, but they were cut out tonight. Then Lisa (Miss Greenbaum) runs on just as Mark comes back on, looking for Teresa. Teresa should have called to him from the wings, but she missed that, and I was about to put her line in when Olga interrupted everything by running across the stage, saying she'd heard something funny. Alex followed her. He found Marguerite, Olga screamed. It was chaos after that."

"And neither you nor Mr Black left the orchestra pit until then?" Ambrose asked, glancing over at Winters who was furiously writing.

"No. I told your colleague earlier that we didn't. We had no reason to. Mr Framilode can back us both up on that. He was standing near us, directing the actors."

"Thank you Mrs Black," Ambrose rose to bring the interview to a close. "We won't need to speak to you again this evening," he smiled. "You can go home now."

"I will wait until Michael is free to take me home," Brenda replied firmly as she left the room.

"We're running out of suspects," Winters sighed after Mrs Black had gone. "She's just given alibis to her son, and Archie Framilode, as well as herself."

"And most of the others were with someone else at the time of the attack," Ambrose agreed ruefully. "Either they're covering for each other, or they're out of the frame too. We need to find someone who was on his own, near the victim and out of sight. So much for me thinking I'd solve this in a couple of hours," he groaned.

"So far, there's just Mr Godfrey," Winters replied, "but he's right that he really wasn't alone for very long."

"That leaves us with Mr Thomas. No one's mentioned being with him at the time."

"Then let's hope he doesn't have a good alibi!"

56

CHAPTER ELEVEN

Ambrose was definitely getting a headache. He glanced at DS Winters who was turning the pages of his notebook, back and forth. "Having difficulty reading your writing?"

"'Fraid so," Winters replied, frowning. "Do you mind giving me a minute to sort things out? Sorry."

"No apology needed," Ambrose assured him. "Everyone's said so much and so fast I'm amazed you've got it down at all. Tell you what, I could do with a breath of fresh air, and I'd like to have a look round the back of this place. See if there's anywhere someone could gain entrance, that sort of thing. I'll be back in a few minutes."

Nodding in gratitude Winters returned to his notepad.

For a few moments Ambrose stood at the back, looking out into the yard. The fog was beginning to roll away. In the light from the open door, he could see the outside toilet and a gated wall beyond it. There was an alleyway the other side of the gate. Crossing the yard, Ambrose tried the handle. As Winters had said earlier, it was locked. Ambrose peered through the bars. A dark shape brooded opposite him – a warehouse perhaps. The alley seemed to come to a blind end on his left, but to the right of him it led off into darkness.

There was a faint smell from the toilet behind him. Ambrose understood Miss Greenbaum's distaste when she spoke of the cast's facilities. Turning back inside, he asked PC Sutton if he had the key to the gate.

It took a few minutes for them to identify the right one on the ring the manager had given them. Ambrose took PC Sutton's torch, and unlocking the padlock, went out.

An empty bottle and a pile of sodden newspapers suggested a tramp slept there, but that night the alley was empty. It led along the back of the theatre, past a couple of windows that Ambrose realised must look out from the dressing rooms. Though it seemed unnecessary, both were heavily wired and secured. No one could have entered the theatre through those windows. Ambrose couldn't believe many people would actually try.

Shining the torch ahead of him, he walked on, the beam bouncing off the theatre's wall to his right. Abruptly, the building came to an end.

Ambrose found himself beside a metal fence enclosing an empty piece of land. The theatre must have extended a good twenty feet further before it was bombed. He played the torch over what remained. A gravelled driveway came from the main road, passing the fire exit and finishing at a set of double doors nearer him; the scene dock he recalled Winters saying. Other than those entrances, both firmly closed, that was it. There was nothing but breezeblock: no windows, no décor, no sign of life or light. Ambrose sighed. Providing the fire exit and scene dock were secure and alarmed, as they had been tonight, no one could have entered the theatre this side.

Ambrose walked on down the alleyway. Beyond the theatre there was another thirty yards or so of vacant space, with all the tell tale signs of a bomb site: jagged bits of concrete sticking out of soil, weeds everywhere, a torn fence where local children had crawled through to play forbidden games. Then he came to the backs of three buildings, each with a wooden gate into a yard.

"Shops," Ambrose thought, recognising the usual seedy flats above, and the dustbins at the back stuffed full of cardboard. A strong smell of cabbage suggested a greengrocers' was nearby. Ambrose doubted if the occupiers of the shops would have any relevant information, but it wouldn't hurt to find out.

Returning, he lingered a few moments looking over the empty space that had once been the side of the theatre. Suddenly a lamp in the street went out, surprising him. There was no moon, and the receding fog covered even the stars. The beam of PC Sutton's torch picked out fronds of dying willow herb outlined against the mist, but without the street light he could see nothing else.

For a second Ambrose felt the old panic swell up inside him. He had to hold his breath to steady it. "Get a grip!" he told himself firmly. He should concentrate; focus on something. He knew from experience that would work.

"What rooms were this side?" he wondered. Yes, that would do. "What was the theatre like before the war?"

A memory returned– when he had come to the theatre with his grandparents. They'd gone into a large lounge during the interval. He must be standing near the site of that lounge now. It had seemed a palace to him then, a room full of red and gold with soft chairs and lots of mirrors. There was a counter where you could order tea or coffee and framed pictures of famous actors around the walls.

Feeling calmer, Ambrose began to retrace his way up the alley, the light from the dressing room windows and the open door beginning to penetrate the blackness. He asked himself what else had been lost in the bombing – more dressing rooms it seemed; certainly better toilets for the cast. And what about the bricked-in area under the stage? He had never been down there of course, but he did recall the orchestra sitting below him with the tops of several bald heads shining in a dim light, and a sunken grand piano where the leader sat. There must have been trap doors onto the stage from that underneath area too. One Christmas he had been quite frightened when there was a puff of smoke and an actor suddenly appeared from nowhere. *Aladdin*, that was it – with the genie of the lamp popping up on stage, to shrieks of startled laughter.

The air was bitterly cold and Ambrose began to walk more quickly. He had been wasting time. At least his head was clearer though. Letting himself through the back gate again, he walked to the men's dressing room to return the key and torch to PC Sutton. As he did so, he noticed the young officer was talking to several of the cast, keeping them company. It was a thoughtful gesture, Ambrose thought, although the fact that one of them was extremely pretty probably wasn't a coincidence.

DS Winters looked more relaxed when Ambrose re-entered the women's dressing room.

"Thanks for the break, sir," Winters said, smiling. "I've rewritten a few bits and sharpened my pencils. My hand's come back to life too."

There was a knock on the door.

"Come in!" Ambrose called.

PC Sutton entered, handed Winters a document, and exited as quickly as he could without being impolite. Ambrose wondered if the young PC was scared of him. With a wry smile, he realised the PC was more likely to be scared of Winters.

"What's that you've got there?" Ambrose asked.

"It's the medical report, sir." Winters handed it over.

"Let's have a look. Hmm, so the victim is Marguerite Monroe, date of birth 11th March 1900."

"Gosh, that makes her older than Archie. By the sounds of things, she's doing pretty well for her age," Winters interjected, "although she must need a lot of makeup to look as young as Grace Kelly!"

"I'd like to remind you that we're not all decrepit you know, just because we're older than you," Ambrose retorted. "Anyway, she's 5'8", that's rather tall for a woman, and very thin. She weighs only just over 8 stone. Yes, she was hit with something large but with no obvious corners. No, they can't be more helpful than that. Most of the blood was from her nose when she fell, but the real injury is to the back of her skull."

"I knew pretty much all of that before you arrived," Winters complained. "Isn't there anything useful?"

"Well, the doctors who examined her at the hospital found no evidence of poison or alcohol. They've also confirmed that the injury to her skull was from behind and slightly above. They're working out the angle she was attacked from and will let us know," Ambrose added.

"One or two of our male suspects are quite tall. Frank Thomas and BJ Godfrey must be about six feet. Would they be tall enough to cause the injury?"

"We can't be sure until we're told the angle," Ambrose replied. "Perhaps we ought to have another look at where they found Miss Monroe. Given she's still alive, I don't suppose anyone marked her position on the floor, did they?"

Winters flushed slightly. "They'd moved her to the ambulance by the time I arrived. Initially no one at Dispatch realised it was an attempted murder so I wasn't notified until it was too late to secure the scene. I guess about half the cast, a doctor and two of the ambulance chaps tromped around the area she was found." Ambrose groaned. "But I can assure you none of the suspects were able to leave the theatre at any time after they called the ambulance," Winters continued. "Our very own version of Miss Marple saw to that."

"And which of our lady suspects, exactly, is going to solve this mystery before we do?" Ambrose grimaced.

"Miss Olga Greenbaum was exceedingly efficient, sir. After she'd stopped the rehearsal, she took control of everyone until the ambulance and police arrived. She has assured me, though, that she has no intention of trying to solve the crime and says she doesn't even know how to knit."

Ambrose shot Winters a glance, then made his decision.

"Get Mr Baker-Smythe and WPC Meadows to accompany us to the stage. I want to see exactly where he found Miss Monroe. In the absence of the lady herself, WPC Meadows will have to stand in for her."

"No problem, sir. I'm sure she'll take any excuse to lie down on the job!" Winters grinned and left the room before Ambrose could reply.

Alex Baker-Smythe was quite happy to help. He led them from the men's dressing room, down the grey corridor that Ambrose so detested, to the stage door. He took them through the gap in the curtains to the bloodstained floorboards.

"With apologies to your nicely ironed skirt, would you mind being our victim, WPC Meadows?" Winters pointed to the floor.

Glancing at Ambrose for confirmation, WPC Meadows placed herself gingerly on the floor, her head nearest the stain.

"Now, Mr Baker-Smythe, if you could just tell the constable which way to move, that would be useful." Seeing Alex hesitate, Ambrose made another suggestion. "If you find it easier, why don't you just move WPC Meadows into the right place?"

Alex looked uncertain as moved towards the 'body' on the floor. Carefully, he moved her head slightly to her left. Then he pulled gently on the sleeve of her right arm, so her hand was forward, above her head. He manoeuvred her legs by holding her shoes, moving her gently to avoid laddering her stockings, so the right leg was bent away from her body. Finally he picked up WPC Meadow's left arm by her sleeve.

"Erm, this hand was under Marguerite's body," Alex explained, "but I'm not sure I can put it in place without hurting your constable."

"That's fine, thank you," Ambrose replied. He and Winters stood looking down at WPC Meadow's position on the floor.

"Any comments, Winters?" Ambrose asked.

"Well, I'd say the lady was definitely facing towards the gap in the curtain when she was hit. The question is which gap she was heading for. Either she planned to go back on stage, or to go out the stage door we came in through."

"My thoughts exactly," Ambrose responded. "You can get up now," he added to the 'body'.

Brushing herself down, WPC Meadows looked long and hard at Alex, who turned away from her stare. Ambrose was miles away, looking down at the stage floor, but Winters noticed Alex's discomfort.

"So how on earth did she get here?" Ambrose was thinking out loud.

"Round the back, I expect." It was Alex who'd replied.

"But that would mean she'd have to exit the stage door round the other side, run round the corridor, back in this side, then turn around again to go out. That doesn't make any sense," Ambrose replied.

Alex looked surprised. "Knowing Marguerite, she'd have used the other way round the stage."

"What other way?" Ambrose demanded.

"I think I know what he means, sir," Winters called out. "Look back here. There's a gap between the curtains going all the way round the stage. I bet if we follow this we'll end up at the other side. I can't believe we didn't spot this earlier, sir, although it is pretty dark round here."

"That's what I was trying to tell you," Alex confirmed. "There was no need for Marguerite actually to leave the stage area. Instead of going out the stage door, she could have gone round the back of the stage between the curtains, to this side."

"So, that would explain why she was facing the exit, but not why she was round here in the first place," Ambrose noted.

Alex shrugged. "I'm afraid I don't know."

"Well, Mr Baker-Smythe, you've been very helpful. If you could go back to the dressing room and ask Mr Thomas to join us next, in the interview room, it would be most useful. You can then leave but we will need you to sign your statement tomorrow. Please arrange a time with PC Sutton before you go."

Ambrose waited until Alex had left them before he continued. He wasn't even aware that he still had an audience of two.

"So, we know that normally Marguerite stands near the stage the other side to do her line. Tonight, Frank Thomas exits as normal eventually followed by Marguerite, but by the time Alex goes to join her she's gone."

"There's no way anyone could carry Marguerite round the back of the stage against her will," Winters noted. "We know she wasn't drugged and it's quite a narrow gap. She'd have had to be careful not to move the curtains when she came round. She'd also have had to do it at quite a pace to get here in time for her next line. I bet she was waiting to do her line when she was clobbered from behind."

"That's a possibility," Ambrose agreed. "But it still gets us no nearer working out what on earth she was doing round here. She'd have had to run round the instant she left the stage, otherwise Alex Baker-Smythe would have seen her when he came off."

"True," `Winters replied. "Is there something you have on your mind, Constable Meadows?" he suddenly demanded. Ambrose turned in surprise to face the young WPC.

"Well, it's just a hunch, sir. I've no real evidence," Meadows replied, quietly, facing Ambrose rather than Winters.

"I know from experience that instincts can be very helpful. I've heard it said that a hunch is just your subconscious working something out. Tell me what's troubling you," Ambrose replied encouragingly.

"It's just Mr Baker-Smythe. People say he's such a hit with the ladies, a real ladies' man."

"And you don't find him attractive?" Winters jeered. Ambrose cut him off with a wave of his hand.

"Go on," Ambrose prompted.

"Well, it's just that I got the feeling, when he was moving me around earlier, that I'm not his type, if you get what I mean."

"You mean he likes older ladies?" Ambrose was confused.

"No sir, that he might not be that way inclined at all."

Ambrose paused. "That's interesting. Thank you very much for your views."

Winters waited until WPC Meadows had disappeared between the curtains.

"You don't mean to tell me you're going to take notice of a woman's *intuition*, sir?" he demanded.

Ambrose remained calm. "There's no difference between a woman's intuition and your gut instinct, which I know you rely on quite heavily. If WPC Meadows is right, it would certainly explain Alex's odd response when I asked about how he gets on with Mr Framilode."

"Yes," Winters conceded, "I spotted that too. I'd been wondering earlier what he meant."

"And it might also explain why he was so uncomfortable when I touched him," Ambrose reflected.

"Well," Winters replied. "I'm afraid the ladies of the cast would be rather disappointed if they knew their beloved Alex is a *poof*. I'm presuming that they don't know."

CHAPTER TWELVE

Winters was determined not to show how tired he was. He consulted his list. "Now for the interesting one!" he said loudly. "Frank Thomas. As you said earlier, so far nobody's said they were with him."

Ambrose looked up, hoping Winters hadn't seen the yawn he had just stifled. "Let's see how he accounts for his movements," he agreed. "Maybe he'll give us our break-through. *Someone* must have been near the victim at the time. I don't believe she took hold of a shovel or whatever it was and whopped herself on the back of her own head."

"Unless she was a contortionist in the past," Winters remarked dryly.

Winters was finding it hard to judge how old Frank might be. His skin suggested he was in his late forties but the deep lines around his eyes and the flecks of grey in his dark hair made him look older. He stooped slightly but was probably over six feet if he stood straight.

Ambrose began this interview: "Good evening, Mr Thomas," he said, indicating the empty chair, which Frank took slowly. "Thank you for waiting so long."

"That's all right," Frank replied. "You have a lot of people to interview."

Ambrose continued. "Your date of birth is?"

"6th of June 1911."

"And your address, please?" Winters added.

"Er, well I live at 311 Quinton Avenue, but I'd rather you didn't publish that information if you don't mind." Seeing Winters' surprise, Frank added quickly, "I like my privacy and I have a lot of valuable books in my workshop. I don't want too many people knowing where I live."

"We won't publish your address; your books are quite safe," Winters reassured him.

"You're a bookbinder I gather," Ambrose noted. "I'm intrigued. What sort of books?"

"Antique and rare books mostly. I restore the leather where necessary and put pages back into place. That sort of thing."

"And there's enough work?" Ambrose asked, interested.

"I do well enough. I also bind small specialist print runs: autobiographies, poetry, memorabilia … the sort of books people want to give as special gifts."

"I see," Winters commented, not really sure that he did. It sounded a chancy way to earn a living. "How long have you been a member of the Chalk Heath Players?"

"Five years."

"And where were you tonight when Miss Monroe was attacked?" Ambrose asked.

"In the men's dressing room."

Winters looked up from his notes. "Why weren't you in the Green Room, with the others?" he asked.

"I preferred to be quiet and read my book," Frank replied. "Besides, I wasn't going to be needed for half an hour or so. I would only have been in the way."

Ambrose tried to remember the order of entrances and exits: "Why was that?" he asked.

"I have only a small part in the scene being rehearsed."

"And yet you still had to spend the whole evening here," Ambrose commented. "Didn't that annoy you?"

"No. If you're to get a scene right, you have to have all the characters present. Besides, most of my work is done on my own, and I live alone. It can get lonely. I like to be out in the evening."

Ambrose nodded. "Of course," he agreed. "We're trying to work out where everyone was when Miss Monroe was attacked. Please describe to me how you came onto the stage, when you left it, and where you went afterwards."

"I walked to the stage with Alex," Frank explained "and when it was my cue, entered with Marguerite – Miss Monroe. As soon as I'd done my bit, I left the stage and walked to the dressing room."

"What route did you take?"

"Past the Green Room …."

66

Winters interjected, "Sorry to interrupt, but did you see anyone in there? "

"Sara was there. I think I waved to her. I saw she wasn't alone but I couldn't really ..." Frank paused, as if slightly embarrassed, then added, "I couldn't see past Sara so I can't say who else was there."

Ambrose nodded to show he understood. "And then," he asked, "where did you go?"

"Past the storerooms and the technical room."

"Did you see Mr Moody?" Winters asked.

"No. I'm afraid I deliberately looked the other way, in case he collared me. Doug is very clever but I find him – a little off-putting. He's always so full of complaints."

Ambrose smiled. He could imagine it. "So you can't confirm whether Mr Moody was in his room?" he asked.

"I am afraid not."

Mentally, Ambrose was ticking off the cast list. "Did you see anyone besides Sara Worsley?" he asked.

For a few seconds Frank paused in thought. "I saw Heather at her sewing machine in here –" he replied finally, "by the door. BJ and Larry were in the men's dressing room when I entered, but they left soon afterwards."

"And you were on your own after that?" Ambrose persisted.

"Yes."

Winters looked across at Ambrose significantly. "Can anyone confirm you were in the dressing room at the time of the attack?" he asked.

"Unfortunately, no," Frank admitted. "I realise that this may look bad but I see no point in lying about such an important matter. I sat on my own and read '*The Old Curiosity Shop*'. Then I heard a lot of shouting in the theatre, and went to see what it was all about. I'm sorry I can't be of more help. I'd like to be. I respected Marguerite, and I hate the idea that someone wanted to hurt her. Have you heard anything from the hospital? How is she? "

"I'm afraid we have no news," Ambrose said. "Thank you Mr Thomas."

He was about to let Mr Thomas go home but changed his mind. Instead Ambrose asked PC Sutton to escort the witness back to the other dressing room.

Afterwards Ambrose sighed. "Damn it!" he said. "There goes another likely suspect."

"Why, sir?" Winters asked. "He doesn't have an alibi for the time of the attack. He's the only one who can't account for his whereabouts. I'm glad you decided to keep him here a bit longer." Winters was insistent.

"I know, but I have a feeling he was telling the truth. He could have invented an alibi otherwise. His body language suggested honesty, too. No looking away, or touching his face – you know, the sort of gestures that tell you someone's lying."

"Perhaps ...."

Ambrose recognised the tone. "You're not convinced?" he asked.

Winters shook his head. "I've got a funny feeling about Mr Thomas," he admitted. "He's too nice – too bland. Actors aren't usually bland. The rest of this lot certainly aren't. Besides, he isn't nervous enough. I'll bet you he's had dealings with us in the past. When people are being interviewed for the first time they either talk too much or get aggressive. We've had both already. But Mr Thomas was too calm. With your permission, sir, I'd like to do a check on his background."

"Is that your gut instinct talking there?" Ambrose said rather pointedly, but he knew Winters too well to argue. "If you think it's worth checking him out, go ahead. Do some digging about Miss Monroe too. We're missing something, probably because we've not been told it – yet."

CHAPTER THIRTEEN

Once again there was a knock on the door and PC Sutton peered in nervously.

"Sorry to disturb you, sirs," he said, "but I've got Miss Greenbaum here, wanting to speak to you again. She says you asked her to tell you if she thought of anything else, and she has. Thought of something else, that is. Can she come in?"

Ambrose glanced at DS Winters but he merely shrugged in reply. Olga Greenbaum was clearly sensible, however, and unlikely to bother them with trivialities. "Tell her to come in," Ambrose said, though inwardly he groaned. He had hoped they were almost through the interviews that night.

Somehow Olga still managed to look immaculate, even after so long waiting around in a darkened, and by now very cold, theatre. She had wrapped a large Victorian shawl elegantly around her shoulders. Presumably it had come from a props box. "I am so sorry to disturb you," she began in her slightly clipped accent. "You asked me earlier about tensions in the Players. I am not sure whether this will be of interest to you, but it might be."

Ambrose nodded. He was having trouble focusing on what the woman was saying. His mind kept telling him that he was very tired and longing for a cup of tea.

"If you think it's of interest, then I am sure we want to hear it," Winters smiled. He could be charming when he liked someone and he liked Olga Greenbaum. He was also aware that his superior was very tired, though no one other than a close colleague would have known.

Opening her bag, Olga took out a pack of booklets wrapped in a large rubber band. She pulled two out. "I have done a lot of paperwork while we have been waiting," she began briskly. "Until now, I have not had chance to read the final programme for our forthcoming show. Perhaps I was not concentrating when I read the proof," Olga shrugged, "or perhaps Sara added bits after I had approved her draft," she continued. It was quite clear from her expression which of the two she thought had happened.

"But I am worried by what has come from the printers. I can see why she did it, but if she had consulted me, I would have warned her that others might not see the joke. You may hear comments about Sara that you do not understand. I am sure she is not malicious, even if she may appear to be. But this will make matters so much worse. I have not shown this to anyone else. Some of the Players will be extremely unhappy when they read this."

Puzzled, Ambrose took the programme Olga offered him, and glanced at it. Winters also took a copy.

It was a cheaply produced booklet, made up of quarto pages folded down the middle and sewn together, but the design on the front was attractive: a montage of a stately home, dancing figures and silver bells. In the middle was a summary of the scenes, and a cast list, the same as the one Archie Framilode had handed over earlier. A page of biographical details followed, each player having provided a small black and white photograph. Clearly, most had been taken at least five years ago, in some cases probably ten. Opposite the biographies various shops were thanked for providing cigarettes, hats and flowers. The rest seemed to be mainly advertisements.

In amusement, Ambrose read the local butcher's proud statement "The best sausages in town", right next to a picture of the 'Neigh Away' Pony Sanctuary. Perhaps not the best place to put the two adverts, he felt. He doubted if the local ironmonger really did provide "Every tool you could ever need". The hat shop's claim to be 'Milliner to the stars' was almost certainly inflated too. There weren't that many stars in Chalk Heath and Ambrose doubted they'd need to change hats too frequently. Even so, he could not see why Miss Greenbaum was so concerned.

"It's at the beginning," she explained. "The part headed 'Chatter'. For each show Mrs Worsley writes notes on the production, life of the composer, things like that: enough to fill a few pages. People want a souvenir to read later, or they won't pay. We can make money by selling programmes, so it's worth giving them what they want, and Sara writes well. She is often amusing. Her summary of *Pirates* was very funny," Olga paused. She seemed uncomfortable but she carried on.

"But this time Sara has gone too far. She will have given offence, and it is too late to make changes. A thousand copies have been printed, at Archie's expense. He will be furious. I blame myself for not checking the final proof, but I thought we had agreed what was to go in...."

"Thank you for drawing it to our attention," Ambrose replied, wondering why an apparently sensible woman should worry about the proverbial storm in a teacup. Thinking of which, he was still longing for that mug of tea. "We'll read it through later," he assured her. "You mentioned checking the proofs. Are you the secretary, then?"

Olga frowned. "I am indeed," she replied. "BJ is the treasurer, Michael arranges all the music and Archie writes the libretto. This time Alex helped with the play writing too. We each have to do as much as we can. I cannot arrange music or choreograph dances, but I can make sure the theatre is booked and that everyone knows the rehearsal dates - boring things the others would rather forget."

"You sound as though your role isn't easy," Winters commented.

Olga sighed, with a gesture of resignation. "Every group needs someone like me," she admitted. "But not everyone wants to hear the reasons why you cannot do something they think will be fun. Or why I must enforce the smoking ban backstage so rigorously."

DS Winters was having difficulty listening. Sara Worsley's programme notes had caught his attention. Forcing himself to stop reading, he looked up.

"I imagine you've been quite worried about copyright with this show?" Ambrose suggested.

"Indeed. We have had to make several changes even in rehearsal, so that we cannot be accused of plagiarising '*High Society*'. It is a risk adapting a film that is so recent, too. There are bound to be comparisons. That, I am sure, is why Sara wrote as she did - to show we are aware of the issues. I do not think anyone else has seen a copy yet, but people like Archie and Michael - even Alex possibly - are bound to be offended, and Kathy will be upset too. As for Marguerite ... Well, that is irrelevant now." Unexpectedly Olga smiled. "I should not say this," she admitted, "But Sara is correct. Miss Monroe is no Grace Kelly."

Intrigued, Ambrose looked down at the photograph beside Marguerite Monroe's biography. It was certainly flattering, probably taken when she was no more than forty, but the comparison with one of Hollywood's most beautiful women was unfortunate.

71

Winters suddenly had a flash of inspiration. "Hasn't she got an understudy?" he asked.

"Of course: Julie, a very pretty student at the Secretarial College. With exams coming up, she will not be able to rehearse enough to take over the lead by next week. But if we can give her more time, she will be good, and I think the theatre may let us change our booking with the local brass band. We helped them last year, and I will ask if in return they can bring their concerts forward a week. Tomorrow I will telephone their leader, and the Theatre Manager, and see if we can sort something out."

"Would Julie be better than Marguerite?" Ambrose asked, suddenly wide-awake.

Olga's reply was calm, but she looked away. "I feel very disloyal saying this," she admitted. "But Julie is far more suited to the part. At the moment everyone in the cast is very upset, but I think soon they may see that there is, how do you say? - a silver lining. We have never had a failure, but I fear *Wedding Belle* might have been one. We are not ready. Even if we were, the critics might have made unkind comparisons, and that would have kept the audience away. Now we may be able to rehearse a little longer, and to have a younger and prettier lead. I am very, very sorry for what has happened, but it is almost a relief."

"Do you think that could be why Miss Monroe was attacked?" Winters asked, following Ambrose's line of thinking. "So that the understudy can take over?"

Looking him directly, Olga replied firmly, "No. I do not believe any one of us is capable of attacking anyone, much less one of our own. We are friends - as I have said. Julie wasn't even here tonight. She cannot possibly have been involved. It is true she has many admirers, but I cannot see them hurting Marguerite to give Julie the lead role. Besides, some of her suitors are just too, well, too *old* to be of any interest to a seventeen-year old girl! Even the most deluded of men would not attack someone just to impress Julie."

Winters wondered if BJ was one of the 'deluded old men' Olga was referring to.

Olga sighed heavily. "Sadly it is clear there are tensions I was not aware of when I spoke to you earlier. That is why I have brought you this programme to read. I will have to destroy all the copies. Perhaps

I can tell Archie it had too many mistakes and we had to reprint it," Olga was thinking out loud. "But then he will insist that the printers do not charge us again. That would not be fair on them. And the Players don't have the money to pay for a second print run. I could insist that Sara pays but I don't believe she could afford it either."

A pause then Olga exclaimed. "I know! I shall ask Frank to help us out. He is in the book business. He may be able to arrange cheaper printing. If I tell him the truth, I know he will keep the confidence. Now I will leave. I do not wish to waste your time."

"You've been very helpful," Ambrose assured her. "Do you mind waiting in the other room a bit longer? We might need to ask you questions about the business side of things. I promise it won't be more than another hour."

"If it is necessary," Olga replied. "You must be getting very tired yourselves - and in need of refreshment. I will see what I can do. Please do not tell Sara that I have talked to you about the programme. She would be very upset."

"We won't unless it's relevant," Ambrose agreed.

"So what do you think she meant by all that?" Winters asked softly after WPC Meadows had escorted Olga Greenbaum back to the other dressing room. "I'm not sure what she thinks is most important: the programme or the bit about the understudy."

"I'd say the first was used as an excuse to talk to us about the second."

Winters nodded. "What do you reckon then? Our esteemed director clobbered his star to save the show?"

Ambrose smiled wanly. "It would be nice to think so," he said. "Unfortunately Archie Framilode was in full view in front of the stage when the attack took place. And virtually everyone else seems to have been accounted for." He rubbed his eyes tiredly. "Including Olga Greenbaum. There's no way she could have been involved. She was on the stage when Marguerite was attacked. It's a shame though. If there's anyone in this lot who has the resolution to attack someone, just to save the show, I'd say it's her."

"And she'd do it for the very best of motives," Winters agreed. "It does beg a question, though, sir. Did our assailant know that the understudy would be absent tonight? It seems every other rehearsal 'young Julie' has been in the wings watching Marguerite's every move. That would make it rather difficult to attack the leading lady, wouldn't you say? Unless Julie was the target? Now there's a thought."

When Ambrose didn't reply, Winters looked down at the programme again.

"Have a look at Mrs Worsley's notes, sir," he advised. "I can see Olga's point too. If you're in the audience, it might not mean that much to you, but the Players will all know exactly who is who. Some of the comments are a little close to the mark, I'd say. I certainly wouldn't want to be on the receiving end of Mrs Worsley's infamous wit. Can you imagine what she'd put if she wrote about everyone at the Station?"

In silence they read for a few moments:

"CHATTER

Hello, Darlings, Lady Tulkington-Browne here. It's so nice to see you all again. I do hope you'll join us on a super trip we're taking tonight. We've been invited to a party in Chalk Heath – one of those delightfully English villages. You know – roses around the door, and lots of bowler hats and umbrellas, that sort of thing.

I've asked Thompson to get the limousine ready, and Harris has laid out my evening dress (the black one with the pearls and the long fringe). I'm sure I'll look absolutely divine (as usual!). Well, of course I'll have to check that my darling friend Lady O*** isn't wearing the same outfit. She does have rather a habit of copying me. But then, that's hardly surprising is it? I mean; one can't expect a foreigner to know how to dress properly, can one?

That terribly nice woman Mrs Laud has invited us to her daughter's wedding, you see. It will be a really big affair, one long party in fact, as there's a little celebration we're all going to beforehand. Just about anyone who is anyone will be there. I'll be the first to admit it's not the highest Society. One just can't get the right standard of people these days. My beloved Frank Sinatra and dear Bing Crosby are out of town, but there'll be some interesting theatrical sorts there.

You really must meet K***, an exotic young thing if ever there was one. It's her first year 'out' although they probably don't worry about that too much in America these days. And she's just so modern *too. You know I swear she looks better in trousers than most of the men. I'm told she's meant to be a superb musician too.*

Oh and I'll be able to introduce you to our handsome young solicitor. He's quite a heartthrob, though of course I personally prefer someone who has actually started shaving! Still, he's far more attractive than the average member of the legal fraternity. He's half the average weight, for starters, not to mention still having all his own hair. Of course, he's terribly new, but given time, I'm sure he'll learn to fit in eventually.

The bride's a hoot, quite a turn. I hope I'm half as good at her age. Come to think of it, I am half her age! I'm afraid she doesn't look anything like a film star. Still, if we all use our imaginations, I'm sure everything will be fine (and perhaps one of our famous thick fogs might help too!).

Our host says there'll be lots of lovely music. They've hired a clever musical chap who's adapted some songs by that American fellow, Cole Porter. I went to some of his shows with his Lordship. 'Anything Goes' was great fun, and I adored 'Kiss Me Kate'. You've never heard of Cole Porter? My dears, he was a child prodigy at ten, came from a good family, went to Yale, lived it up in Paris, all that sort of thing. Mind you, he seems to have had problems with his mother and married to get away from her. Musicians often seem to, don't they? I'm told his wife very much ruled his roost. You could say she wore the trousers in the family! Nothing changes, does it darlings?

Now I'm sure you've heard some of the songs. My absolute favourite is 'Who wants to be a millionaire'. Well of course I did – I wouldn't have married Lord Tulkington-Browne otherwise! I'm quite fond of 'True Love' too, although I'm not sure I've ever actually seen any. What about 'You're Sensational' – that one must have been written for yours truly, don't you think? Of course, that's just a few of the show stopping numbers you'll hear tonight. I'm starting to hum them already.

There'll be some dancing at the party too, so bring your soft shoes. Of course, there are those of us who have to be a little more sedate these days. It just wouldn't do for someone in my position to be cavorting around and my lovely friend L**** isn't up to much on the dancing-front these days either. Still he is such a gentleman, that one can forgive him.

75

Luckily Sir B* more than makes up for it – he's a mover if ever I've seen one. He can dazzle you with the speed of his feet. Perhaps that's why he's never been able to settle down? None of the ladies have been able to catch him! Oh and dear F**** is a very capable dancer too, if a little staid for my tastes. A lady does prefer to be swept off her feet, doesn't she?

I must say I'm really looking forward to letting my hair down out of the tiara. Oh, and if you're really interested in Cole Porter, there are some notes on his life and work on the next couple of pages. Now where did I put my glass of champagne? Cheers!!"

Ambrose rolled the programme up gently and put it in his pocket. He had to share it with his wife, although the comments wouldn't mean so much to her without knowing the people. Still, she'd find it interesting anyway. He'd show 'Chatter' to her when he got home. If he ever did get home that is.

CHAPTER FOURTEEN

Winters looked at the drawing of the theatre for at least the tenth time. A deep frown was etched between his pale eyebrows.

"Problem?" Ambrose asked. "Other than who could have clobbered our victim, while being in full view of everyone else?"

Winters nodded, turning the map upside down and then back again. "I just can't get my head round who enters where and exits when," he said. "I keep looking at Mrs Black's evidence to see if that helps, but it doesn't much, and neither does this dratted map. I suppose every world has its own language, but the theatre seems to be particularly mystifying."

"The actors probably do it to sound clever," Ambrose suggested. "Tell you what, why don't you go and ask Mr Framilode if he'll do an outline of all the entries and exits, like he did of the players? I'm sure he'll be only too pleased to prepare you another of his 'documents'."

"Yes – why not?" Winters agreed, looking more cheerful. "And now to Mr Black. This should be a quick one. He at least must be in the clear – sitting at the piano the whole time."

Michael Black entered the room. He was about 5'9", slightly built with dark hair, receding at the forehead. A pair of heavy glasses obscured his brown eyes. Michael confirmed his date of birth as 22/7/1914.

"Good evening, Mr Black," Ambrose started. "You are the musical director for the Chalk Heath Players?"

"That's my title, yes, but – well - it's a bit of an overstatement," Michael smiled, embarrassed. "Really I'm a music teacher and accompanist. It's only when the professionals come in that I do much directing, and to be honest, I find that the hardest part. Most of the time I accompany the rehearsals on the piano, and do a bit of arranging. Usually that's just when the singers can't reach the top notes, or find a line too difficult to hold. This time I actually arranged the whole score, from the film music." He sounded proud.

"Do the singers often have problems?" Winters queried.

"No more than in any amateur group. You've got to adapt your production to the skills you have. I mean – sometimes I'd love to be up on stage rather than stuck in the pit, but no one else could do the music so I do it, or there wouldn't be a show. Well Kathy obviously could if she wanted, but she'd far rather sing. She does enough thumping the piano during lessons, she says. Kathy's my wife, or do you already know that?" Michael looked from Winters to Ambrose.

"Yes, your mother told us," Winters confirmed. "Tell us a bit about the Players. You must see a lot from the piano. Do people get on well with each other?"

Michael shrugged. "Most of the time, yes. There are a few frictions, particularly when everyone's getting nervous before a show, but never anything serious. I don't think Marguerite and Sara get on very well, but they're both professional enough not to make it obvious."

"Would you say the Chalk Heath Players are a successful group – as amateur groups go?" Winters continued.

"Definitely. There are some lovely voices among us, even if – well – other things aren't quite so good."

"Such as?" Winters persisted.

Michael looked uncomfortable. "I wouldn't want to name anyone in particular. Let's just say one or two of us have trouble dancing and don't really look the part, but can sing very sweetly, whereas some of the others are the opposite, if you see what I mean."

"I do," Ambrose reassured him. "Your mother told us you were in the 'pit' during the whole rehearsal tonight. Is that correct?"

"Yes."

"You never left the piano – not even for a short break?" Winters looked up from his notes.

"No. We were doing the one scene over and over. I'll admit I was getting a bit fed up, playing the same piece again and again. I started fluffing a few notes myself but I doubt anyone would have noticed. Well my mother would have done, of course, but she'd have saved ticking me off until later," Michael smiled wanly.

"And your mother was with you the whole time?" Ambrose lent forward, scrutinising Michael.

"Yes. She was acting as prompt and turning the pages for me," he replied.

Winters smiled. "Do you find that helps or hinders? I'm not sure I'd want my mother turning my pages."

Michael laughed. "Well – actually – I'd far rather she didn't, but she likes to help. My mother was a much better pianist than I'll ever be, as she frequently reminds me."

"And you could see Mr Framilode the whole rehearsal too?" Ambrose queried.

"Yes. He was directing the action from just below the stage, at the side of the pit."

It was Winters' turn. "Can you think of any reason why someone might want to hurt Miss Monroe?"

"No. Honestly I can't," Michael looked upset. "We all respected her. She knew more about the theatre than any of us. She'd been on the West End, did you know? Yet she always encouraged us, made us believe in ourselves. I simply can't believe one of us would even want to do her any harm. It must have been an outsider."

Ambrose rose. "Thank you. That will be all," he said, showing Michael to the door. "You may leave now," Ambrose added.

Michael's face lit up. "That's excellent news. I need to take Mother home; she's very tired." He suddenly stopped, half way out the door. "What about Kathy? Can she come home too?"

"I'm afraid we haven't interviewed her yet," Winters replied.

"Oh dear," Michael looked confused. "I had better wait for Kathy, obviously I can't go home without her. That wouldn't be right at all. But Mother is certain to want to leave now. Oh what a bind."

As Michael left the room, PC Sutton popped in to hand over another document. Ambrose smiled at the PC's rapidly retreating back. He idly wondered whether to delay PC Sutton deliberately next time, just to see his reaction.

"It's the report on the angle of attack, sir," Winters explained. "It says that, as we knew, Miss Monroe was attacked from behind and above. This is interesting though. They calculated the weapon (whatever it was) would have hit her at about an 80 degree angle."

"That is interesting; that's almost horizontal," Ambrose commented. He turned to Winters. "You're about the same height as the victim, so can you stand in front of me please."

"Certainly sir, as long as you don't clobber me over the back of the head!"

"Perish the thought, you're quite safe. Well for now anyway," Ambrose added laughing. "I reckon I could just about hit you from that angle to cause the injury, but only if I bend into a very strange position."

"We don't have any suspects who are as tall as you, sir," Winters pointed out.

"True, but I can't see how someone smaller than Miss Monroe could have caused that injury. Not unless the assailant was standing on something. That might make it easier to hit her from just above the horizontal."

"I can't imagine anyone bringing a box with them to stand on, in between all those curtains, sir. There was certainly nothing to stand on when we got there," Winters noted.

"Well I think we should have another look at the scene of the crime."

They returned to the bloodied floorboards and looked around.

"You're right," Ambrose sighed. "There's absolutely nothing here anyone could stand on."

They both looked up. In the dark, Ambrose could just make something out above his head. "That's interesting, there's a lighting gantry here. Perhaps our assailant sat or lay on this, before clobbering Miss Monroe. Get someone to check this out, will you?"

"Will do," Winters replied, staring up. "Look, the gantry goes all around the back here, sir."

"Yes, it does," Ambrose mused, "but I think you'll find this is the only bit where it would be dark enough for an assailant to wait without being seen."

"I suppose this means we need to find someone with enough strength to lower the weapon to head height, hit our victim and then pull the weapon back up again."

"That might explain our second mystery noise, don't you think?"

"The bell-like metallic sound you mean? You mean when the weapon was pulled back up? It certainly could, sir."

80

CHAPTER FIFTEEN

Olga Greenbaum had been busy. She'd brought a pack of biscuits and cajoled everyone else to look in their bags for things to eat and drink. When she finally persuaded PC Sutton to raid the theatre bar, the combined haul included: a loaf of bread, 2 tins of sardines, 4 packs of biscuits, a small pork pie, 1 cream puff, a large meringue and enough beer to float a ship on. Olga was now sharing it all out amongst both witnesses and police.

"I can't imagine who we have to thank for the puddings, given what BJ told us about Sara Worsley," Winters laughed, as he and Ambrose balanced their spoils on the interview chair.

Ambrose was concentrating on placing two small sardines on a slice of bread. "Hmm," he commented. "Does this remind you of something?" Seeing Winters' blank face, Ambrose expanded. "You know, sharing bread and fish amongst the masses…"

"Ah, I see," Winters replied wiping cream off his upper lip. "I hope you're not suggesting that one of our suspects is the Son of God?"

"Daughter of God would presumably be closer," Ambrose joked then noticing Winters' reaction he hurriedly added, "besides I don't think fish were tinned in Biblical times!"

As soon as they had finished, they returned to the final interviews. The remaining witnesses ought to be allowed home sometime, Ambrose mused, suddenly feeling better. Eating always helped revive his spirits. If no definite suspect emerged soon, they would have to suspend the investigation for a few hours and call people back into the station in the morning.

Winters looked at his notes. "Well we ought to see Mrs Worsley next," he suggested. "She has young children. I'm sure she's got a husband but she'll want to get back to them soon anyway." He thought again about his own young family. They'd all be long asleep by now. He wondered if he'd be back home before they woke up.

They ushered Sara Worsley into the interview space. Winters had been polite earlier, Ambrose noted. Sara Worsley was more than ample. She was extremely over-weight, huge in fact. Her presence made their corner of the dressing room feel like a small cupboard.

Winters recorded that Sara was of medium height, around 5'5". She'd pinned back her shoulder length blond hair. She was wearing a pink gingham check dress with matching pink satin shoes. Her sparkling green eyes suggested she had been a very pretty girl in her younger days. Sadly, Winters thought, Sara now resembled a rather large pouffe under a tablecloth.

"Good evening," Winters began. "I believe your full name is Sara Jane Worsley and your birth date is 2nd February 1924. That is correct?"

Sara nodded. "You can call me Sara if you want," she invited. "It's pronounced 'Sarah' not as if it rhymes with Sahara," she corrected Winters.

Ambrose managed not to smile. "Thank you, Sara," he said. "And your address please, for our records."

"71 Heath Avenue," she replied proudly.

Another posh address, Winters thought to himself. Sara's husband must be doing well to afford a house on Heath Avenue.

Ambrose continued. "First of all, what part do you play in this production?"

"You might well ask! I'm Marguerite's mother! I mean, Marguerite's old enough to be my Grandmother. And to think she's meant to be Grace Kelly! Quite why she always gets the part of the young heroine I've never worked out. Perhaps she could sing and dance once, but she can't now, and her acting isn't brilliant either. You'd think there was a dummy on stage sometimes."

"Really?" Winters replied in surprise. "I gathered she'd been professional when she was younger."

"That's what she tells everyone, but I've never seen any evidence of it. I mean you'd expect her to show off her cuttings and playbills – stuff like that. Usually you can't stop people getting their photographs out, but Marguerite never even says what parts she played. And I don't think it's down to modesty either. She's not shy about anything else. She acts like she was half her age – still plays up to the men and dresses in the latest fashion." Sara barely paused for breath. "I rather admire her for that, to be honest," she went on. "Mind you, sometimes it doesn't look right. She changes her hairstyle every few weeks and this last one is awful - makes her look like a man. I know she's taken quite a fancy to young Alex, haven't

82

we all, but I can't see the point in trying to look like his older brother. Oh dear – I shouldn't speak ill of her, should I? Not now she's been hurt. That's terrible. I wouldn't wish that on her."

Ambrose glanced across. Winters was clearly struggling to get it all that down. Ambrose paused deliberately before carrying on. "I gather you have little liking for Miss Monroe," he remarked.

"Don't get me wrong. I really, truly, wouldn't wish any harm to her. Like I said, I admire her in some ways, never giving up. It's just that she's a bit of a fraud if you ask me. Several of this lot strike me that way, always on about how good the Players are, and the shows they've done in the past. I suppose they don't really have anything much else in their lives. Someone younger like me, with a family and a life outside, must be a bit of a threat. That's why I end up with the worst parts I'm sure. Of course, they'd never admit it. I've got to serve my apprenticeship, Archie says."

"Are you new to the group, then?" Winters asked.

Sara sniffed scornfully. "I've been with them two years now," she replied, "and I'd done ever such a lot before. I used to be one of the Principals with Westfield Amateur Opera. You should have seen me dance then. Of course that was before I had the children and started having glandular problems. As soon as I get myself sorted out I shall go back to the WAO. It was much better than the Chalk Heath Players. Even Archie admits I can sing better than most of the other women. Kathy can't even hold pitch, for all she's supposedly such a good musician. You should see Michael wince sometimes. Mind you, he'd never dare say anything. He's thoroughly henpecked, poor man. Talk about frying pan to fire!"

"Why do you keep coming," Ambrose asked, "if you feel you're not getting your fair share of the parts?"

Adopting a confidential air, Sara leant forward. "To be honest, it's a way of getting out, and leaving the children with my husband," she explained. "He likes me to keep my singing up. We met through the WAO, you see, and he's always encouraged me. Most of the time I enjoy coming in any case. We usually get on well. BJ always makes me giggle. He pretends to be a real ladies' man but I think he'd run a mile if any woman actually showed any interest back. Mind you, he pays us ladies some lovely compliments. Last night he said I was a pretty face in an ample wrapping! You should have seen Olga's expression! Thoroughly disapproving. Mind you, I reckon she's quite lively herself on the sly. I like her, though, and Archie. And as for Alex, he's a sweetie; everyone has a soft spot for him - even Marguerite. I'm sure that's why she kept making him sing his song again tonight so that he'd have to kiss her again. Mind you, you won't believe how many times he forgets his lines. You'd never believe he actually wrote the libretto!"

Winters could barely keep up and wrote furiously for a few seconds while he could remember it all: "Really?" he said at last. "You're obviously very observant, Sara. Tell me. What did you mean about Mr Black a minute or so ago? You said he'd gone from 'frying pan to fire'."

"Did I? Oh yes. Poor Michael. You can tell he's been bossed around by his mother all his life, and only married to get away from her. Kathy was one of his mother's pupils, you know. A really talented child, she was. Although thoroughly spoilt too I'm sure. She used to win the local piano competition every year. Of course, it caused quite a stir when Michael married her. He's old enough to be her father! There must be at least 20 years between them. But if he thought he was going to have an easy life, he was very much mistaken. I mean, Kathy's a very sweet girl, but she can't half fly off the handle. I don't think she stands much nonsense with her pupils either, now she teaches piano. A proper disciplinarian so I hear, even though she's not much more than a child herself. Mind you, you have to be strict nowadays, don't you? It's not like it was in my day. When I was younger, we always respected our elders."

Sara didn't notice Ambrose's grimace of recognition. She ploughed on. "Of course, everyone presumed that there had been, well, an *accident* when Michael married Kathy so quickly. I'll bet Brenda even started knitting booties. Not that she likes Kathy all that much, but I'm sure Brenda would have loved grandchildren. Still it clearly wasn't what we all thought. They've been married nearly a year now and there's absolutely no sign of a bump in Kathy's costume, I can tell you. Plus of course there's the question of her, well you know, *parentage*. That can't help."

"I'm sorry, her parentage?" Ambrose was surprised.

"Haven't you met Kathy yet?" Sara breezed on. "I suppose some would find her attractive. She's very petite with lovely dark hair. But that's the problem, don't you think?" Sara turned to Winters. She knew *he'd* seen Kathy already.

"To be honest, I'm not quite sure what you're getting at," Winters replied as diplomatically as he could.

"Well, it's just that her mother is light haired with blue eyes and her father's as red as you are," Sara replied knowingly. "So how did they have a dark haired daughter with brown eyes? And Kathy does look very tanned, don't you think? All she has to do is stand outside in the sun for five minutes and she's as dark as the ace of spades."

Ambrose wasn't sure what to say or indeed if he needed to say anything at all. Sara settled the matter by carrying on.

"You see," Sara lowered her voice slightly, "there's a suggestion, and I mean it is only a suggestion, that Kathy's father may not be her father at all. He was injured very early on during the war. So he was back in Chalk Heath, but he may not have been up to much, if you get what I mean." Sara glanced behind her as if to check Kathy wasn't standing there.

"But there was a rather handsome American Lieutenant stationed in Chalk Heath at the time. He was arranging for his troops to come over. We had absolutely hundreds of American soldiers here by the end of '42. If you believe the gossip, which of course I would never pass on myself, the Lieutenant showed rather too much attention to Kathy's mother. And, in case you hadn't guessed," Sara leaned towards the two policemen. "The Lieutenant was *coloured*!" she exclaimed.

"Of course, Kathy is really touchy if you mention it so I wouldn't dare say out loud what everyone else is thinking." Sara paused, then continued. "But I'm sure it's alright to tell *you*. You're the police. After all, you need to know everything don't you, and I'm sure you won't break any confidences," she smiled sweetly.

"Of course it explains why Kathy does such a wonderful American accent," Sara carried on. "I mean I have no problem with accents myself, with my experience, of course. But for all Marguerite is meant to be an old pro, she just couldn't do American. She sounded so *odd* when she tried. More Welsh or Irish. Poor Archie had to tell her she just wasn't up to scratch."

Intrigued, Winters made a note to himself to look into this further, although he couldn't quite see how it was relevant to the attack on Marguerite. "You sound as though you know the Black family quite well," he commented.

"Michael and Kathy live near us, so I see them around the shops as well as here. Mrs Black used to give piano lessons to my sister Dulcie, only we knew her by her teaching name, Miss Liversedge. I got a real shock when she turned up as Prompt a few weeks ago, and I realised she was Michael's mother. She was quite a famous concert pianist in her day, and she still gives lessons sometimes although Kathy has taken over most of them. Still I suppose it's natural for Michael to think a lot of his mother." Once again, Sara leant forward confidentially. "I'd love to be able to hear her thoughts, I can tell you," she admitted. "For all she fawns all over her son, even Mrs Black must realise he's a pretty dreadful music director. The music arranging isn't bad. I suppose he has to be quite talented to write it all down from the '78 but he's so hard to follow when he conducts. Besides, it's a good job Mrs Black is here. We'd really been struggling with getting the lighting cues right. I don't believe for one minute that Michael would have told Archie to try without the lights, just once, unless his mother put the idea in his head. I was certainly very grateful for that suggestion, I can tell you."

Ambrose was getting tired. "Can we get back to tonight's events, please?" he asked.

"Sorry – I do go on, don't I?" Sara smiled and plumped up her hair. "What do you want to know?"

"Where were you just before Miss Monroe was attacked?"

"In the Green Room."

Ambrose nodded. "Who was with you?"

"Kathy. Then she went out to wait for her cue. We both come on Stage Right you see, after Alex and Olga go off, but Kathy goes on before me, and likes to stand in the wings for a while, ready, so I didn't follow her straight away. I wanted to finish a story I was reading in my magazine. Then I heard Olga shouting and came out to see why."

"Did you see anyone then?" Ambrose continued.

"Other than Kathy? Yes. Larry - Mr Lyndon. He looked like he was heading my way when the chaos started."

Ambrose paused again for Winters to catch up, then asked, "One last question – we've heard that Miss Monroe had an argument tonight. Do you know what that was about?"

"An argument? No not really …Oh yes, she had a bit of a go at Heather about her costume being too tight, and Heather said she'd made it to the measurements, only Marguerite had put on weight. That didn't go down too well I can tell you!" Sara laughed.

"Was that all it was?" Ambrose probed.

"Yes. Just a bit of a spat."

"Thank you for your time," Ambrose brought the interview to an end. "You're free to go home now," he added. Sara looked delighted as she left the room.

"Phew!" he said afterwards, leaning back in his chair. "Did you manage to get all that down?"

"Just about," Winters replied, stretching out his hand and rubbing his fingers. "I think I'd better check my notes, if you don't mind. I need to see if I can read everything!"

Ambrose sighed. "So much for the 'We're just one happy group'!" he remarked. "There seem to be enough motives in that lot to keep even Agatha Christie going …" He looked at his watch. "I don't know about you, but I could do with another stretch."

"And I need to find out what's happening with the checks on those gantries. Excuse me for a few minutes please, sir. Won't be long …"

They were interrupted by a knock on the door. Mr Framilode had brought the list of stage directions Ambrose had asked for earlier.

List of entrances & exits from rehearsal

(left hand side)   _(right hand side)_
                                            1) Geoffrey & Teresa enter arguing
                                            2) Mark enters

3) Geoffrey exits in a huff
Mark & Teresa talk
Mark sings "You're a sensation!"
Mark kisses Teresa
[Offstage singing omitted from tonight's rehearsal]
4) Teresa runs off*
5) Mark runs after her*
[Scene change omitted]
6) Mark re-enters looking for Teresa

[Teresa calls to Mark from wings – this call was missed]
[Rest of scene halted due to need to call emergency services – if it
had continued the following entries/exits should have taken place]
                    8) *Mark runs off**
9) *Diana and Dudley enter*
Dudley talks to Liz
[Mark calls for Teresa from wings]
More dialogue Lisa & Dudley
[Uncle Wally calls from wings]
10) *Lisa runs off*
11) *Mother Laud enters*
                    12) *Diana exits – sent home*
Mother Laud & Dudley sing
13) *Mother Laud exits*
                    14) *Uncle Wally enters*
Uncle Wally & Dudley talk
                    15) *Dudley exits*
16) *Lisa runs on & off at sight of Uncle Wally*
17) *Uncle Wally runs after her*
18) *Mother Laud & Seb enter*
                    19) *Seb rushes off for champagne*
[Servants enter & scene changes to poolside]
20) *Teresa enters, by pool*
21) *Mark enters & sings to her again*
[End of scene]
Those exits marked * indicate that the actor usually waits in the
wings, to deliver a line off-stage or to re-enter quickly.

"Typical lawyer, eh?" Winters smiled. "Giving you information you don't need and didn't ask for!"

"You mean the stage directions after the attack?" Ambrose nodded. "But the earlier bit is interesting," he noted.

"Miss Monroe really didn't have much time before her next line, after she left the stage, did she?" Winters agreed.

"Yes, that's what I was thinking. Which makes it even stranger that she'd choose to run around to the other side of the stage for just one line, don't you think?"

"It also begs a rather obvious question, doesn't it sir?"

"You mean, how on earth did our killer know that Marguerite was going to run to the wrong side of the stage?" Ambrose queried.

"That's exactly what I meant, sir."

CHAPTER SIXTEEN

Winters came back, scowling. He looked decidedly displeased. Ambrose raised an eyebrow in enquiry.

"Well we've finally found the weapon!" Winters exclaimed.

"That's good news, surely?" Ambrose was puzzled.

"Yes, but I'm not impressed sir. It was in plain view the whole time and they've only just got around to checking it."

"Really? What was it?"

"A fire extinguisher, sir. It was in its place near the stage door to the alleyway. It's bright red, heavy, made of metal with no obvious corners and no one thought to check it until now. When I ask for a thorough search, I expect it to be thorough."

Ambrose thought, not for the first time, that he was glad Winters worked for him and not the other way around. He had no doubt the other officers were well aware they hadn't met Winters' expectations. The phrase 'doesn't suffer fools gladly' was a huge understatement. DS Winters' intolerance of mediocrity and failure was legendary at the Police Station. Ambrose, however, was one of the few who actually knew what lay behind Winters' exacting standards.

DS Winters had been far more relaxed when he'd first joined the force, so Ambrose heard. A fellow Inspector had told Ambrose the story. It was back in 1953 and the hunt for the Teddington towpath murderer was at its height. Winters was a newly promoted sergeant, not long out of the Royal Military Police Corps. Winters and a young PC had chanced upon a possible suspect, a man behaving rather oddly not far from where the two girls' bodies had been found.

Ambrose could imagine Winters' elation when they discovered a blood soaked axe in the suspect's car. What happened next wasn't Winters' fault. There was nothing wrong with Winters asking his younger colleague to put the axe in the evidence locker. There was no way Winters could have known that his colleague would take the axe home to chop firewood.

It's not as if the mistake hampered Winters' career. The suspect, Alfred Charles Whiteway, was hung anyway. Forensics had linked blood on his shoes and on the axe (once it had been rediscovered) to the murders. Whiteway's confession confirmed it.

Ambrose grimaced as he recalled the station gossip. He never had found out whether Whiteway was forced to confess. There was certainly a suggestion, at the time, that two of Winters' colleagues had been rather heavy handed.

Winters had been mortified when he'd heard the ugly rumours. He never again fully trusted his colleagues. Never once did he let evidence, once located, out of his sight until he knew for sure that it had been properly dealt with. And he always took the greatest of care with his suspects.

Unaware of where Ambrose's mind had wandered, Winters handed him a short report.

"Ok, so the extinguisher has a very small amount of blood on it plus what looks like a trace of skin and hair," Ambrose read out loud. "That sounds like a bit of scalp if you ask me. Be fair, these traces wouldn't be visible to the naked eye. They're checking the blood type against Miss Monroe's but I think we can safely presume it's a bit of her scalp and no one else's. I'd like to think we'd have spotted a second victim. Oh, this bit is interesting."

"The bit about the fibres you mean?"

"Yes I do. So the extinguisher has two types of fibre on it, near the neck. One seems to be from a coarse rope and the other from a rough black material. Probably a cotton-nylon mixture, although they'll be doing further tests."

"I wondered if our assailant used rope. He could have swung the extinguisher down towards Miss Monroe from the lighting gantry."

"Good thinking. That would make it a lot easier to pull it back up again. The momentum would also add to the impact of the blow."

"Which means we may not be looking for someone with a lot of strength after all? Perhaps some of our daintier suspects could have done it?"

"It's possible," Ambrose conceded. "Can you show me where the infamous fire extinguisher was found?"

Winters led Ambrose out of the interview room, turning right into the corridor. They reached the end of the corridor. The door leading to the outside toilet and yard was to their right. Just to the left of that door, in the corner, Ambrose saw a metal clip where the fire extinguisher had been. The extinguisher itself had been removed for forensic tests.

Ambrose looked around him. The extinguisher would have been in plain sight, so how could someone have returned it there without anyone noticing? Could the assailant have waited until everyone was rushing towards the stage, to the stricken Marguerite, before calmly replacing the extinguisher? Ambrose doubted anyone would have spotted it wasn't in its clip earlier.

"We'll have to go over everyone's movements again carefully," he noted. "There must be someone who could have had enough time to replace the extinguisher. And let me know as soon as we've heard from forensics on those fibres. In the meantime, we still need to work out who would want to do away with Miss Monroe."

CHAPTER SEVENTEEN

"Who are we interviewing next?" Ambrose sighed and stretched in his chair. It had been a long night already.

"Larry Lyndon, sir. He plays the part of Seb Laud, according to this sheet from Mr Framilode."

"Oh yes. We need to check where he was. BJ Godfrey said that Mr Lyndon was on his own when Marguerite was attacked."

Larry was escorted into the room. He walked slowly to the chair then lowered himself down carefully. Larry was about 5'11" but starting to bend slightly at the shoulders. His hair was now entirely grey, with the exception of jet black eye brows. He was trim but not thin.

"Could I please have your details for my notes," Winters started.

"Certainly, young man. I was born on 7 January 1889. I am retired. I live at 114 High Street," Larry replied pleasantly.

"Isn't that the Surgery?" Ambrose was surprised.

"Yes I live in a lovely flat just above," Larry confirmed. "My replacement has a large family and didn't want to move in. Since I didn't particularly want to move out, it's worked out nicely all round wouldn't you say?"

"You were the local GP?" Winters asked.

"I was indeed," Larry nodded. 'I retired four years ago. I have absolutely no idea why I didn't do it earlier. Life is just so much better when one doesn't have to listen to people describing their ailments all day," he laughed gently.

"I can imagine," Ambrose nodded. "I'm sorry it's taken us a little while to get to you, sir."

"Not at all, Inspector. I'm sure you've been extremely busy investigating this unpleasant business. Might I ask how Marguerite is doing?"

"We're still waiting to hear from the hospital, sir, as to how the operation went," Winters replied.

"Yes, dear me, that would have been rather a tricky procedure," Larry frowned. "I've always been glad that I became a GP rather than a surgeon. One got to see far less blood that way. Well apart from stints in the two Wars, of course. One obviously got to see a large amount of blood whilst in the medical corps."

"Can you tell us your movements this evening sir."

"Well, I arrived more or less perfectly on time for the rehearsal as my flat is only a short walk from the theatre. I don't think I've been on my own for more than five minutes ever since. Do you need to know where I was before I got here?" Larry looked over at Ambrose.

"Not for the moment, sir," he replied. "I do need to know exactly where you were during this last rehearsal please."

"Yes of course. Where was I when the attack took place? The truth is I'm not entirely sure, unless you can tell me the exact time poor Marguerite was injured? No? Never mind, I'll describe everything and you can work out what is important."

"That's very kind sir," said Ambrose.

"When the rehearsal started I was in the men's dressing room. I was speaking with BJ, Mr Godfrey I mean. Neither of us was needed until later in the scene, so we decided to stay out of everyone's way. It can all get a bit chaotic, as I'm sure you can imagine. It was rather pleasant having a brief moment of peace and quiet in the dressing room. Of course BJ will have complained to you about not being able to smoke. I have to admit I am rather glad of the ban personally. It does make the air backstage a lot easier to breathe."

"Did you see anyone else in the dressing room, sir?" Winters interjected.

"Yes of course. Frank joined us after his few minutes on stage. I don't think his appearance at the start of the scene actually lasts very long. Not that he'd complain about it, I should add. We left him there reading a book. Something by Dickens I believe," Larry smiled at Winters.

Ambrose continued. "So you left the dressing room at the same time as Mr Godfrey? Did you see anyone else near the dressing rooms?"

"I am afraid not, but I wasn't really looking. I walked to BJ's right, so the only things I could see beyond him were grey breezeblocks. They're not exactly a wonderful sight," Larry sighed.

"Yes I know what you mean," Ambrose said quickly. "How far did you walk with Mr Godfrey?"

"We walked together until we reached the corridor behind the stage. BJ walked towards Stage Left and I walked towards the Green Room. Before you ask, yes I did see someone else. Olga passed me, going the other way. I presume she was going from the Green Room to Stage Left, which is where she goes on stage."

"Did you get as far as the Green Room, sir?" This came from Winters.

"No I am afraid I did not," Larry conceded. "I was a few feet away when I heard Olga shouting. I fear I am not as quick as I used to be, sadly. I have developed a joint problem that causes me quite a bit of pain if I move quickly. I suspect that someone younger would have been sitting in the Green Room having had a cup of tea by the time I got there. I saw Sara coming out of there before I reached the door. She must have heard the hullabaloo and come out to see what was happening."

"And you play the part of Seb Laud, is that correct?" Winters continued.

"Yes it is. I'm glad I don't have to do too much running around in this scene. I have to do a little bit of dancing in an earlier scene but as long as we take it slowly, it's fine. Sara is very kind to me; she knows I can't go at things too quickly. I know some people make fun of her, with her being so buxom, but I find she is very understanding."

Ambrose asked the final question. "Can you think of anything else that would be useful to us, sir? Such as why someone would want to attack Marguerite?"

"I am afraid not," was the reply. Then as an afterthought, "it's such a shame young Julie wasn't here tonight. I'm sure she'd have been able to tell you exactly what happened to Marguerite."

"Well thank you sir for your time," Winters rose to escort Larry to the door. With a nod from Ambrose, Winters added, "You may go home now, sir, but please speak to the Constable on your way. He will fix a time for you to sign your statement at the Station tomorrow."

"Certainly," Larry said, as he stood slowly. He hesitated, causing Ambrose to look up.

"Would it be in order to ask your constable to run me home?" Larry asked diffidently. "My old bones aren't too good this time of night. I fear it would take me forever to walk back. I know it's not far," he added quickly, "but if it's not too much trouble?"

"Of course, of course," Ambrose was only too happy to agree. He stood to pass on the request, but Larry pre-empted him.

"I will speak to your constable, there's no need to interrupt your interviews. I'm sure you're keen to wrap everything up quickly."

Ambrose nodded his thanks, watching as Larry walked slowly towards the door. Winters returned to his chair and started looking through his notes.

"Oh, I'm confused," he frowned and looked up at Ambrose.

"Well that makes two of us. Is anything in particular confusing you?"

"Yes there is, sir. Mr Lyndon said that he left BJ Godfrey near Stage Left, before walking down the corridor towards the Green Room. He also confirmed that he saw Olga Greenbaum going in the opposite direction to him, from the Green Room, and that she was also heading to Stage Left."

"Ah, I see what you mean. How can that be right, given that the Green Room is almost opposite the left hand entry to the Stage?"

"That's exactly what I was wondering."

"Well," Ambrose looked thoughtful. "I guess we had better ask someone who knows all about the theatre. Can you ask our director to pop in to explain all?"

Winters fetched Archie from the waiting room. He was only too happy to explain.

"It's simple, really" he assured Ambrose and Winters. "You have to look at it as if you're an actor. So if you're standing on the stage looking at the audience, Stage Left is to your left and Stage Right is to the actor's right. Likewise, downstage means the part of the stage that is nearest the audience and upstage is the back. I know a lot of people get it all the wrong way round initially."

Winters looked back at the list of entries and exits that Archie had given them earlier. "But what about this list?" he asked. "This seems to be the opposite way round."

"That's right," Archie agreed. "I did the list for you as if you're the audience. The entries on the left are Audience Left, which is the same as Stage Right. Likewise, Audience Right is actually Stage Left. I do apologise if that confused you."

"So what you're saying," Ambrose replied with a sigh, "is that your list of entries & exits is actually back to front?"

"From the actor's point of view, yes, that's exactly right," Archie responded cheerfully.

Thanking him, Winters escorted Archie back to the dressing room.

"Well I think I understand now, sir," he said, "but I'm not sure if it's important."

"I think it could well prove very important indeed," Ambrose replied.

CHAPTER EIGHTEEN

"I'd better ask WPC Meadows to draw another map, sir," Winters said, ruefully looking at the various documents he'd spread out on the chair in front of him. "This one's out of date already. It doesn't show those curtains at the back. While she's at it, she'd better mark Stage Left and Right like Mr Framilode said. Then we might be able to see what's been going on."

"I was going to make the same suggestion," Ambrose agreed. "If we finish the first round of interviews, we may be able to leave the theatre for the night. I'm beginning to see some possibilities."

Winters glanced up. He recognised Ambrose's expression. They were getting somewhere at last.

"Who's next on your list?" Ambrose asked.

"The rather intriguing Kathy Black, sir."

PC Sutton was sent to bring Kathy in. She was really very pretty. Petite with extremely striking brown eyes and long dark hair, Kathy was the kind of girl who made men's heads turn as she walked down the street. She was clearly having that effect on PC Sutton.

"My full name? Katherine Ellen Black. My date of birth is 3 November 1939."

Ambrose replied. "I'm sorry to keep you waiting so long."

"That's alright," Kathy smiled. "We've been well looked after by your constable. I was getting worried about my cat, that's all. I had to come here straight after teaching at a pupil's house. If I don't feed Clara soon, she'll be eating the curtains."

"We'll let you go home as soon as possible, Mrs Black," Ambrose assured her.

"Call me Kathy, please. 'Mrs Black' makes me feel like I'm my mother-in-law." She laughed slightly. "I'm not quite used to being 'Mrs' yet I'm afraid."

"All right, Kathy it is," Ambrose smiled. He recalled his wife saying something very similar when they were first married. "Tell us where you were just before Miss Monroe was attacked."

"In the Green Room, with Sara," Kathy replied. "We were discussing one of those silly magazines she loves. Sara had been reading out the Agony Aunt pages. I realised it was getting late and went to the stage door ..."

"Sorry to interrupt, but which side did you go?" Winters interjected.

"Stage Right, ready to come on as Diana," Kathy explained. "I like to be in position early. Normally Archie joins me there and we come on together. Of course, we never got that far."

"Did you hear anything while you were there?" Ambrose queried.

"Olga gave a little scream – not loud but I knew something awful must have happened. She's not a woman to scream lightly. Then she shouted 'Stop the rehearsal' several times."

"Was there anything else?" Ambrose persisted.

Kathy reflected, before replying. "I heard a funny noise a few moments before, like metal clanging against metal, but I assumed someone had dropped something. I didn't hear Marguerite fall or cry out."

Winters changed tack. "I believe you're a relatively new member of the Players?"

"That's right," Kathy agreed. "I joined when I married Michael. He's been the Music Director for absolutely years."

"It's been suggested to us that you're unhappy with the parts you have to play," Winters continued.

"Who said that?" Kathy asked hastily. "No - of course you won't tell me. I know - it's confidential. I'll admit I'd have loved to play the lead. I know I don't sing brilliantly, but my voice isn't as bad as some might have you believe. Besides, I'm definitely no worse than Marguerite and she doesn't look at all right for the part. The understudy Julie would be so much better. And she really can sing. I'm being petty though. My silly gripes aren't important," she smiled ruefully.

"Your gripes may help us understand other people's – and why Miss Monroe was attacked," Winters pointed out. "Have you noticed if there are any tensions in the group?"

"We wouldn't be human if there wasn't, but there's never been any serious trouble between us. Not that I'm aware of anyway. It's dreadful to think that Marguerite could have been attacked, and by one of us…"

"Why do you say that?" Ambrose asked quickly.

"You obviously think so, or you wouldn't be interviewing us all," Kathy replied. "Besides, I can't see how a complete stranger could come in, attack Marguerite on the stage, and get out again without being seen."

Ambrose smiled at Kathy's logic. "It would be most helpful if you could give us an insight into some of the tensions you've noticed. Is there ill feeling about Miss Monroe playing the lead all the time?"

Kathy shrugged. "There are mutterings sometimes, and about Archie always being the hero, but then they did set the group up. Most people accept they get the best parts in return. Except Sara of course. She thinks she should be the star. She has a lovely voice and people put up with her because of it. Although she is *such* a gossip, honestly sometimes I think she's deliberately trying to upset people."

"Why do you say that?" Ambrose prompted.

Kathy sighed sadly. "I know we all love a good story, but I swear Sara makes things up. You know I overheard her talking to Archie once, telling him that I'm an American soldier's daughter. I mean, I ask you. Have you ever heard anything so ridiculous?" Kathy's laugh sounded slightly strained.

"I would have challenged her but there's no point. The whole thing's too silly for words. It's not as if there were any Americans around when I was born; they arrived years later. Besides, the only so-called proof Sara has is that I'm darker than my parents. But she hasn't met any of my mother's family. My grandparents were from Malta and my aunt Vera's complexion is really dark. In fact, it's my mother who's the odd one out."

Kathy tossed back her lovely hair and carried on. "To be honest, I don't want Sara to know I overheard her. I'm sure it's better to ignore her idle gossip completely. It's not as if I give any credence to what she has to say!" Kathy's voice was firm. "Besides what's the point in telling her the truth? I'm sure Sara would just raise doubts about my mother being so fair instead!" Kathy laughed, more freely this time.

"What about the others?" Winters asked.

100

"Well, BJ can be annoying, always messing about, but he's deadly boring when he's serious, so most of us prefer him when he's joking. He does make rather a thing about chasing after the women but he doesn't mean anything by it. Larry's a dear – what my father calls 'a gentleman' – and he's still a very good actor, so everyone makes allowances for him getting so slow. Frank's a bit of a loner, but he's probably the most capable amongst us, always quietly professional, so nobody minds if he keeps to himself. As for Alex - everyone likes him. He's so easy to talk to and understands how you're feeling." Kathy started to redden. 'But he has trouble remembering his lines and cues. Doing the same scene again and again because of his mistakes was causing friction tonight. Olga is always quite sharp but perfectly pleasant. I haven't noticed any other 'tensions', as you put it."

Winters asked the next question. "You haven't mentioned your husband and your mother-in-law. Do you find it difficult having them around all the time?"

"Michael and I met through music and the Players have been pretty much our life outside work since we married. I'll admit I wasn't pleased when his mother volunteered her services. We see enough of her at home, without having her at the one nice thing we share together."

"I thought your husband invited her to help out?" Ambrose queried.

Kathy smiled grimly. "Brenda has a way of making it impossible not to invite her."

"I gather you don't get on with your mother-in-law." Winters observed.

"Put it this way, no woman would have been good enough for Michael in his mother's eyes. She's made it very clear that she's disappointed with me. She tries to rule his life and I don't see why she should. My own parents are so different, just giving me support when I need it, but Brenda wants to know what Michael's doing, and where, like he's a boy still. She's very proud of him, but she smothers him, and freezes me out. I suppose it's with his father dying so early, and him being an only child, but I find it very difficult sometimes," she admitted.

"And you share your feelings sometimes with Alex?" Winters asked.

Kathy went very red. "Occasionally, but not like you're thinking! Alex and I are just friends, however silly that sounds."

"No criticism was meant, Kathy," Ambrose reassured her. "We're just trying to work out relationships within the Players."

"Alex and I are not in any sort of relationship - and we're certainly not having an affair!" Kathy answered hotly. "It's just that Michael's so involved in his work he doesn't notice much beyond it. Some days I feel a bit down and talking to Alex helps. Please don't repeat that to Michael. It would hurt him deeply, and I wouldn't do that to him for the world."

"Nothing you say will be repeated to him, or anyone else in the group," Ambrose smiled paternally.

"Thank you." Kathy suddenly sounded tired and very vulnerable.

"How do Mr Moody and Mrs Broomhead get on with the rest of you?" Winters changed the topic.

"Everyone respects them, I think," Kathy sounded a bit brighter. "They're both very good at what they do. Heather can make a ball-gown out of an old sheet, if needed, and Doug knows a tremendous amount about lighting and props. I'm sure the Players couldn't stage productions without them, but we don't have a lot to do with them socially. They're always too busy."

"One last question," Ambrose smiled again. "Can anyone confirm you were outside the stage door at the time of the attack?"

Kathy looked astonished. "Sara would have seen me as she came out of the Green Room."

"Thank you, Kathy. That will be all. You've been very helpful. You can go home now," Ambrose took her arm gently as he led her to the door, dwarfing her petite frame.

"Interesting," Winters said as he stretched out his fingers and rubbed his wrist.

"Very," Ambrose agreed. "If it was Brenda Black or Sara Worsley lying with her head bashed in, we might have had a clearer suspect."

"Or if Kathy had been attacked, I'd put my money on Mrs Black senior being the culprit any day!" Winters agreed.

He stood and stretched his back. "There's no love lost between those two women," Winters continued. "Do you think there is anything between Kathy and Alex? She's newly married, but she's clearly a lonely young woman."

"I think they probably are just friends. If they're more than that, we have a whole new set of motives, but with the wrong victim." Ambrose frowned, considering possibilities. "No," he said at last. "That idea merely confuses things. Kathy Black's probably the most straightforward of them all. Mind you, she is extremely attractive – the more so because she doesn't seem to realise. It's a shame her husband hasn't noticed either."

CHAPTER NINETEEN

WPC Meadows had been watching for a gap in the interviews. Taking her opportunity, she gently opened the door that Kathy had just closed.

Winters looked up wearily. "Sorry to intrude, sirs," Meadows started, noting how tired her superiors both looked. "I've been given a note for you." She proffered the small piece of paper. It had been folded over and over, just like the personal letters she and her girlfriends used to pass round at school.

"Who gave you it?" Ambrose sounded surprised as he took the note.

"Mrs Worsley, sir," came the reply. "She was most insistent that I give it to you. She said it contained important information. I did suggest she pop in to speak to you direct, but she said she had to rush back to her family. She thought her husband would be really worried, what with her being home so late."

Winters managed a dry laugh. "I don't think I've ever been given a note before like this. Still, it'll be far quicker reading this than listening to Mrs Worsley, wouldn't you say?"

WPC Meadows smiled as she closed the door carefully behind her. She made up her mind to see if she could find further refreshments to help the detectives get through the night.

Resignedly, Ambrose unfolded the paper, and smoothed it out. He had expected a long wandering story and was surprised how succinct the message was.

"Dear Police,

I think I ought to tell you that I'm sure Miss Monroe was very unpleasant to Dr. Lyndon a few weeks ago. No one will want to say ill of her now she has been so hurt, but she could be very difficult if she did not get her own way. Dr. Lyndon is the nicest, kindest of men, and he wouldn't tell you himself. Marguerite knew about something in his past, and threatened to tell everyone. You are bound to find out what it is at some point, so I hope you can ask him now and let him tell you about it himself. Larry (Dr. Lyndon) would never, ever have hurt Marguerite, but if you talk to him you might understand better why someone else might. Please don't tell him I sent you this note.

Sara Worsley"

Intrigued, Ambrose passed the note to Winters. He read it, shook his head in bewilderment and passed it back. "I would suggest we'd better call the man in but he'll have gone home by now," he noted.

Ambrose nodded and sighed. "Gossips often have the occasional bit of useful information amongst the chaff," he observed. "And Mrs Worsley probably knows more about our suspects than they do themselves. There may well be something Dr. Lyndon preferred not to tell us."

"Shall I just check he isn't still here?" Winters suggested.

Seeing his colleague nod tiredly, Winters popped his head round the door to speak to Gregory Sutton. Surprised at not finding the junior officer, he found another PC at the door to the men's dressing room. Peering into the room at the remaining suspects, Winters was even more surprised to find Larry still sitting there. Obviously there was a delay in getting the car ready. Presumably that was why PC Sutton had disappeared.

Larry Lyndon was understandably irritated to be called in again.

"I've told you everything I can," he said. "Really, it's getting very late, and I'm not so young as I used to be. I would appreciate it if you'd ask me whatever it is you've suddenly thought of and then let me go home. I'm sure the car will be ready for me soon."

Ambrose had worked out what he hoped was a tactful opening, but it was difficult to get an interview started when he had so little information.

"We've been doing background checks on everyone," he bluffed. "I think there may be something you haven't told us, Dr Lyndon. Something Miss Monroe knew."

With a gesture of annoyance, Larry Lyndon leant back in his chair. "I prefer to be called Mr Lyndon now I've retired," he said firmly. "And I don't think a case twelve years ago is of interest. Besides, I was completely exonerated."

"Miss Monroe thought it important," Ambrose replied vaguely, fishing for something he could get his interview teeth into.

"I'm afraid Miss Monroe sometimes says silly things."

"You mean she threatened to tell other people what she knows?" Winters asked quickly, suddenly catching on.

"Perhaps," Larry acknowledged and eased his position in the chair. He was clearly in some pain. Sitting around so long had made his joint problem worse.

Ambrose began to regret acting on Mrs Worsley's note. It was probably just a silly letter from a silly woman. Still, his instincts told him to persist.

"We'd like to know more about Miss Monroe's recent behaviour," he explained. "It could indicate a motive for the attack. Did she try to blackmail you too?" He hoped adding the word 'too' would make Larry more forthcoming.

"I would have said 'put pressure on me," the old doctor replied. "Blackmail's too strong a word."

"Then tell us your experience, so that we can judge for ourselves," Winters suggested.

"If you think it's important."

Ambrose sighed inwardly. They were not getting far. "Yes, we do," he insisted.

Trying to find a comfortable position, Larry Lyndon shifted twice in the chair. "Very well," he agreed reluctantly. "When rehearsals for *Wedding Belle* started going badly, a few of us felt Marguerite wasn't – well - suitable – to play Teresa Laud. The part is just too demanding. I suggested that, just once, she should stand down, while there was time for her understudy to learn the dances. Julie is much younger, you see, and much better looking too. Marguerite was furious and said some silly things. I gave in. That's all there is to it."

"You gave in because of something Marguerite said? Or was it something she threatened to say?" Ambrose was intrigued. He glanced significantly towards Winters, who began to take notes.

"It wasn't so much a threat as an implication."

"I think you'd better tell us everything," Ambrose insisted.

"I fail to see the point," Larry Lyndon retorted, sharply. A mixture of pain and tiredness showed him in a different light. The rather jolly former GP they had met earlier was clearly not used to being questioned. "You'll have it all on record," Larry continued. "It belongs to a particularly difficult period in my life; one I prefer not to recall. Hanging around here half the night is bad enough without these old wounds being reopened."

In surprise, Ambrose tried to think how to proceed. What he had thought was just Sara's idle title tattle was clearly more serious than he had expected. "We'd like to hear your side of things," he replied.

"Very well," Larry said curtly. "If you must." He stretched his left leg out gingerly and rubbed his knee. Then he moved his leg back, as though nothing eased his discomfort.

"Before I moved to Chalk Heath I was a GP in Jenners Park. My dear late wife hated the place. It was very run-down just after the war - it isn't that much better now as it happens. Sadly Rose became rather depressed. In those days there was little sympathy; you were just told to 'pull yourself together'. Fortunately there's a bit more understanding now …"

Larry paused, realising he had strayed from the immediate question. Patiently Ambrose waited. Winters looked up, wondering if he should say something, but seeing his superior's expression, he looked quickly back at his notes.

"Of course, you don't want to know that," Larry added, briskly. "Except in so far as people may say that Rose's well, *condition*, affected my professional judgement. I can assure you it did not. When a boy was brought to me after a bad fall, I examined him thoroughly. I could see nothing more than bruises. I suggested his parents might take him to the hospital for a thorough check, but said I thought he was all right. I did warn them that if he became sleepy or complained of a headache, they were definitely to take him to the Emergency Room. Unfortunately Mr and Mrs Reynolds took the boy straight home, where he went into a coma during the night and never regained consciousness. He died two days later; from a brain haemorrhage."

Ambrose was beginning to see the link with their current investigation. "And the parents blamed you?" he suggested.

"They made an official complaint. There was an enquiry and I was suspended. It was all very unpleasant. The family tried to get the local paper on their side, by telling lies, but in the end I was cleared. The poor child had an unusually thin skull. No one could have known without an X-ray and sadly his family didn't do anything when he said his head was hurting. His parents wouldn't accept the judgement though, and brought a private case. They lost that too, but they wouldn't give up. I'm afraid some people can never accept that life itself is cruel. They must have someone to blame."

Ambrose nodded. "And Miss Monroe knew about the case?" he prompted.

"Of course. She sees a lot of cases through working at the courts. Most of the time she's very discreet about what she knows, but when she's angry or has had a bit too much to drink, she can let things slip or hint that she might do so."

"Why should it matter?" Winters remarked, puzzled. "You were exonerated."

"That was my reaction at the time," Larry agreed. "What concerned me was not what Marguerite said – which seemed to me rather silly – but what it showed about Marguerite. She was so desperate to keep the lead that she was making silly threats. As I said earlier, I backed down. I said she should keep the part if she wanted it so much."

"Why *did* she want it so much, do you think?" Ambrose asked, genuinely curious.

"Perhaps to prove that she could still do it. We all fear old age, but for an actor that fear can often be even greater. There are not many parts for old men, and even fewer for women - except for the Witches in *Macbeth* or dotty old grandmothers in pantomime, and even then those parts are often given to men. I think she realised this could be the last time she had the limelight."

Ambrose nodded thoughtfully. He found this new view of the victim interesting. Whether it was any help in the investigation was another matter. "You did right to ignore her threats," he commented.

"Actually, now I've thought about it more, I realise she could have hurt me," Larry admitted. "People in Chalk Heath gossip, especially about anyone they put on a pedestal – the Vicar, the local doctor ... people they respect but secretly envy."

"I can imagine," Winters muttered softly, thinking of his wife's annoyance at being labelled 'foreign' when they first came to England. "Those how you say, neighbours?" she had complained furiously. "They call me names. Not good enough for you!" He'd always presumed she was exaggerating, but now he was beginning to wonder.

"Rose and I moved to Chalk Heath to get a fresh start," Larry continued, "but it didn't help. Poor Rose was very affected by the hurtful things people said. She never really did recover. My dear wife died eighteen months ago." Larry was clearly still upset. Winters wondered what Rose Lyndon had died of but didn't feel it right to ask.

Larry was carrying on. "Rose would turn in her grave if all that *unpleasantness* started again. Even now it could affect my reputation, at least at places like the golf club." Unexpectedly Larry smiled. "I'm learning to play, you know. My doctor said it might loosen me up."

Ambrose began to feel sorry for keeping the man so long, especially when he was in pain. "You've been very helpful," he said. "Just one more question. Did anyone else in the group hear Miss Monroe talking to you?"

"No."

"Are you sure?"

"There was no way they could," Mr Lyndon said firmly. "We were in the Copper Kettle – the café over the road. Marguerite invited me there after a rehearsal, for what I thought was a friendly cup of tea."

Mystified, Ambrose tried another tack. "Do any of the Players know about the case?"

"Sara does. She lived in Jenners Park at the time. Her family was on my practice list and gave me a lot of support. Rose and Josie – Sara's mother - were friends. It was through Josie in fact that we came here. She let Rose know that there was going to be a vacancy in the High Street practice. Sara won't have told any of the other Players, though."

Incredulously both Ambrose and Winters stared at Larry. Seeing their faces, he relaxed a little and laughed.

"Oh, I know she's a complete gossip," he acknowledged. "She can talk the hind leg and the tail off a donkey. But once she's given a promise she keeps it, and when she joined the Players I asked her not to tell anyone she'd known me before. Not because I was afraid, but because I didn't want Rose to be upset again. Sara kept her word, even when my wife died."

An expression of understanding suddenly came to Larry's face. "Ah – I see," he said, and let out his breath in amused exasperation. "Sara asked why I had changed my mind about who should play Teresa Laud. I said Marguerite had been very unpleasant, and it wasn't worth antagonising her any more. I expect Sara put two and two together, knowing that Marguerite had worked in the courts. Presumably she then suggested you should talk to me."

Rather uncomfortably Ambrose and Winters laughed. "Something like that," Ambrose admitted.

"It would be from the best of motives," Larry assured them. "Sara means well, poor girl! She was so lovely before she had the children, but she's bored and unhappy now. She eats, and gossips, for comfort. Then she puts on more weight and feels worse. The sooner her boys are old enough for her to go out to work again, the better for the whole family, though it will horrify the neighbours. She used to be a receptionist at the Chalk Heath Hotel, you know, and misses it terribly. When she's ready, I'll see if there's a job as a Doctor's receptionist somewhere. She'll be good at that."

Ambrose smiled in disbelief. "I think she'd have a problem with confidentiality," he remarked.

"Not at all. Sara's not stupid. She'd know she'd lose her job if she ever talked about the patients, so she'd keep quiet," Larry replied firmly. "Meanwhile, I've tried to persuade her to write for the local magazine. I'm sure that fertile imagination could be put to good use and they're always looking for stories. If nothing else, she could probably make up the letters to the Agony Aunt! Now that we've sorted things out, can I go? I'm getting very stiff. It's the cold. I'm sure your constable will be ready to take me home by now."

Thanking him for being so co-operative, Ambrose helped Larry to the door. Afterwards he remained standing, to stretch his back. Winters had stood up too, stamping his feet to try to warm them up. The theatre was getting colder and colder.

"What do you reckon?" Winters asked. "The whole lot wanted to bump the victim off and hired an assassin?" He was only half joking.

"It may not be such a daft suggestion," Ambrose acknowledged. "The trouble is, there's no way anyone could have got in and out of the theatre. I checked. Unless …" An idea began to suggest itself. "Unless they've been here all the time, hiding somewhere."

"Where? In one of the props boxes," Winters asked, "and everyone takes turns to sit on it, so we don't notice?"

"Come on, let's go for a quick walk," Ambrose suggested, laughing. "We need a stretch and we're almost through for tonight. Besides, there is one place I didn't look: under the stage."

Explaining to a surprised WPC Meadows that they were going to check something for themselves, Ambrose and Winters left the female dressing room. They walked down the corridor, past the electrician's room and the props store. They glanced into each and paused at the green room next door. There were clearly no places to hide an assailant in any of these rooms. They turned left, along the corridor that went behind the stage. The screens were immovable. Though flimsy, they hung heavily and could only be pulled from above. "No one could hide behind this lot," Ambrose thought to himself.

Going through the stage door and the gaps in the curtains, they went on to the stage. Winters examined the floorboards, and rapped his knuckles at different places to check if there were any changes in sound. Everywhere gave a dull, hollow, sound in reply. Then he tried feeling around the floor to see if there were any trap doors. The boards were all unbroken. The stage must have been rebuilt after the War, Winters mused. There was absolutely no way through the floor now.

For a few moments Ambrose stood looking out into the auditorium. The theatre was in total darkness, except for a couple of safety lights around the stage. Their glow reflected palely onto the small grand piano below. "They must have rebuilt this stage on top of the orchestra pit," he commented, echoing Winters' thoughts. "Pushing everything forward if you see what I mean. Presumably the bomb damage was too bad to put the stage back where it was."

"That makes sense of what Mr Framilode told me at the beginning," Winters agreed. Their conversation seemed weeks ago now. "I think I told you already that a Buzz bomb hit the place, sir."

"You said it hit to the right of the theatre," Ambrose recalled. "Of course, that must be true; otherwise the whole place would have gone. When I went outside earlier I saw the gap where the buildings next door used to be. Looks like space for two or three shops to me. Presumably the right hand side of the theatre went with them."

He suddenly felt an unexpected admiration for the Chalk Heath Players and all the other amateur groups who had decided the show must go on – for the theatre owners, too. They'd patched the place up, as best they could, and got on with entertaining the town.

"Well, there's nothing more to see here," he said aloud. "We'll look at where the orchestra entrance used to be, and then go back."

They reached the bricked-in area behind the screens, but Ambrose seemed reluctant to get too close. Leaving his boss standing a few feet away, Winters approached the wall, tapping to see if there was any difference in sound. Where the breezeblocks replaced the red bricks, the sound change suggested a stairwell, but there was no way anyone could enter it. Nor were there any trap doors in the corridor.

"Unless there's a secret tunnel from a smuggler's cave by the river," Winters joked, "there's no way any one could hide under this stage, sir."

"No indeed," Ambrose agreed from behind him. "Pity. That means we're back with the cast, and no one but the cast."

CHAPTER TWENTY

"That just leaves us with Mrs Broomhead," Ambrose said. His head felt heavy. "At least the end's in sight," he added.

"Hopefully," Winters agreed. "The way I see it, if she was in the ladies' dressing room the whole time, then BJ must be lying. On the other hand, if BJ did see her returning to the room, where'd she been?"

"Bring her in," Ambrose agreed, "and we'll put the question to her."

Before Winters could get up, however, there was a knock on the door. "What is it now?" Ambrose called in annoyance. They wouldn't be finished before dawn at this rate.

The door opened a little. "Sorry to disturb you," WPC Meadows said through the gap. "But can I have a word?"

"Two minutes," Ambrose agreed wearily. The young WPC was unlikely to interrupt without good reason.

Pauline Meadows came into the dressing room. "There's a reporter hanging around," she explained. "I was walking through the foyer and he banged on the outer door. I wouldn't open it, but he kept shouting that he wanted to speak to you. Said his name's George Miller and that you'd know him."

"Who tipped him off?" Winters demanded.

"No one, sir. I imagine he saw the theatre lights and our cars outside. He's still out there, hanging around."

Ambrose smiled inwardly. He did indeed know George Miller. Three years ago that young man was covering 'Matches and Dispatches' for the weekly *Advertiser*. Now he was crime correspondent for the *Chalk Heath Gazette*. In a few years he'd be working on a National. Until then, he could be very useful, passing leads on to Ambrose in return for the odd exclusive. He could also be a thundering nuisance, though. He would never give up once he'd smelled a story.

"Tell him to call at the station tomorrow afternoon," Ambrose instructed, "I might have something for him - so long as he goes away now. If he doesn't, I'll have him up for interrupting police business."

"Yes sir," WPC Meadows replied. She glanced nervously at DS Winters. "I've done the map you asked for, sir," she said.

"Let's have it then," Winters snapped.

Flushing slightly, Pauline Meadows handed it over and went out hurriedly.

Ambrose frowned. He didn't like tension between members of his team. "Is it just Meadows you dislike?" he asked Winters outright, "Or all WPCs?"

In surprise, Winters looked away. His superior could be a difficult man to work for. He was too quick. He noticed things other men might miss. "Just Meadows," Winters replied, adding quickly, "I have my reasons."

Ambrose could tell it was best not to press for an explanation. Sighing, he spread the map on the dressing table in front of him.

Winters began to feel uneasy, wondering if his reply had been correct. Was it just WPC Meadows he resented?

He came to an uncomfortable conclusion: he didn't think that much of women, Women Police Constables included. Perhaps during the early years of the war he had lived too long without female company. When they did arrive on the base, he resented them. Like many of the other servicemen, he felt they were an interruption to their male domain. The NAAFI was suddenly full of screaming girls, and they didn't seem to have the same spirit of comradeship that existed among the men. They simply didn't fit in. Unless, he thought suddenly, he and his male colleagues just didn't let the girls fit in?

"This looks very useful," Ambrose was saying. With a start, Winters returned to the present.

Leaning forward, he examined the map. "I asked Meadows to concentrate on the stage area," he explained, "but we can refer to the earlier drawing for the names of the rooms and so on."

[WPC Meadows' second hand-drawn map; back stage & stage area only]

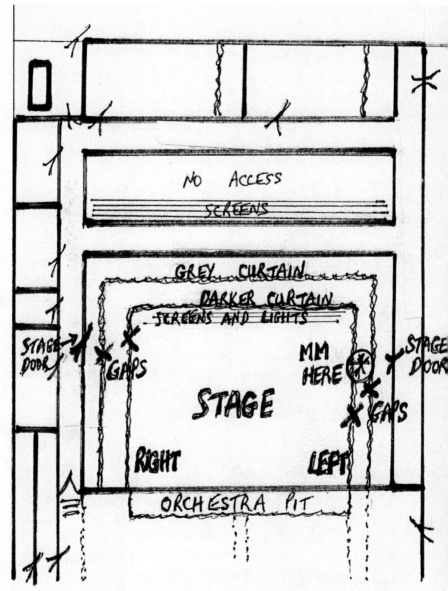

"This is great," Ambrose said.

He looked up as Mrs Broomhead was brought in. She was about 5'6", thin, round-shouldered with dark blond hair tied in a bun. Her long grey skirt was unfashionable and almost touched her ankles. She was wearing a grey cardigan and half-moon glasses.

As Heather came towards them, both men were surprised by the strong smell of lavender, as if she'd covered herself from head to toe in scent.

"My date of birth?" Heather scowled at Winters' query. "I can't see how that is in the slightest bit relevant," she retorted. "How is my age connected in any way to what happened this evening?"

"It's just for our records," Ambrose intervened. "We will keep your details in total confidence," he added. He wondered if she was particularly concerned about people knowing her age. Perhaps she was just cross that she'd been left to last, he reflected.

"Oh well I suppose I understand," Heather replied. "My date of birth is 1st September 1907. Since you're sure to ask, I live at 11A Holly Road and I'm a seamstress. I own 'Sew and Sew' – the alterations shop in Chalk Heath," she added.

"Thank you for waiting so long," Ambrose started.

"I'll admit I was beginning to get worried," Heather replied. "I have to be at the shop by 8 tomorrow morning. Or is that later this morning? Anyway my eyes play up if I'm tired. Still, you have to do your job, and I suppose there are a lot of us to talk to," she sighed.

"We'll try to be as brief as possible," Ambrose assured her. "First of all, where were you when the attack took place please?"

"Well, I'm not sure when Marguerite was attacked but it doesn't make any difference. I was in here, working on the costumes, the whole rehearsal."

"You were here the whole night?" Winters looked at Heather closely.

"Yes. I was sitting at the sewing machine there, by the door. I like to see people come and go."

"Thank you, now what can you tell us about Marguerite?" Ambrose said with a glance at Winters.

Winters understood Ambrose was changing tack. They'd come back to this line of questioning later.

116

"I didn't know her that well, to be honest. She seemed nice enough. She was always very polite to me," Heather took off her glasses and started polishing them on her cardigan.

"I heard she had a bit of a go at you earlier," Winters pointed out.

Heather looked surprised as she replaced her glasses. "Now you mention it, I suppose she was a bit short with me."

"What caused that?" Ambrose persisted.

"We had a bit of a disagreement about the outfit I made for her. I followed the measurements exactly, I know I did, but she flew at me for getting them wrong. She's put on weight I'm sure but she almost bit my head off when I suggested that to her. She couldn't possibly be wrong, could she? I shouldn't speak ill of her, not when she's been so hurt, but she forgets I don't get paid." Heather looked angry. "I make their costumes because I enjoy doing it and to help the Players," she added, as an afterthought.

"That's very good of you, I'm sure," Ambrose smiled.

"Do you ever do a bit of sewing on the side, as it were?" Winters asked.

"Occasionally I do when I have some spare material. I got a roll of black cheap at the market. It's not pure cotton but it wears really well. It's got one of those new synthetic fibres in it. I used it for the men's trousers and some of the ladies' outfits. They were all pleased with it. Doug asked me to make him a pair of trousers and Sara got me to make a skirt for her – poor girl, she can't get nice ready-mades her size. I often do a bit of tailoring on the side for the cast. They pay me for it, of course, but I give them a good discount," she added quickly.

Winters continued. "I believe you've been with the group about ten years. You must know everyone well by now. Can you think of any reason Miss Monroe might have been attacked?"

"No. None at all, even if she can be a bit, well, demanding at times. How is she?" Heather frowned.

"There's no news yet I'm afraid," Ambrose replied. He made as if to stand up, before sitting down again suddenly. "Before you go, can I just check one point with you?" He fixed Heather with a stare. "Are you sure you never left this room until you heard Olga stop the rehearsal?"

"Of course I'm sure," Heather replied quickly, but she didn't look Ambrose in the eye.

"Not even to stretch your legs or go to the Ladies?" Winters joined the attack.

"No. I had a lot of sewing to do," Heather shifted uncomfortably on the chair.

"Are you sure you didn't pop out for a moment or two? Think a bit before you reply, Mrs Broomhead," Ambrose sounded grave. "If you lie to us it could be a serious offence. Remember, we've interviewed everyone else already."

Heather started then looked around her, as if to see if anyone was standing behind her. "I don't want to get into any trouble. It's just that ... I'm not sure. I may have gone out for a minute," she mumbled.

Winters could sense they were nearly there. "Could someone have seen you outside this room?" he asked.

Heather looked extremely uncomfortable. "Perhaps I did pop out – but it was only for five minutes."

"Where did you go?" Ambrose maintained his stare.

Heather was completely flustered. "To the back door, for a breath of fresh air," she stuttered. "And to go to the toilet."

"Now that's interesting," Winters replied. "Did you see anyone else there? It's just possible the assailant came in that way."

"No," Heather was starting to stammer, "but I wasn't there long, really I wasn't."

With a smile, Winters felt sure he was on the right track. "It's just that we found some cigarette butts outside that door. Could it be that you went out for a quick smoke?"

"There's no harm in admitting it," Ambrose joined in. "I imagine several of the Players smoke when they're not on stage. And we know the theatre won't let anyone smoke back here."

"I don't smoke. Honestly, I just went to the toilet!" Heather nearly shouted.

"Then who was smoking out there?" Winters persisted. "Some of the cigarette ends we found had lady's lipstick on them."

"But I don't wear lipstick," Heather replied. Winters could see she was clearly telling the truth. He didn't think Heather was wearing any makeup at all.

Ambrose put on his most charming smile. "I promise you we'll keep anything you tell us confidential, if we find it's not relevant to the attack on Marguerite."

Heather paused, as if uncertain what to say. With a sigh, she continued. "I popped out the back just the once. I've already told you: I only went to the toilet. I wasn't away more than 10 minutes, at the most."

Winters was confused. He'd been expecting Heather to admit to meeting someone out there. He thought back to the cigarette butts. He'd been convinced Heather was responsible for some and her mystery man for the rest. It looked like he was on totally the wrong track.

"I don't understand: why all the secrecy?" Winters asked finally.

"I don't like talking about personal issues," Heather replied, reddening.

"Did you see Douglas Moody in his room when you popped out?" Ambrose continued.

There was another long pause before Heather replied. "That's funny. I'm not sure. I could hear his kettle boiling but I don't remember him sitting at his work desk. He must have been bending down, or at one of the cupboards. Still, I rushed out and back again, so I wasn't really looking that way. Besides, I would have heard him leave his room. He always make such a noise with all those keys in his jacket."

Ambrose rose to escort Heather out. "Thank you, Mrs Broomhead. That will be all," he said. "You're free to go home but we will need you to sign your statement tomorrow." Ambrose gestured to the PC on the door, noticing with surprise that PC Sutton was still absent.

"Thank you, Inspector," Heather replied. At this range, Ambrose was struck with the full force of the lavender. He wondered if Heather even gargled with it.

Winters waited just long enough for the door to close, then scratched his head. "So what was that all about?" he asked.

"Maybe Mrs Broomhead had a bit of a, well, problem," Ambrose replied delicately.

"You mean a problem in the toilet department?" Winters smiled. He was startled by a knock on the door. WPC Meadows was cautiously opening it, peering in at the two detectives.

"Sorry, sir," Meadows started. "I've found something you might find interesting," she continued, glancing down at the hessian bag in her hands. She was surprised it was Winters who beckoned her in.

"So what have you found?" Ambrose looked at the young WPC.

"It was just a hunch, sir. My grandmother was exactly the same. I mean all the lavender. When I smelled Mrs Broomhead, I just wondered if the scent was to cover something else up."

"Go on," Winters prompted.

WPC Meadows seemed to gain in confidence. "Well I checked the outside lavatory. Did Mrs Broomhead admit she'd been out there this evening?"

"She did indeed. Eventually," Ambrose replied. "That's hardly a crime though," he smiled.

"No, I dare say no crime has been committed at all," Meadows conceded. "But Mrs Broomhead may have been out there quite some time."

"What makes you say that?" Winters was curious.

"I found this sir," Meadows opened the bag to reveal its contents. "It was in the cistern. I've dried it as best I can but it's still a little damp. You can tell someone had stood on the rim of the toilet. I'm about the same height as Mrs Broomhead, sir, and I was able to reach it quite easily."

Winters started laughing. Leaning forwards, he took the large bottle of whisky from WPC Meadows.

"So all we need to know is how quickly Mrs Broomhead drinks and whether this bottle was full to start with," Winters opened the bottle and sniffed its contents. He wrinkled his nose with displeasure. "Then we'd be able to work out how long Mrs Broomhead was out there for."

"I can help on the second point sir," Meadows replied. She handed Winters a receipt. "I found this in the waste paper in the lavatory. I'd say the bottle was full when Mrs Broomhead bought it earlier this evening."

"So she's had about two inches in total," Ambrose noted. "That must have taken her a little while. Isn't it any good?" he asked Winters, who was still trying to get the smell out of his nostrils.

"Let's put it this way, sir," Winters replied. "I'd rather drink Mrs Broomhead's lavender water!"

"That's what put me on to her," Meadows admitted. "My grandmother would use perfume as a mouth wash to hide the smell of alcohol," she explained.

"I thought you Methodists were meant to be teetotal," Winters pointed out, but with good humour.

"Granny was a Baptist," Meadows replied with a smile.

"I wonder why Mr Moody told us Mrs Broomhead was in her room all the time?" Ambrose mused.

"Because he knew she liked a quick tipple and wouldn't want people to know?" Winters suggested.

"Perhaps …" Ambrose stood, turning the bottle slowly as he pondered. "By the way," he said suddenly. "Where *is* PC Sutton?"

"Ah, well, yes," WPC Meadows seemed lost for words. With a quick intake of breath, she decided the best idea was just to come out with it. "He's taking Mr Lyndon back to his flat. He would have done it earlier, but he had to take Kathy Black home first."

Seeing Ambrose's look of surprise, WPC Meadows explained. "When you'd finished with Miss Black, she went to find her husband to drive her back. It's quite a walk to her house and it's far too late for someone as pretty as her to be walking the streets on her own."

"What happened to her husband?" Ambrose asked, confused.

"It seems he had to take his mother home first," WPC Meadows replied, meaningfully.

"You mean he took his mother but left his wife here to get home by herself?" Winters was astonished.

Meadows nodded. "Miss Black was really upset, I'm afraid. She was going to wait for her husband to come back, but well, we thought it would be easier for one of us to run her home. We hadn't realised that you'd also want us to take Mr Lyndon to his flat. Fortunately he was happy to wait for PC Sutton to return."

"And PC Sutton kindly volunteered to take the fair Kathy home first," Winters noted drily. "Let's hope he doesn't forget that she's Mrs Black, not Miss Black."

"If her husband carries on like that much longer, he may find he's single again very soon!" Ambrose replied.

CHAPTER TWENTY-ONE

Winters entered with two slightly chipped mugs of tea.

"You're a marvel," Ambrose breathed in the aroma. "Where on earth did you find tea at this time of the night?"

"Well, to be perfectly honest, you owe your thanks to WPC Meadows. She heard that there's a kettle in the technician's room and made a brew."

Ambrose was indeed grateful. "So where are we now? We've interviewed everyone I believe."

"That's right, we have. I'm not sure if we've quite finished with everyone though," Winters replied.

"Probably not," Ambrose agreed. "But we can't keep them all here much longer. I don't suppose WPC Meadows made tea for everyone did she?"

"Of course, sir," Winters smiled. "We take good care of our suspects, even if one of them did try to commit murder."

"Quite. Sadly we're no nearer to understanding why someone would want to bump off Miss Monroe. She's clearly disliked by some and others feel she was nowhere near as good an actress as she'd have them believe. But I can't really see that being enough to try to get rid of her. Besides, all her attempts at 'blackmail' seem pretty amateurish."

"I'm also not sure we know exactly how that fire extinguisher was used to bash her head in," Winters mused. He looked up as PC Sutton entered the room.

"Oh so you're back now, are you?" Winters demanded.

"Don't be so hard on the boy," Ambrose intervened. He felt so much better with a mug of tea in his hands. "He was just doing young Kathy a good service." He turned towards the PC. "Has her husband reappeared yet?"

PC Sutton shook his head. He handed Winters a document without saying a word.

"Perhaps the background checks will help, sir," Winters said as he passed the dossier over.

Ambrose started flicking through the pages, vaguely aware there was an additional presence in the room. Surprised, he looked up at PC Sutton.

"Sorry sir," the PC looked embarrassed. "It's just that some of the others are asking when I can drive them home."

"Really?" Ambrose looked amused. "We're not offering a taxi service. Perhaps you can kindly tell everyone that we should hopefully be finished here in about an hour." He paused then changed his mind. "No, tell them they can go home now, but I will need them all to be present at the station tomorrow morning to sign their statements. Make sure they know where to go and fix a time with each of them."

Ambrose glanced at his watch. As an afterthought he added, "You can drive the women home. The rest are perfectly capable of getting themselves back."

"The only woman still here is the rather indomitable Olga Greenbaum," Winters noted. "She's probably more capable of looking after herself than some of the men!"

"Offer her a lift anyway," Ambrose smiled.

PC Sutton hurried out to pass on the news, banging the door on his way out. Ambrose didn't look up. He was now engrossed. "Hmm, I don't recall asking for background checks on Archie Framilode or Douglas Moody." He raised both eyebrows.

"Ah sir, didn't you?" Winters feigned surprise.

"No, I didn't. But I'm rather glad you did. Look at this."

Winters peered over. "So, Mr Moody has rather large debts does he?"

"Hmm, our technical expert likes illegal gambling," Ambrose replied. "It seems he's quite a regular at that warehouse down on Wood Street. You know the one with the poker games and casino that we keep trying to close down. Mr Moody was picked up in two of our raids last year. This bit about our director is rather interesting too. The Law Society struck his father off for embezzling client funds. Oh dear, oh dear."

"That is rather embarrassing for an upstanding pillar of the community, wouldn't you say?" Winters noted. "I bet he doesn't tell everyone about it."

"I suspect not," Ambrose agreed. "Goodness!" he suddenly sat bolt upright.

"Are you ok sir?"

"You were quite right there was more to Frank Thomas than he was letting on. Listen to this. His name is actually Frank Thomas Lucas. He dropped the last name after he was prosecuted five years ago."

"What was he up for?" Winters asked.

"He was accused of killing twenty people in the Dagenham West crash. He was the train driver."

"And he was let off?" Winters was surprised.

"He was found not guilty," Ambrose corrected him. "It's not clear why."

"That is extremely interesting, sir. Perhaps we'd better ask him. Particularly given he's our suspect with the closest thing to absolutely no alibi."

"Quite. I suggest we speak to Mr Moody, Mr Thomas and our director again tomorrow, under caution, to see what they have to say for themselves."

"Should I let them know?" asked Winters.

"No, just let them think they're signing their statements like everyone else. I don't want to warn them, just in case any of them makes a bolt for it," Ambrose replied. "I don't think there's any risk of that at present though."

They both looked up, surprised, as the door flew open. Michael Black was standing in the doorway, out of breath and slightly dishevelled.

"Can we help you, Mr Black?" Winters asked politely.

"Where's my wife? I can't find her," Michael gasped.

Ambrose walked over and laid a hand on Michael's arm. "It's alright," Ambrose assured him. "One of our PCs ran her home earlier. She's probably safe in bed now. Hadn't you better drive home and join her?"

"Oh that's a relief," Michael blurted. "It's not my fault, really it isn't," he seemed eager to explain. "Mother insisted I take her home after my interview. I told her we had to wait for Kathy but Mother was feeling ill. I had to wait with her for the GP to arrive. I couldn't leave Mother all on her own," he finished.

Winters raised an eyebrow. "You ended up leaving one of the women in your life on her own, sir."

There was silence. Michael looked dejected.

"Yes I know. Mother always thinks she's more important than Kathy," he admitted. "I'm really not sure what to do about it."

"Go home," Ambrose said, not unkindly. He wasn't sure he was the right person to start giving out marriage advice.

They waited while Michael left the room. He was clearly distressed. Ambrose turned back to the papers he'd been reading.

"There's also some information here about Miss Monroe. Can you read it out?" He handed Winters a single page document, then sat back rubbing his weary eyes.

"Hmm, well Marguerite Monroe has only been her name for the last eleven years. She changed it by deed poll. I wonder if Archie was the one to deal with that," Winters queried.

"That's quite possible."

"The best bit is her previous name. I can see why she changed it." Winters added. "Betty Fagg doesn't have quite the same ring to it as Marguerite Monroe does it?" He was amused. "This bit is interesting too. Between 1932 and 1945 Betty Fagg worked as a secretary at the Law Society."

"Did she now? Was she a professional actress before that?" asked Ambrose.

"Well, she worked at Drury Lane theatre between 1916 and 1932 alright," Winters paused for dramatic effect, "but not as an actress."

"Really? What did she do?"

"She was a seamstress," Winters grinned.

126

CHAPTER TWENTY-TWO

"Didn't think we'd be seeing you again tonight," Sgt Bob Hurst said as WPC Meadows signed in at the desk. "Been some trouble at the theatre, I hear." He stubbed out his cigarette in the glass ashtray.

"The leading lady's been attacked," WPC Meadows confirmed, unbuttoning her jacket. After coming in from the November night, the 'nick' was comfortingly warm and snug.

"What happened? Someone threw a tomato at her? Was she really that bad?"

Meadows smiled, glancing up at the clock. It was exactly two am. She had another four hours of her shift left. Hopefully there would be no more calls. She'd like to write up her notes and then take things easy. She was also looking forward to breakfast at the Copper Kettle. With any luck she wouldn't be eating on her own. Perhaps PC Sutton would be able to join her.

"It must have been something heavier than a tomato," she replied. "It stove her head in. And it was at a rehearsal, not a performance."

"Blimey! Those theatrical types do get carried away, don't they?" Sergeant Hurst grinned. He was a good desk sergeant: always ready with a joke and a cigarette, even on a foggy November night, yet efficient and reliable. "You'll be needing to write up your report I suppose?" he hinted. "If you want a bit of quiet, Cell Two's vacant. Not much else for you to do at the moment."

Nodding, WPC Meadows opened the charge book. It had been a slow night. Most people were safely tucked up at home away from the fog. There was a 'Drunk & Disorderly' in Cell One sleeping it off, and two of her colleagues had gone out to a 'domestic' on Park Street half an hour ago.

Sergeant Hurst saw her reading the entry. "Neighbour rang," he explained. "Reckoned she could hear a bloke shouting he'd kill his so-and-so wife. Jennings and Hemmingway have gone up to sort him out. We're a bit short-handed tonight, what with Jim Parsons off sick."

WPC Meadows nodded. "Give me a call if you need me," she said, and went down the corridor towards the cells. As she passed, she peered through the grill into Cell One. A dishevelled old man was lying on the floor, snoring, a battered hat squashed over his eyes to keep out the light. He wasn't going to cause trouble for a while. She should be able to get her report done quickly.

For half an hour Meadows sat on the bench in the empty cell, smoking and writing up her notes of the events at Chalk Heath Theatre. Twice the telephone at the desk rang. She heard PCs Hamilton and Jenkins returning and then going out on another call: a break-in at one of the warehouses.

For a few moments longer she smoked quietly, thinking about the attack on Miss Monroe, and the members of the cast she had spoken to. She thought in particular of Alex Baker-Smythe and wondered if she had been right about him. She hoped she hadn't done the man an injustice. He really was good-looking and very pleasant. As her mother often said, it was always the way – the nice ones were spoken for or not available. Not that Mum had much hope of her ever finding a husband. "What man would want to marry a police woman?" she had demanded only last week. "He'd be afraid you were going to arrest him. And he'd be too nervous to say anything in case you used it in evidence against him!"

Smiling, Meadows remembered the family's horror when she had announced that she wanted to join the police force. And as for the training! Her mother was certain no woman could learn self defence without turning into a Russian javelin thrower.

"What *would* she say if she knew I was on another murder case?" WPC Meadows wondered wryly. "Not a suitable subject for a young woman!" or something equally damning. If she knew just half of what her daughter had done during the past year...

"And loved almost every minute," WPC Meadows added, to herself. She would love it all if only some of her male colleagues would stop treating her like the little woman at home or a threat to their egos. She was definitely not a real part of the Force as far as they were concerned. And she was getting fed up of always being the one to deal with bereaved women or children who'd become separated from their parents at the market. DI Winters, now ... she had definitely got off on the wrong foot with him. Still, she had to admit that some of that was partly her fault.

Outside, the telephone was ringing again. Realizing that she must be the only officer left to respond to a call, Meadows went to the front desk to see if she was needed. Sgt Hurst put his hand over the

128

mouthpiece and beckoned her forward. "Traffic accident," he whispered, "near the old Chalk Heath Arms."

Sgt Hurst was scribbling rapidly. "Yes, ma'am," he said twice. "Yes, I've got that. From the window? I see. Thank you for telling us. The ambulance will be on its way by now. I'll send one of our officers out and you can tell her what you saw."

He turned to Meadows. "Sorry," he said, "You're the only one left. Corner of old Chalk Heath Road and Meadow Lane. Near the pub. Two cars side on. The landlady at the Arms phoned it in. The bang woke her up and she saw the mess out of her bedroom window. Her husband's giving first aid until the ambulance arrives. I've told her you'll take a statement, but if she didn't actually see what happened it won't help much. Still, you'll make her feel better."

At once WPC Meadows did up her jacket again. She looked at the keys of the only remaining car. "Can I drive up there?" she asked. "It's a bit far to cycle."

"Go on, then," Sergeant Hurst nodded. "I know you'll be careful with the car. Just don't let PC Sutton anywhere near the driving seat!"

Smiling, she popped the keys in her pocket.

"Go up to the hospital afterwards, if you think it's worth it," Sgt Hurst called as she went though the door. "Have a chat to the two drivers if they're fit enough. Why they can't avoid each other at two thirty in the morning on an empty road, God only knows!"

Leaving the Station car park behind her, WPC Meadows drove though the darkened town. As cars weren't allowed in Victoria Park, she couldn't drive that way, not even for an emergency. Instead she turned right onto Moor Lane, taking the long route towards the old village, the heath brooding darkly to her left. Streetlights had been switched off by now and great pools of shadow lay beyond the car's headlights. At night, the heath was a black, foreboding space that seemed to return to the wild whenever the citizens of Chalk Heath slept. Clumps of gorse crouched like animals by the side of the road.

The new town hadn't yet stretched this far, adding to the sense of emptiness beyond the fringes of urban development. Very few people lived this side of the open country, most having chosen to move into the houses clustered around the railway station, shops and businesses built in the 1930s. The few occupied houses in old Chalk Heath were in total darkness, their inhabitants sound asleep. Once, this had been the centre of life in the area, but now the old village was marooned on the wrong side of the heath. These days it was nothing more than a quaint place for a Sunday afternoon stroll or drink at the pub.

Watching out for stray dogs or foxes, WPC Meadows drove on towards the Chalk Heath Arms. The road ahead was even darker, heading towards the eight miles or so of open country before Jenners Park. WPC Meadows was very glad she had the security of a car around her. When she got there, however, the Chalk Heath Arms was ablaze with light, the door wide open and curtains pulled back. An ambulance had arrived, casting an eerie blue glow to the hedges either side of the junction. The crew was already dealing with the two drivers. Both were wrapped in blankets and sitting on the pavement outside the pub. Mercifully neither seemed badly hurt. One was even fit enough to protest, several times. "It was that idiot's fault," he insisted, "not mine. He should have seen me!"

As Sgt Hurst had predicted, the landlady's evidence was not actually a lot of use. She had not seen the impact, only heard its result. So, after taking her statement, and thanking her for her co-operation, WPC Meadows set off to the hospital. She had found before that it was a good idea to speak to drivers involved in an accident straight away, if they were able to talk. You had more hope of finding out the truth then, before they had time to invent excuses. Sgt Hurst had said she could go if she wanted. It was nice to think that he trusted her judgment.

Meadows drove behind the ambulance, watching its revolving light dancing on the road ahead. The crew hadn't turned on the emergency bells. There was no point waking up the neighbourhood for these two 'patients'; they weren't sufficiently injured.

The accident and emergency department at Chalk Heath Hospital was busy, even at three thirty am. The drivers were taken to a waiting area, and after they had been checked over and declared non-emergency, they were left to wait their turn, lying on trolley beds. It was fortunate that they were in separate cubicles, for by now both had regained enough strength to be very angry.

"I was just driving back from a meal out, minding my own business, when this fellow flew round the corner, straight into me," Driver One, Mr Jones, declared when WPC Meadows was allowed to talk to him. He was dressed in a suit, still in his jacket and tie, and had appearances on his side. Meadows detected a faint smell of whisky on his breath, however, and made sure she jotted that down in her notes.

Driver Two, Mr Morton, was equally insistent that he had been minding his own business, driving home, when this stupid idiot slammed straight into him. Ruined his new car too. He looked far less respectable than Mr Jones, a faded duffle coat covering baggy flannels and an open necked shirt. He smelt of menthol rather than alcohol. "Catarrh," he explained. WPC Meadows had her doubts about him too. When she found a roll of menthol cough sweets in his pocket, with the wrapping evidently hurriedly torn open, her doubts increased.

"How on earth is a magistrate going to decide between them?" she asked herself. "I'll bet they've both been out drinking somewhere." Which raised an interesting question: where could either man have bought alcohol in the early hours of the morning, long after closing time? Unless of course they had both been to private parties …

She was still considering the issue when she saw a man come into the waiting area, supporting an older woman. "We need a doctor," he said urgently to the nurse. "My mother's having a heart attack!"

Immediately the nurse was running to the woman's assistance, almost pushing people out of the way. A buzzer sounded. Another nurse appeared from behind a screen. A doctor came striding through a pair of swing doors.

Impressed, WPC Meadows stood watching their efficiency, being careful to keep out of the way. She hadn't yet finished interviewing the two drivers but the woman seemed familiar. And so did the man with her.

Suddenly she recognized them both. It was Michael Black, and his mother, Brenda. Only a few hours ago she had been talking to them at the theatre.

Though she ought really to be continuing taking statements from the two drivers, WPC Meadows walked across to Michael. She wanted to speak to him, to check that he and his mother were all right. She saw Michael look up and recognize her in return.

It took no more than ten minutes for Mrs Black to be admitted to a ward and for her son to be left outside. Meadows guided him towards one of the seats in the corridor. His face was grey with tiredness and worry.

"Your mother will be ok," Meadows assured him, sitting down beside him. "She's in the right place now. What happened? She seemed fine when she left the theatre with you."

"She wasn't," Michael Black insisted. "Or at least she said she felt ill as soon as I took her back home. I had to call the doctor. That's why I was too late to take Kathy home." He rubbed his hand across his forehead in a weary gesture. "I should have stayed with her then," he continued. "She has angina, you see, and stress often brings on one of her attacks. But the doctor said she was just tired, and I couldn't leave Kathy on her own much longer ..." His voice tailed off in despair.

"Is Kathy on her own now?" WPC Meadows asked. She was beginning to feel as much sympathy for the young wife as the husband.

"Yes. Mother rang half an hour ago and woke us up. She said she was much worse, and needed me to come at once."

"Why didn't you call an ambulance?"

"Mother said she didn't want to make a big fuss and I should bring her myself. The taxi service wouldn't have come out this late at night. And honestly, I didn't think she was that bad – not until we came in through the door just now. She seemed to get a lot worse suddenly."

Glancing at the man beside her, WPC Meadows began to visualize a marriage made up of three people: the husband, new wife, and husband's mother. She wondered just how ill Mrs Black really was, or whether her 'turns' were a way of continuing to control her son.

"It's the stress I suppose," Michael added. "She's always worse when she gets upset about things. I should have realized she'd be very disturbed by what had happened to poor Marguerite. Having you lot around won't have helped. You have to do your job, I know, but tonight's not been very pleasant."

"Even less pleasant for Miss Monroe I imagine," Meadows pointed out quietly.

"Yes – oh, I know... Please don't misunderstand me," Michael apologized. "It's just that I'm so worried about my mother."

A nurse came out to speak to him. "Your mother seems fine now," she said. "Probably just a bit of indigestion. When you've got angina it's easy to panic and think you're having an attack. Still, we'll keep her in for the night, under observation. You go home now and get a bit of sleep. Ring up in the morning and we'll tell you what time you can pick your mother up. It'll depend on when the consultant does his rounds."

As if half asleep, Michael Black got up obediently and looked round for his jacket. WPC Meadows went with him to the door. "Do you think you're fit to drive?" she asked.

"I'll be fine," he assured her. "Once I get out into the cold air I'll be wide awake. I need to get back to Kathy. She'll be worried and upset too."

"Furious, more like", WPC Meadows added to herself. "I would be if my husband left me alone twice in one night, to see his darling mother." She kept her thoughts to herself, however, merely checking that Mr Black did indeed wake up once the cold air at the front door had hit his face.

Before she could leave the hospital herself, she still had a couple of questions to ask the drivers. There was a stop sign on Meadow Lane. Had Mr Jones seen it? And what about the twenty-mile an hour limit on the bend in Chalk Heath Road, just before the junction? What speed did Mr Morton think he was doing as he came down the hill? That should tell her whether either driver (or both) was paying enough attention.

It took her only a few moments to go back to the two drivers and ask her questions. By now both were calmer. Mr Jones was almost dozing. Mr Morton complained about how long they were being kept waiting for a doctor to see them. He had broken his leg he was sure, though he showed remarkably little sign of pain.

As WPC Meadows was leaving, she paused. Then, on an impulse, she went back towards the ward where Mrs Black had been settled for the night. Curiously, she glanced through the glass doors, trying to see where the woman had been put. Most of the beds were occupied by sleeping forms, some propped up on pillows. There was movement beside one of the beds near the door, however, and Meadows recognized Mrs Black sitting up against the iron bedstead. She was talking to a nurse, and seemed to be asking her to do something. Then she reached in her handbag and took out a small envelope. Quickly, the nurse put it in the pocket of her uniform, under her apron.

It seemed such a strange thing for a nurse to do, and ducking back so that she could not be seen, WPC Meadows lingered, still watching. Mrs Black reached into her bag again, and this time took out her purse. At that angle it was impossible to tell what she took out of it, but it could well be a bank note. The nurse took that too, and pushed it into her pocket. Then she turned towards the door.

Only just avoiding being seen, WPC Meadows darted to one side, and through a nearby door marked 'Gentlemen'.

Fortunately there was no gentleman inside, and after a quick glance outside to see no one was watching, WPC Meadows came out, and walked briskly back down the corridor. That was most interesting, she reflected. She must tell DI Ambrose what she'd seen.

CHAPTER TWENTY-THREE

DS Winters turned his key slowly, grimacing at the noise it made. At once the front door swung inwards with a creak. He had been meaning to oil the hinges for weeks but had not yet found the time. Every nerve in his body was screwed tight, his hearing so acute it almost hurt.

After such a long shift, Winters' whole body longed for sleep. His co-ordination had long ago deserted him. His fingers were stiff with cold. It would have been far easier to ring the doorbell, but that would have woken everyone, and he just *had* to get to bed silently. The consequences of making too much noise didn't bear thinking about. Praying that the door would not swing back as usual, he managed to shut it quietly behind him. Tip-toeing through to the lounge, he breathed a cautious sigh of relief.

His relief was short-lived. No matter how hard he tried to be quiet, it seemed his house - even his clothes - were against him. One of his shoes clumped to the floor when he eased it off. His keys rattled as he placed them carefully on the sideboard. His coat slid off the banister, the buttons clanking on the bare linoleum. Hastily he hung it back up, desperate not to jangle the coins in his pockets. At each and every sound, Winters flinched, and paused to listen to the silence around him.

The bottom stair groaned slightly as he put his foot on it. "Jerry built!" Winters thought angrily. The house might be only two years old, but it was all show. The rather grand hallway, with its fancy glass panel above the door, was far too large. It made the other rooms seem disappointingly small. His mind leapt sideways for a second or two. Now if you could just keep your guests in the hallway, he thought, they might be impressed. Mind you, the lounge wasn't bad. His sister had been really impressed with the bay window. She didn't see the way it leaked after last year's snow, though. At least his little house on Blenheim Terrace had good floorboards and solid wooden doors that fitted properly, even if it had become far too small for a growing family....

It was probably inevitable. Lack of concentration caught up with him. Winters trod on the fourth stair without thinking about it. The stair that always creaked on its way down and snapped back as your weight left it. The stair that could act as a guard dog, he'd frequently joked. Except now he wasn't laughing. He paused with his foot in the air, not even noticing that he was holding his breath.

Suddenly there was the sound he had dreaded. First a small grizzle or two, then a cough, and finally a full-scale wail. The baby was awake.

Immediately there was the pad pad of his wife's slippered feet on the landing above him, and a boy's voice calling to her, "Is Dadda home?"

"Sshht!" he heard his wife whisper angrily. "Go back to sleep, Patrick."

"Caitlin woke me -" Patrick complained.

"And me!" little Seann added from the depths of his eiderdown in the next bed.

The boys' older sister Bridget suddenly appeared at the door of the bedroom she shared with Caitlin, holding her hands over her ears. "Can't you make her shut up?" she asked bitterly. "I'm fed up with being woken when she cries! It's the third time tonight."

Caitlin was in the process of waking the whole street, wailing like a small banshee. Winters could almost hear the lights going on in nearby houses and the tutting neighbours turning in their beds. Since he could hardly have caused more chaos if he'd tried, he walked normally upstairs and into the bedroom. Too tense to get straight into bed, he sat on the edge of the mattress with his head in his hands, listening as the wailing slowly turned back to a grizzle, and then to silence. He heard Bridget grumbling as she got back into bed and the two boys settling down again to sleep.

He was still sitting there when Francesca returned and closed the bedroom door. "What time you call this?" she demanded. The last word was stretched to 'thisse' by her strong Italian accent. Winters used to love the way she spoke. Now it irritated him. She ought to have learnt to speak decent English by now he thought. They'd been married and living in England for nearly ten years now.

"I'm sorry, Fran," he began softly. "A case came in just as I was about to leave - a woman had been attacked. I had to go."

"Why?" his wife whispered back. "Why you not able to go home like any other man? Why you not able to see your sick baby?"

"DI Ambrose -" Winters began but was cut off immediately.

"DI Ambrose," Fran mocked. "DI Ambrose, that is all I hear. You not marry him and bring him to a foreign country! He is your boss, not your wife, or your children!"

"Look I'm sorry," Winters said again, almost pleading. "I tried so hard not to make a noise, but that bloody stair always creaks. You know what it's like." He could almost see the funny side of the situation but knew better than to smile now. Tomorrow perhaps his wife would laugh with him, but not now.

"Why you always working?"

"Because I have to do over-time," he pointed out. "so that we can afford this house." He knew that always won any argument with Fran. She knew the fragile state of their finances probably better than he did.

"How's Caitlin been?" he asked, trying to smooth things over.

"Cry, cry, cry," Fran retorted. "Not that you would care."

"Did you call the doctor?" Winters asked, ignoring the gibe.

"She no need Doctor. Just sleep," was the sullen reply.

Winters found his concern making way for irritation. "You should call the doctor if you're worried," he insisted. "You know it's free in this country, and he won't make you feel like a foreigner, or inferior; that's just your imagination."

"Imagination!" Fran repeated furiously. "The man is, how you say? a snob. If Mama were here she would deal with him." Her voice was rising in anger and distress.

"Shush-" Winters whispered. "You'll wake the little 'un again." He put his finger gently to his wife's mouth, but she dashed his hand from her. She was too angry to be pacified.

A wail rose from the next room and they looked at each other in despair. "Not again," Winters said resignedly.

"She's got a cold. She not breathe properly. You go to her this time," his wife insisted. "You make her to sleep." Getting back into bed she pulled the blankets over her face pointedly.

Sighing, Winters went into the other room. He dared not switch the landing light on, or it would wake the two boys by now asleep again in their bunks in the little box room. There was no moon that night and the lamps in the street outside had gone out, so he had to feel his way through the doors into the bedroom Bridget and Caitlin shared. There, a small nightlight was burning in a dish, and he could just about see what he was doing. Careful not to wake his elder daughter in the bed near the window, he took his baby out of her cot.

Awkwardly, he rocked her, trying to soothe her. He felt as if she might break in his arms. He was no good with babies. Women were good with them, as Nature intended, not men. When he was young, his mother had had a new baby almost every other year, but if they cried he had always had a sister to push him out of the way with a cheerful "Here, let me..." Winters loved all four of his children dearly, but he had to admit he coped far better with the older ones now they were becoming people. This fretful little one, so often sick, almost frightened him. He did not know what to do with her.

Finally, though, the grizzling did stop, and Caitlin was asleep in his arms. Very carefully, Winters laid her back in her cot. Then he tiptoed back onto the hall, careful not to wake any of his children, now all happily asleep.

Though the candle in the other room had only given a pale glow, it took Winters' eyes a moment to adjust to the darkness on the landing. He dared not switch the light on, in case it woke Fran when he opened the bedroom door. As he felt his way forwards, he tripped over the pillow and blanket left in front of him. Stumbling, he cursed under his breath as he tried the door. Fran had locked him out.

"Fran!!" he whispered hoarsely, but there was no answer. Any louder and he would wake all four children again. He had no choice but to gather up the bedding and trail it downstairs into the lounge.

For several minutes, Winters sat on the settee, with the blanket wrapped round him, too angry to lie down. He would be on duty again in a few hours, trying to look as though he was fresh and efficient, while his head pounded for lack of sleep. What he'd have done if Fran had finally opened the door he was not sure. Many men would have hit their wives with far less provocation. He had often been called out to 'domestics' that proved to be about almost nothing – a dinner that wasn't cooked properly or a quarrel over the housekeeping. He would never lay a hand on his wife, but the fury would have been hard to hold inside him.

Gradually though, Winters calmed down. "Try to see it from her point of view" he told himself. That always helped. It couldn't be fun, coping with four children under eight in a foreign land, with no family to help. He knew she missed her Mama dreadfully, but there was no way they had space for his mother-in-law to stay with them. He wasn't sure he could face the endless Italian chatter and pasta for long either.

The English winter was also so different to what Fran was used to. The fog of the last few days would have made everything even more depressing. How must she be feeling now? She would not be asleep however much she pretended. No, she would be crying quietly into her pillow. Whenever they had a row like this, her eyes would be red and puffy by morning. And he had to admit he still loved his exotic wife, despite her temper.

Finally Winters started feeling less sorry for himself. He would have to take Fran back to see her family next summer, even if that did mean more over-time. Her family had never seen little Caitlin, apart from a few photographs. Settling down on the settee, he tried to sleep. He must get at least a few hours or he wouldn't think straight the next day. DI Ambrose didn't suffer fools lightly.

"Count sheep or something," Winters told himself. Instead, he found his mind going over how he and Fran had met, and how his heart had felt it would burst with love for her. She was so beautiful and so brave, hiding British soldiers in the loft while the Nazis searched beneath. Not just once, but several times, helping the Patriots to smuggle them out to Switzerland. And after the Italians surrendered, she and her family had been so good to the exhausted soldiers waiting for fresh orders near them, though it had caused trouble with the priest, and the Signore at the Palazzo above the village.

He had never forgotten his Francesca, and he had kept his promise to come back for her, though it had taken him five years to save up the money to travel back to Italy. She had braved the suspicions of his family: the jokes about 'Ities', and the lies about Italian soldiers only knowing how to retreat. She had done her best to settle into English suburbia, too, though he knew she hated it. He too detested the twitching curtains and the neighbours who sniffed when he and his family set off to Mass each Sunday.

To his surprise, Winters found himself looking back to the war almost with pleasure. It was a terrible thing to say, he admitted, but it was the happiest time of his life. Signing up as a Regular was one of his best decisions, but joining the Military Police had been a stroke of genius, even if he did say so himself. Being an MP had given him a bit of control over what he did, and over others; not like the poor conscripts, sent wherever their officers wanted. And joining the police force as soon as his service ended, that had been another good decision, however long the hours, and even if he had just spent half the night questioning a lot of daft theatrical types.

He ought to be thinking about the case, Winters reminded himself, not about the past. It would look good if he could come up with some new ideas for DI Ambrose in the morning. Now, which of the suspects had the most likely motive? Frank Thomas perhaps? Or Douglas something. Moody, wasn't it? That was it, Moody by name and moody by nature. Or was it the Olga, the striking super-efficient German? Or Archie what-was-his-name? Dramiflode? No, that wasn't right.

The names began to jumble in Winters' mind until, stretched out on the settee, he fell asleep.

Act 2

CHAPTER TWENTY-FOUR
21st November 7.24am

A smell of cigarette smoke and bacon hit Winters as he opened the door to the 'Copper Kettle'. He breathed in the aroma, the café's warmth welcome against the bitter early morning air. Stallholders hurried past him towards the market, their breath billowing in small wispy clouds. Making his way to the counter, Winters nodded at the young girl clearing tables.

The owner, Doreen Stanley, fixed him with her usual smile. Her long dark hair was held back by a headscarf, wound like a Sultan's turban. Glancing him up and down she laughed gently as she passed him a steaming mug of camp coffee. Nodding with gratitude, he poured in the warm milk, using a teaspoon to stop the skin falling into his mug.

"Late night or early morning, love?" Mrs Stanley grinned, wiping her hands on her frilly apron.

"Both," Winters sighed heavily.

He ordered his breakfast and glanced around the café. He could just see Doreen's husband Les in the kitchen, a blue stripy tea towel tossed over his shoulder, turning endless sausages and flipping the fried eggs.

Looking out of the windows next to the door, Winters could see the Chalk Heath Theatre, now in total darkness. He groaned quietly as he recalled that he'd been there only four hours earlier. Turning to his left, these windows looked over the sleepy market, now slowly awakening. He could see stallholders rubbing their hands for warmth, their voices carrying crisply above the din of metal frames being dropped into place. Shutters were being opened, floors washed, produce displayed. He'd have to pop in there later to buy some flowers for his wife, he realised.

He was perching on a stool at the counter when he spotted them. WPC Meadows and PC Sutton were sitting at the back of the café. Two empty plates showed they'd been there some time. They were now sharing a pack of cigarettes. Winters walked over.

"Mind if I join you?" he asked, pulling back a metal chair as he did so.

"Course not, sir." It was PC Sutton who replied.

Placing his mug on the Formica table, Winters sat down then rubbed his weary eyes.

"Haven't you been home, sir?" WPC Meadows looked at him with concern. Her shift was over now and she was looking forward to a good sleep.

Winters shrugged. "Briefly," he replied. "But I wasn't exactly made welcome." Seeing his two companions' surprise, he explained.

"I woke the baby when I got in, she started screaming, then she got everyone else going. My wife probably won't speak to me for a week!" he sighed. "I grabbed forty winks on the sofa and a change of clothes, then came out for breakfast."

"That's tough, sir," PC Sutton said with feeling.

Winters looked up as young Gladys brought the most welcome sight in the world: his breakfast. Grabbing the ketchup bottle, he smothered his sausages, egg and bacon with his favourite red sauce. Picking up the bread from the side plate, he suddenly stopped mid-bite, unsure whether he was being impolite.

"You carry on, sir," Meadows encouraged him. "It'll do you the power of good!" She decided to stub out her cigarette while he ate. Taking her lead, PC Sutton followed suit.

Munching happily, Winters relaxed. Suddenly everything was right with the world. He cast an eye round at the clientele. He could see the usual early morning crew; Reg the lorry driver (by himself at the table near the door), two coppers from the night shift he didn't know too well plus Eric the market inspector, smoking at the counter.

Winters smiled at the flowery wallpaper, probably once pure white but now a more yellow-brown colour. He took in the scratches on the black Lino floor, the way the steam condensed on the windows behind the grey lace curtains. He grinned at the blackboard with that morning's specials, complete with chalk smudges and spelling errors: "Bacon Sanwich, Ham & Eggs, Fried Bread and Full English Brakefast". He didn't know why they bothered with the board: the menu was the same every day. And they really must teach Gladys to spell, Winters mused. She must surely be the only girl to leave Chalk Heath Secondary Modern without having learnt a thing. In fact, he doubted she'd pass the 11+ even now, at the age of seventeen.

His companions seemed content to let him eat in peace. Pauline Meadows was sipping cocoa. Greg Sutton was stirring sugar into bright orange tea, taken from the big teapot kept warm on the gas stove. Clearly it was time for a new brew. It looked like Sutton's tea would dissolve his teaspoon, if he left it in too long.

It was PC Sutton who finally broke the silence.

"So what's it like working with a hero?" he asked somewhat shyly.

Winters was bemused. Pausing between bacon and egg, he frowned.

"You mean DI Ambrose?" he asked.

Sutton nodded vigorously. "I mean I know the DI is super intelligent, always solving cases and so on, but I was just wondering if he ever talks about *that* day?"

Not sure how to reply, Winters made a show of chewing his sausage. Sensing his discomfort, WPC Meadows decided to intervene.

"He never mentions it at Chapel, so I don't expect he says anything at all about it when he's on a job," she opined.

Grateful, Winters nodded. "He's a very private person," he added quickly.

"But surely he says something, every now and then?" PC Sutton persisted. "I mean I don't even know the full story."

A piece of bread suddenly occupied Winters, so Meadows had to help him out again.

"Look, I'm not sure it's something he really feels that comfortable talking about," she said. "I don't think the DI sees himself as a hero. He was just furious, so I hear, that he was ordered not to go into the hospital after it had been bombed."

Seeing she had both men's rapt attention, Meadows explained.

"Well, this is what I've heard from Stacey Morris at Chapel, who said she got the story from the DI's mother-in-law herself." WPC Meadows paused for a mouthful of cocoa.

"It was in 1944, the DI was living in London. He'd been married just over three years, but not told anyone at first. You see his wife Mary was working on some top-secret code translations at Whitehall and she knew she'd be sacked when she wed. Seems rather stupid to me, if you've got someone as talented as her, a fluent German speaker too, but that's the way it was in those days."

Another swig of cocoa, now almost entirely cold, and Meadows carried on her story.

"Anyway, when Mary was expecting their son in 1943, there was obviously no hiding it towards the end so she had to stop work. She fell pregnant again a year later. She was in the maternity hospital for her final check up before the birth, when a bomb landed. It was almost a direct hit. No one survived above ground but fortunately when the air raids got really bad a few weeks before, they'd moved the delivery suite and examination rooms into the basement. Those below ground were ok but there was a problem: they were all trapped by rubble. Including the pregnant Mary Ambrose and their 11-month old baby son."

"Oh my God," PC Sutton interrupted. "How did they get out?"

"Well DI Ambrose (or Sergeant Ambrose as he was in those days) was on duty that day and he heard the emergency call come through. He knew straight away his family were in the maternity home. The fire brigade had told everyone to keep out but Ambrose couldn't just leave his wife and son trapped in there. So he ignored his orders and went over to the hospital to rescue them, taking a few of his colleagues with him."

A swill and final swig of cocoa, then: "The story is that there was a small transom light into the basement, but those inside were struggling to reach it, what with all the rubble. The fire brigade didn't want to go in for fear the basement ceiling would collapse. Pretty much everything above ground had been destroyed already. So DI Ambrose, despite being the biggest of all the men there, crawled through the window to see how many people were trapped. He found three midwives, four babies with their mothers, and two pregnant women, one of whom was Mary. And as I said, she had her little boy with her too. Anyway, the DI passed his son and the other babies to his colleagues. Then he got those who could make it out the transom light to safety, but there was no way he could get the pregnant women through."

"Gosh!" PC Sutton exclaimed unnecessarily.

"Quite," Meadows agreed. She carried on. "So the DI went looking for another exit and found an old coal hole. It had been boarded up but that didn't stop Ambrose. Not that he'd ever tell you himself, but by the sounds of things it's a good job he's so strong. I don't think many men could have torn the nails out of wooden planks like that."

"Anyway, it was all going fine at first. Ambrose found some old steps in the coal hole, going up to the back yard. He was helping Mary and the other pregnant woman climb out when there was a massive crash. No one's quite sure what happened: it could have been the vibration from another bomb dropped near by. Whatever the reason, suddenly a wall collapsed, completely covering them with bricks. Ambrose was a bit behind and able to get clear, but the women were trapped. The other woman died and Mary was badly injured. And there was no way Ambrose could get up the stairs to carry her out."

"How long were they both trapped like that?" Sutton couldn't help asking.

"Nearly three hours," Meadows replied with a shudder. "Imagine, Mary Ambrose was bleeding heavily, she needed medical help quickly, and no one could get to where she was lying. The fire brigade didn't dare use their machinery, in case that made more debris fall. So the DI had to dig his way to her with his bare hands – and the only light was what came through the rubble! But it was harder than he thought and his skin was almost falling off his fingers when he finally broke through to Mary. They say he still can't stand the sight of grey brick walls."

"That's true," Winters noted, pleased he could contribute. Suddenly things were starting to make sense. Some of DI Ambrose's 'foibles' didn't seem so strange now.

"Anyway," Meadows continued. "DI Ambrose saved Mary's life, but she lost the baby and could never have any more."

"That explains why the DI is so upset with his son rebelling!" Winters exclaimed, realisation dawning on him.

"That's right," Meadows agreed. "Young Joseph has no memory whatsoever of events. I sometimes wonder if he'd have a bit more respect for his parents if he knew what happened. And of course, the Chief Inspector didn't know whether to suspend DI Ambrose for disobeying orders or give him a medal for bravery. In the end, he did neither and no one really talks about what happened that day."

"That's so unfair," PC Sutton almost shouted, drawing Mrs Stanley's attention. Misunderstanding, she came over with a fresh pot of tea.

Embarrassed at the personal service, Sutton took his colleague's cups over to the counter for refills of coffee and cocoa. Somewhat

147

nervously, WPC Meadows leant across the table. She decided to risk speaking to her superior.

"There's something I think I should tell you, sir," she began.

"Oh?"

"I was up at the hospital last night on another case and saw Michael Black bringing his mother in with a heart attack. Only, well...., I wasn't sure how serious it really was. And nor was Michael, I think."

Winters looked up from his toast and marmalade.

"Interesting," he commented.

"What I saw afterwards was even more interesting, sir. I popped back to check how Mrs Black was doing and I saw her give something to one of the nurses. It looked like an envelope but I can't be sure. I was peering through the glass doors. Whatever it was, the nurse hid it in her pocket. Then Mrs Black took a note out of her purse – it could have been a quid but more likely a fiver. She seemed to be paying the nurse to do something with the envelope. I'm not sure whether it's important, but I thought I should tell you."

For several seconds DS Winters considered what the young policewoman had said. She watched his expression anxiously. Finally, he nodded.

"I think it might be very important," he said, "though I don't know how yet. Thank you."

WPC Meadows flushed, intensely relieved. Afterwards, Winters looked almost bashfully at her.

"Look," he said quickly, making the most of PC Sutton's continued absence. "I'm sorry I've been a little, well, *short* with you on occasion."

Meadows smiled wanly. "It's my fault. I sometimes don't think before I speak," she admitted. "I shouldn't have said anything to DI Kirk that day. You know, in that Henley Street poisoning case. I mean it was really none of my business who you interviewed."

"No, you were right," Winters found himself saying. "I hadn't thought things through. I should have realised that the neighbour was a suspect. It's just that I was so certain that the victim's wife was guilty."

He stopped in surprise. He wondered what that said about his thought processes, or for that matter about his marriage. Putting such thoughts to one side, he ignored PC Sutton's return and asked "But how did you know the old dear next door did it?"

"I didn't, not for certain," Meadows replied. "It's just something she said that made me wonder. I took out a pile of books on poisoning symptoms from the library in July. I decided it would be useful to know a bit about it. Before then, I wouldn't have had any idea what it actually looks like when someone dies from arsenic. The neighbour just seemed to know too many details for an innocent little old lady. And then when I found out that two of her dogs had died mysteriously, I realised she'd been practising on the poor animals."

"Disgusting!" PC Sutton interjected, as he put their drinks on the table.

"That case was an eye-opener, I can tell you," WPC Meadows smiled.

"Well, I've learnt something too," Winters said quietly into his new coffee. "Always listen to your colleagues, just in case they spot something you've missed!"

PC Meadows nodded happily. Mystified, PC Sutton glanced at his colleagues. He sensed that the atmosphere between them had eased.

"I'll drink to that!" he said, raising his fresh cup of tea.

CHAPTER TWENTY-FIVE

Chalk Heath was quite attractive by daylight, Ambrose reflected, as his car drove slowly through the town. He could see why families would want to move there from nearby Jenners Park. A series of smart shops, all apparently doing well, surrounded the central square. Although it wasn't yet nine thirty in the morning, the pavements were busy. Clearly, most of Chalk Heath's male population was at work, but housewives hurried along, ready to fill their bags with that day's fresh produce.

A few late scholars ran towards the school, almost colliding with mothers returning from dropping their children off at the front gates. Many of the women were pushing perambulators. There seemed to be a rule Ambrose noted: 'the smaller the baby, the bigger the pram'. It all seemed so pleasant and innocent; a world away from last night's mysterious attack in the darkened theatre.

As PC Higgins drove down the main street, Ambrose asked him to pause briefly. He wanted to look at the Theatre from the outside. Though ending abruptly to the right, the facade was bright and welcoming. Billboards announced next week's show: a vaguely familiar comedian on a national tour. Audiences were warned they might die laughing. "He ought to carry a Ministry of Health Warning," the poster quipped. Several smaller notices anticipated the forthcoming production of *Wedding Belle*: "A brand new show by our very own Chalk Heath Players".

The bombsite next door was far less threatening than it had seemed the previous night. A few pieces of concrete and twisted metal poked from the soil, but the area had mainly been flattened. The driveway along the side was neat and graveled. The missing buildings were clearly going to be replaced; trenches were being dug ready for new foundations. Even the line of remaining shops looked a lot tidier from the front than they had from the alley behind. One was indeed a greengrocer; its displays of fruit colourful and inviting.

Despite having had only a few hours sleep, Ambrose felt refreshed. He knew from experience that the tiredness would hit him in the afternoon. If he was lucky, he might get a nap in his office. Even ten minutes would help.

"Straight down Main Street," he directed PC Higgins, "then keep your eyes on the right. Manor Road isn't on the map yet. It's too new. Mrs Trevellyan said to look for a bus shelter, then turn immediately after the pillar box."

Ambrose checked his handwritten notes again. He wondered who on earth had decided to use the same name for all the roads in a brand new housing estate. It was all far too confusing.

"Then take the next turning into Manor Avenue. Manor Crescent is second on the left, after Manor Close."

"Right you are, sir," PC Higgins said cheerfully.

Ambrose glanced at his watch, hoping they would find the house quickly. As it was, he was going to be late back at the Station. DS Winters would have to hold onto the witnesses they wanted to interview again.

Ambrose began to wish he hadn't decided to come in person. PC Higgins could have gone alone. Higgins was one of the station's oldest and most reliable constables. He wouldn't get promotion now before he retired, but he probably didn't want it. Ambrose knew the PC would have interviewed Julie Trevellyan tactfully and come back with readable notes.

Yet Ambrose had said that he knew the case better. That he might think of questions his junior officer would not know to ask. In reality that was just an excuse. Truth be told, Ambrose wanted to meet Miss Monroe's understudy himself. After hearing so much about Julie from the other Players, she intrigued him. There was also the crucial question: why wasn't she in the wings watching the performance that night?

They found the bus stop and the post box then turned into an area of newly built houses. Most were in semi-detached pairs, but the occasional detached property catered for wealthier families. Each house had its own small garage and a sizeable front garden, complete with standard roses and a newly planted privet hedge. At the end of the street another cul-de-sac was being laid out with wooden markers. Chalk Heath was clearly developing.

"Nice," PC Higgins said with appreciation. "My missus'd love one of these." He sighed. "You'd need more than a PC's salary, though."

Ambrose had been right to be concerned. With every road being called Manor something-or-other, it took them five minutes to find the Trevellyans' house, despite the detailed directions. This property too had its neat front garden and freshly painted door.

Mrs Trevellyan had insisted that they must not park in front of the house. "Think what the neighbours would say!" she had said on the telephone. "Park right out of sight please. And don't come in uniform! I won't let you in if you come in uniform."

Ambrose had been tempted to offer to come dressed as a tramp but he dared not risk a joke. Julie Trevellyan had not even been at the theatre when the attack took place. He had little grounds to demand to interview her and, as she was under eighteen, he needed her parents' co-operation.

"Drive on past the house," he directed PC Higgins. "It's hardly fair to park outside somebody else's either," he added. "Go in front of that bit of open land. We'll walk back."

Even so, net curtains twitched as the police car drove past. Ambrose could almost smell the relief as they passed each house without stopping. On a smart estate like this, a visit from the police could mean only one thing: bad news.

Higgins parked the car as directed. Ambrose was surprised to see a large derelict house occupying what he'd thought to be empty land. Wire fencing had been erected around it to keep local children out. Numerous roof tiles were missing, but even so, it was an impressive building. A dozen windows looked out onto what had once been gardens and a long driveway. Above them, three sets of chimneys suggested many rooms and a whole squadron of servants needed to look after them.

"The old Manor," Higgins commented. "The one the streets are named after. All this land must have belonged to it once."

As they got out of the car, they looked though the mesh at the once splendid house.

"Pity," Ambrose said sadly. "Probably taken over by the war office, and not fit to live in afterwards."

"Or the son and heir died in action," PC Higgins agreed. "They say a lot of the nobs are having to sell."

Turning back from the house, Ambrose nodded. Part of him was sad to see such a grand place derelict, all its lovely gardens disappearing under roads and bricks. Still, it was good to think the nobs, as

Higgins called them, were at last being cut down to size. He was wasting time, though. They needed to get this interview over quickly.

As they walked, Ambrose briefed PC Higgins. "You're welcome to put in a question if I've missed something," he invited. "Let me start though. I think this could be tricky."

He was not looking forward to contending with the mother. Images of Mrs Trevellyan filled his mind. If she were the type to push her daughter on stage, she would make him nervous. He remembered taking his son Joe to play guitar at the summer festival. They had stumbled into the children's singing competition. There was a line of 'theatrical mothers', each with the expression of a woman determined that her little darling should win. As he and Joe entered the room, the whole row had turned round with a smile like a crocodile.

When Mrs Trevellyan came to the door, however, she did not fit Ambrose's image. She was dressed smartly - expensively even. Her hair colour must have taken hours to acquire. Yet something was not quite right. The pleated skirt did not go with the frilled blouse; the white shoes were down at the heel. Even her voice seemed out of keeping with the rather grand hall and stairway. Every word was enunciated carefully, but the accent reminded Ambrose of the barmaid at the 'Queen's Arms'.

As they were led into the front room, Ambrose glanced around him. It was dangerous to form snap judgments, he knew, but the way people dressed or furnished their homes could tell you a lot. The Trevellyans' best room was as odd as the lady herself. The settee was the latest fashion, but the rest of the furniture was wartime utility. China shepherdesses had been arranged around the fireplace, but they were the type you could buy at any seaside resort. A print of Constable's 'Haywain' hung above the fireplace, quacked at from the opposite wall by a flight of pottery ducks. Beneath them, Mr Trevellyan was sitting in a threadbare armchair, with a tin of tobacco beside him. He was dressed in what Ambrose always thought of as 'Sunday best': suit, tie, stiff collared shirt, cufflinks, even a tiepin. Presumably his wife had ordered him to look smart for the police, but his suit had definitely seen better days.

His mother had a phrase for people like the Trevellyans, Ambrose thought wryly: "Fancy hats and no knickers." She was a snob of course, but her judgments were often accurate. The family probably

153

could not afford a brand new house in such a genteel estate. They had decided 'to move up in the world' but they were over-stretching themselves. He began to understand Mrs Trevellyan's concern about the neighbours.

"I hope you're not staying long," Mr Trevellyan said. "Some of us have work to do." Then he took a pinch of the tobacco and began filling a cigarette paper.

Assuring him that his visit would be as short as possible, Ambrose sat on the settee beside Mrs Trevellyan. Higgins had to make do with a very low stool. He had a lot of difficulty finding somewhere to put his legs. Finally he folded them under him, so he was virtually kneeling, and got out his notebook.

When they entered, Ambrose had not noticed Julie Trevellyan standing in the bay window, looking out. She turned now to greet them. Her pretty blue eyes were ringed with red, as if she had been crying. Even so, as she crossed to greet them she held out her hand and smiled pleasantly. "Don't mind my Dad," she said. "He's always grumpy in the mornings. Aren't you, Pops?" She kissed the top of her father's balding head, her blond hair falling over his face.

Ambrose could see why the Chalk Heath Players liked Julie Trevellyan. Slender and pretty, with the figure of a dancer, she had an open, friendly manner and a winning smile. He would have to be careful, or he would forget the questions he had planned to ask. Fortunately PC Higgins seemed immune to charm.

"We'd like to ask you a few questions about last night, Miss," he said briskly.

"It's just routine," Ambrose assured her. He turned to the girl's parents. "Would you mind leaving us to chat to Julie for a few moments?" he asked. "It's about the Chalk Heath Players."

With a disapproving sniff, Mrs Trevellyan got up. Mr Trevellyan, however, stayed put. "Julie's only seventeen," he pointed out. "I'm not having you bullying her into saying what you want."

"I assure you, we have no intention of doing so," Ambrose was astonished at the hostility.

His wife hovered in the doorway. "Dad - Don't be rude," she cautioned.

"You policemen are all the same," Mr Trevellyan insisted. "If you can't prove a case, you'll stitch one up."

Ambrose had to hold his tongue to avoid an angry retort. There was no sense in getting involved in an argument. "We came to ask your daughter a few questions about the Chalk Heath Players," he repeated carefully. "I'm afraid there was an incident at last night's rehearsal."

To his surprise, Julie's eyes filled with tears. "I know," she said. "Mrs Black rang this morning."

"Mrs Black?" Ambrose asked quickly.

"She's been here quite a few times with Miss Monroe," Mrs Trevellyan explained. "We've got a piano."

She nodded proudly towards the far side of the room where a black upright supported a lace cover and a vase of flowers.

"They've been helping Julie with Miss Monroe's songs. Our Julie is Miss Monroe's understudy, you see."

"If you ask me, Julie's been helping Miss Monroe," Mr Trevellyan added.

"That's not fair, Dad," Julie said softly. "Miss Monroe's been very good to me and so has Mrs Black."

"Of course they have. They know talent when they see it," Mr Trevellyan boasted.

"You're not being fair," his daughter repeated quietly. She was clearly embarrassed. "They've been so supportive. The other understudy, Ken, hasn't had private coaching, you know."

"That's because he doesn't have a piano at home!" Mrs Trevellyan crowed.

PC Higgins had begun to take notes, but with so many people speaking almost at once, was uncertain whether to continue. He looked up at Ambrose for direction.

"Please let your daughter speak for herself," Ambrose said firmly, to both parents. "If you don't, I'm afraid I shall have to ask you to sit in the other room." He glanced towards the table and chairs on the other side of a pair of sliding glass doors. "You'll be able to hear everything out there, but not, I hope, keep interrupting."

"Well!!" Mrs Trevellyan said. "There's no need to be so rude." But she kept silent after that. Mr Trevellyan merely humphed and rolled his cigarette.

Ambrose turned back towards Julie Trevellyan. "Mrs Black told you about the attack?" he repeated gently.

"Yes. She rang before eight this morning. She was ever so upset."

"Did she tell you that we've been interviewing all the Players?"

Julie nodded. "I'm not sure why you want to speak to me, though," she replied. "I wasn't there."

"We just want to get a picture of everyone's movements," Ambrose assured her. "Tell us what you did last night."

Mrs Trevellyan began to speak but Julie put her fingers to her lips.

"Shh, Mum," she said. "I can answer. I went to the theatre for nine o'clock, as Mr Framilode asked. I usually go earlier, even though I only have a small part - as one of the servants. I stand in the wings when I'm not on stage, learning Miss Monroe's lines and watching her moves."

"And what was different about last night?"

"They were having a lot of trouble getting one scene right. Mr Framilode wanted to go over it lots of times, and Marguerite knew I have my secretarial exams on Tuesday. So she told him I should come with the other extras later. Mr Harris called for me. He plays the butler and he only lives down the road. We got to the theatre just before nine."

"And then?" Ambrose prompted.

"There was an awful fuss at the theatre," Julie replied. "A police car was parked outside, and Miss Greenbaum was standing with a constable turning us away as we arrived. She looked ever so upset but she wouldn't tell us what it was about. And nor would the policeman."

PC Higgins was writing furiously, having difficulty resting his pad on his knees. Ambrose paused to give him time to catch up.

"So where did you go then?" he asked at length.

"The others were going over to the public house opposite, to wait and see if they would be needed, but I couldn't go in with them," Julie explained. "So Mr Harris brought me straight home. He said he was going to go back to the Queen's Arms to wait with the others and see what was happening. He thought perhaps there had been a burglary. There have been a couple of break-ins from the back alley, sir."

"So you didn't set foot in the theatre at all last night?"

"No, sir. I stayed up practising my shorthand, in case Mr Harris came back for me, but he didn't."

"She's telling the truth," Mr Trevellyan said. "She was back here for nine thirty and sat in the dining room for over an hour afterwards, scribbling away at her notepad."

"You said Miss Monroe had been very good to you," Ambrose continued, ignoring the interruption.

"Yes," Julie smiled. "Miss Monroe can be sharp with the others, but she's always been very nice to me. She wants me to do well she says, in case I have to take over from her. She's taught me a lot - how to speak and make sure I don't turn my back to the audience, things like that. 'Stage craft' she calls it. I want to go on the stage myself you see, I mean professionally. Like Miss Monroe."

Mrs Trevellyan was unable to contain herself. "You'd be far better spending your time doing your secretarial course, my girl," she said. "Get a proper job, earn some money and marry a nice young man. That's what you should be doing!"

With a slight sigh, her daughter bowed her head, as if she had heard it all many times.

"Yes, Mum," Julie agreed. "But that's not what I want to do."

Her tone suggested good advice was never going to dissuade her.

"Have you ever had to take over Miss Monroe's part before?" Ambrose asked.

"Yes; twice during *Pirates*, when she had a bad throat."

"It looks like you'll have to take over again now," Ambrose pointed out, "and for longer this time. Does that please you?"

The girl looked at him in bewilderment for a second or two. Then she sat up straighter.

"If you mean am I glad Miss Monroe's been hurt, the answer's 'no'," she said firmly. "I'm very sorry. I liked Miss Monroe, even if others thought she was getting a bit - well - old for the leading parts. I certainly wouldn't have asked someone to hurt her so that I could

157

have her part. I'm scared stiff of having to play Teresa Laud. There are ever so many lines and songs, and the dances take some remembering too. I've told Miss Greenbaum I can't possibly do it next week and I'm not sure about the week after either."

"Miss Greenbaum's been in touch too?" Ambrose asked in surprise.

"Of course. She rang me soon after Mrs Black, to tell me I was needed. She thinks she can get the dates switched with the Chalk Heath Concert Band."

"It'll be your big break, won't it?" Higgins remarked.

"Perhaps," Julie admitted, turning towards him. "You never know who might be in the audience. There might be some agent from the West End, or there might just be a few dears from the Old People's Home. It'll be good experience though, *if* I can manage it."

Ambrose was impressed. Julie Trevellyan might just manage to get the career she wanted. It was risky though and he could understand her parents' concerns. He hadn't been at all happy when Joe said he wanted to form a rock and roll band. "Rock and Roll's going to be all the rage, Dad, you'll see," Joe had assured him. "We could make the big time ..." Ambrose had poured scorn on the idea but maybe Joe was right. Everyone needed a dream.

Returning to the present, Ambrose was about to draw the interview to a close when he remembered one last detail. "You said Mrs Black's been coming here with Miss Monroe. Did they get on well?" he asked.

"Yes," Julie replied, smiling. "They're very good friends. During the week, Mrs Black paid for a taxi service to bring her and Miss Monroe over here. At weekends she got her son to drive them, although he never came in. Either he'd drive home or he'd sit in the car if we weren't going to be long. Mrs Black played the piano and Miss Monroe and I rehearsed the songs. It's been quite good fun. Mrs Black was ever so upset on the phone this morning when she rang ..."

Breaking off, Julie put her hands to her face. She was near to tears again. "It's awful!" she said. "So awful!"

"You're upsetting her. Can't you see?" Mrs Trevellyan said. "She's had enough."

"I'm sorry," Ambrose apologised. "We'll go now. Thank you all for being so helpful."

Getting up, he nodded to PC Higgins, who managed to untangle his legs and get up slowly, closing his notebook as he did so.

Turning back to Julie, Ambrose offered her his hand. In surprise, she took it nervously.

"Good luck," he said to her. "There's nothing wrong with wanting to follow your dream. I'm sure you'll be a huge success."

CHAPTER TWENTY-SIX

Just as DI Ambrose was arriving at the new Manor estate, PC Sutton was pedaling hard in the opposite direction, trying to keep his helmet from falling over his eyes. He was nervous. If his guess were wrong, his trip would have been wasted. If he was right, the next hour or so was going to be very difficult.

Going to see the next of kin always made him feel a bit sick in the stomach. It didn't get any easier, no matter how often you did it. You never knew how the family would respond. Sometimes it was with floods of tears; sometimes with accusations, as if you were to blame for what had happened to their loved one. He could still remember the first time he had had to make such a call, about eighteen months ago, when he was still in the Midlands. A young boy had drowned in the canal near his home. Well, not exactly drowned, for his friends had fished him straight out. Sadly he had died a few hours later from the foul water he'd swallowed. He might just as well have been poisoned.

PC Sutton had volunteered to deal with that case because he knew the family. Now here he was again, volunteering for a job he dreaded because he knew Nurse Griffiths; well - not exactly knew her, but he had met her before. And because it seemed he was the only one to work out that she was Miss Monroe's niece.

He wondered how she would react. When she had looked after his grandfather, Nurse Griffiths had seemed very pleasant and caring. Was she close to her aunt? She used to come to the Players' shows regularly but then she had stopped coming. PC Sutton couldn't help wonder why. Had there been a quarrel between them, or was it just that her shifts had changed?

Passing the Town Hall and the Library, Sutton took the left fork towards Victoria Hill. Though he was very fit nowadays - cycling a beat every day did wonders for the leg muscles - the hill was steep and he was tired after being up most of the night. He kept up a good pace all the same. He did not want Nurse Griffiths hearing what had happened from someone else first. News travelled fast in Chalk Heath.

A little out of breath, he reached Victoria Park. Sutton had always wondered why part of the heath had been made into a park. It was only recently that he'd learnt it was public land and couldn't be built on. He supposed a park was as good a use for the land as any.

He rode into the park between a pair of imposing iron gateposts standing incongruously on their own. The gates and ornate iron railings that had once secured the entrance had long gone, to help the war effort. Remembering that riding bicycles in the park was strictly forbidden, Sutton dropped down onto the path and continued at a brisk walking pace, pushing his bike beside him. At so early an hour there were few people around: a few dog walkers, and one or two mothers heading towards the playground with toddlers in tow. Seeing him approaching, Wally Yates came out of his hut to greet him. 'Morning," he called. "It looks like the sun's going to break through."

Even though he was in a hurry, PC Sutton found time to greet the park keeper. Wally was an old friend and a useful source of information. After assuring Wally that the police were indeed looking for the little monkeys who tied all the swings in knots, Sutton hurried across the park. As he did so, he saw two boys coming towards him. Both were wearing the navy blazer and cap of Chalk Heath Grammar.

As soon as they saw him they vanished.

"Oh yes?" PC Sutton said to himself. Hopping back onto his bike, he sped across the grass towards a large clump of rhododendrons. A furtive rustle among the leaves confirmed his suspicions. If he had not been in such a hurry, he would have dived in after the boys. As it was, a little joke would have to do. Lowering his voice to its deepest, most official tone, he said, very loudly, "I saw you. I'm coming in to arrest you!"

There was a suppressed squeak underneath one of the bushes.

"You're coming with me to the police station unless you get back to school at once!" PC Sutton boomed.

The squeak became a frightened whisper.

Barely able to control his laughter, Sutton rode around the rhododendrons until the leaves were too thick for the boys to see him, then he doubled back again, towards the road. The boys would have no idea that he had left. How long they would huddle in their hiding place, would depend on their shoes. The earth under the bushes must be damp and cold. Their feet would soon be freezing.

They would probably already be shivering with fright, afraid that he was going to tell their headmaster that he had seen them playing truant. He ought to, of course, except he didn't know their names. He wondered if they were also the culprits of the swing-tying episode. With any luck his little intervention would have helped keep his promise to Wally.

Smiling PC Sutton said to himself. "They probably won't dare play hooky again." He could recall skipping school himself, once or twice, before the classes he hated most - mathematics. It was Wally who had talked sense into him, after finding him near the bowling green. Sutton had a soft spot for Wally ever since.

As soon as he was through the park gates, PC Sutton sped up. King Edward Road was almost empty. A milk float trundled along the road ahead of him, overtaking a boy on a bicycle delivering bread. Despite the need to hurry, he cast a quick glance over the houses as he passed. Relics of a more gracious age, they were far too big for modern families and most had been turned into offices or divided into flats. Several of them were quite seedy and 'things' tended to happen in them – 'things' it was worth an ambitious young PC knowing about. Today, however, everything appeared perfectly quiet.

At the end of the road an even larger house was set back from the road, behind high hedges. "That must be the nurses' home," Sutton said to himself. It certainly fitted Sergeant Hurst's description: "A big, rambling place - looks like a haunted house. It may be, too, if you believe the stories," the Sergeant had added mischievously.

"What stories?" PC Sutton had asked, uneasily.

"About the little old lady in black. The nurses reckon she comes and sits on their beds sometimes. Several of them have seen her. Down-to-earth, no-nonsense women at that, not the sort to imagine things."

"Thanks for the warning," Sutton had replied, trying to make light of it.

As he pulled the old-fashioned bell and stepped inside the porch, he still couldn't decide whether the Sarge was joking.

The inner door had been left slightly ajar and PC Sutton could hear feet crossing the tiled floor, echoing around the entrance hall. The young woman who answered the door was, fortunately, most definitely not a ghost. Wrapped in an apron that could have done service as a tent, she was wiping a pair of very red hands on a tea towel. She was humming softly and smiling at some remembered joke.

Her expression changed immediately she saw PC Sutton's uniform. "Matron!" she called over her shoulder. "Matron! There's a copper at the door."

Through the half-open door Sutton saw an imposing looking woman come hurriedly out of a side room. "Then let him in, girl," Matron retorted. "And show him into my office at once." She retreated into the room she had come from.

As he entered, Sutton could smell bacon and eggs. His meal at the Copper Kettle suddenly seemed a long time ago. "There's no need to be alarmed," he assured the girl.

"This way," she said abruptly. They entered a high ceilinged room that had once been a study or a library and was now filled with soggy armchairs. Matron was sitting at an old fashioned desk near the window. She got up, extending a large hand to PC Sutton. He grimaced as she crushed his fingers in greeting. "Can I help you, officer?" she asked.

"I hope so," Sutton replied. "I need to speak to Nurse Griffiths. She does live here, doesn't she?"

"She does," the woman replied briskly. "Has she complained to the police? She didn't mention it to me."

"No. Not at all. I'm afraid I have some bad news about a relative, though."

"Oh dear. Poor Nancy," Matron said, her manner changing at once from caution to concern. She indicated a chair near her.

"Do sit down. I'm sorry if I misunderstood why you were here. We've been having trouble with some of the neighbours since they turned those nice houses into flats. We've had a 'peeping Tom' here more than once. I've had to move the girls' bedrooms to the second floor. I assumed you'd come about that."

She paused for breath then continued. "I'm afraid Nurse Griffiths isn't in. She was called out to her district an hour ago. One of her patients needed a dressing changing urgently. Can you wait? She shouldn't be long."

Sighing, PC Sutton assured her that he could.

"I'll just carry on with some paper work, if that's all right," Matron replied.

So PC Sutton settled down into a big, flowery old armchair and waited while Matron wrote figures in a ledger and ticked totals. He would far rather be going to bed, but at least he would soon be earning overtime, he reflected. The money would come in handy. He might even afford to take a girl to the pictures next week. Though he couldn't think of anyone to invite - unless ... No. That was being silly ... She was out of the question.

At last, through the window near him, Sutton saw a woman cycle into the back yard. Stopping with an easygoing skid, she propped her bike against the wall and took a large black bag off the carrier. Matron saw her too - clearly there was not much she didn't see. Opening the window, she called through it. "Nancy -- Can you come into my office please? There's someone here to speak to you." Then, tactfully, she got up. "I'll see if there's a pot of tea in the kitchen," she said and walked out.

As she came into the office, Nurse Griffith's expression was already anxious. When she saw PC Sutton stand up to greet her, she did not waste words. "Who's died?" she asked.

"No one - not yet. But I may have some bad news for you," PC Sutton replied. He had found it was kinder to get things over and done with quickly. "Do you have an Aunt called Marguerite?"

"Marguerite? No."

PC Sutton's heart sank. He had been so sure he was right. He'd thought himself quite clever in fact.

"Oh! You mean Betty," Nurse Griffiths added, suddenly understanding. "Marguerite's not her real name, well not really, so I never think of her as that." Then Nancy went rather pale. "Has something happened to her?" she demanded. "Is she all right?"

PC Sutton shook his head. "Come and sit down beside me," he invited, indicating the other armchair.

Reluctantly Nancy Griffiths sat beside him. "I know you, don't I?" she asked.

"Yes. You visited my grandfather when he was living with us." Curiously Sutton looked at the woman beside him. She seemed the same as eight years ago, though she must be in her late thirties now.

Well built, capable and pleasantly attractive, she still looked exactly how he imagined a District Nurse should look.

"What's happened to my aunt?" she repeated. "Don't be afraid to tell me."

"Miss Monroe was attacked last night. She was taken to the hospital straight away, and underwent emergency surgery. I'm afraid she has a serious head injury."

"You said she was attacked?" Nurse Griffiths said disbelievingly. "Who by?"

"We don't know yet. We're investigating at the moment. It happened at the theatre - during a rehearsal."

"Good Lord! Did someone break in?"

"We think it has to have been one of the cast," Sutton replied carefully. "Did she have any enemies among them?"

For a long time Nurse Griffiths sat in silent thought. "I can't believe it," she said at length. "Not here - in Chalk Heath. It's such a dozy place normally. Poor Aunt Betty!"

"Did she have any enemies?" PC Sutton repeated.

"No, not to my knowledge - other than my mother that is, and she's been dead three years." Nancy Griffiths shook her head. "But I'm not really in a position to say," she admitted. "I haven't seen my aunt for a couple of years. We had an argument. Oh Lord! I wish I could take back what I said!"

"What was the argument about?"

"I thought it was time Betty gave up - that she was making a fool of herself still playing the young heroine." Awkwardly, Nurse Griffiths paused. "I don't just mean in the theatre," she added, "but well - with men ... She was lonely I suppose, and liked attention. It never went much beyond that I'm sure. She was far too concerned about her reputation at work. But well," Nancy was finding it hard to explain. "I said my mother had been right about her - and Betty never forgave me for it."

Frowning in bewilderment, PC Sutton asked, "Right about what?"

"About her being all brains and no sense. My mother often used that phrase about her, and it just slipped out of my mouth."

"Your mother and her sister didn't get on well, then?" Sutton prompted.

"No. I think my mother was jealous of Betty's good looks, and of her career. She worked in the West End at first, and that seemed ever so glamorous to us, and then she got a job in the Law, and that was the tops. When I was about eighteen, Mum and Betty had a terrible row and never had any more to do with each other. Awful isn't it? Sisters not speaking."

"Yes," PC Sutton agreed, wondering if he should be taking notes. He tried to remember every word, so that he could pass anything that might be useful on to DI Ambrose. "Can you give me any other details?" he added. "You never know, it might be helpful."

"All right. I'll go back to the beginning." A reflective expression came to Nancy Griffiths' face, making her look younger and more vulnerable. "I was very fond of my Aunt," she explained. "She'd never married - it would have meant giving up her career - but I think she would have loved to have children. When I was little she used to entertain me for hours, making miniature stages out of shoe boxes, or letting me dress up in her old shoes and hats. She had money - compared to us any way - and when I was older she took me to the theatre and concerts. I kept in touch with her after I started nursing, and went to see her whenever she was on stage."

Nurse Griffith's eyes were beginning to fill with tears and she paused briefly. When she continued her voice was unsteady. "I don't know why my mother quarrelled with her so badly," she admitted. "I think she thought my aunt was having an affair with a married man and would bring scandal on us all. When I asked, though, Mum just pursed her lips and said I shouldn't see Betty any more. That was daft, telling an eighteen year old she mustn't see someone. Besides, I knew that whatever my aunt might do, she would never cause scandal. She wouldn't let anything - or anyone - jeopardise her position at the courts, or her being on the stage. They were the two most important things in her life. It was when I tried to tell her that she wasn't young any more, and needed to find other things, that we fell out."

Feeling in her uniform pocket, Nurse Griffiths found a handkerchief and blew her nose. "Do you think she'll recover?" she asked.

"I don't know," PC Sutton admitted. "The hospital will be able to tell you more. I've written the Sister's name down for you." He passed her the piece of paper.

"I'll go at once," Nurse Griffiths replied. "Someone will cover my visits I'm sure." She extended her hand. "Thank you for coming to tell me. Tell me something, though. How did you know to come? I mean, my aunt and I haven't seen each other for over two years, and she'd changed her name."

"One of the cast remembered being introduced to you after one of the shows. She could only remember that you were called Nancy, and that you were a district nurse. I knew a Nancy who was a district nurse. It was a lucky guess."

"Gosh," Nurse Griffiths replied. "You are lucky. There are three other nurses called Nancy just in this home. I hate to think how many there are in total. Thank you again, anyway."

They walked across the tiled hall to the front door together. The smell of the nurses' breakfast still lingered. PC Sutton's stomach turned a little. He was very, very tired, but relieved too. He had been right and the meeting had gone far better than he had feared.

CHAPTER TWENTY-SEVEN

Back at the Police Station, Winters took Ambrose a cup of tea. He updated him on what WPC Meadows had said.

"That's curious," Ambrose commented. "The understudy said Mrs Black telephoned her this morning. There was no mention of a heart attack or angina."

"She must have called from the hospital," Winters replied. "Clearly she was fit enough to walk to the public telephone in the lobby."

"It's no wonder," Ambrose reflected, "that WPC Meadows wasn't convinced Mrs Black was really ill. Poor Kathy," he added.

Bringing himself back to the task at hand, Ambrose watched as Frank Thomas was brought into the room. Winters was looking at the man curiously, trying to assess his mood. He appeared calm but a tightness about the mouth suggested he was nervous. Winters had known murderers appear just as cool, before boasting about appalling crimes, but Mr Thomas did not have their cold, emotionless eyes. Strangely, his eyes had a boyish openness that made it difficult to imagine him as responsible for so many deaths.

But Winters had been wrong before about killers, he reminded himself. And perhaps it was easier to murder just one person, Winters thought, once you'd already killed nearly two dozen.

Ambrose was silent, preparing himself for a long session. It would start with denials of course; probably even end that way, but they might be able to get to the truth that morning. Thomas certainly seemed the most likely suspect.

ooOoo

"Interview beginning 9.35am," Winters said for the benefit of the young WPC doing short hand in the corner. "Interview with Mr Frank Thomas Lucas. Present: DI Ambrose and DS Winters."

"Thank you for coming back in to talk to us, Mr Lucas," Ambrose began. "You do not have to say anything but anything you do say may be given in evidence. Do you understand?"

The man in front of him sighed. His shoulders slumped and his face took on a tired, defeated expression. "Yes," he replied. "Is it possible for you to call me Frank Thomas please? It's my legal name now."

Ambrose nodded. "If you wish," he agreed. "We have some further questions we would like to put to you."

"I presumed you would have, although I thought it might be last night."

After even just half a night's sleep Ambrose felt fresher and more alert. "It appears you haven't been entirely honest with your co-Players," he remarked.

Frank Thomas looked away. "Would *you* tell everyone that you'd been driving a train that killed twenty people?" he asked quietly.

Ambrose was surprised by the reply. "No. I suppose I wouldn't," he admitted. "But you're not trying to hide it now?"

"I'd be foolish to deny it. I'm sure you have the full story in your notes. It won't tell you how it happened, though, or that it really wasn't my fault. And it won't say I've spent the last five years wishing I could do things all over again differently." Frank sighed heavily. "I bet you're just like everyone else: convinced I'm to blame even though I was acquitted."

Winters, too, was puzzled by Frank's directness. In his experience, guilty people rarely admitted anything straight away. "So how did it happen, Mr Thomas?" he asked.

"Because it was foggy. Because I couldn't see the signal. And because I was careless," he replied. "It's not as if I was the first driver to go through a red signal," he added, defensively.

Pausing, he stared into the past. "There'd been two near misses just a few months before. We all knew that bend was a problem. It was just too difficult to see the signal on the approach to the station."

There was another long pause. "Go on, Mr Thomas," Ambrose prompted.

"Well that night we were rushing. My engineer was ill and he'd turned up late." Frank sighed. "Now I wish he hadn't turned up at all. I wouldn't have been able to drive without an engineer. I wouldn't have been able to kill twenty passengers if I hadn't driven the train. One of them was only four years old, you know."

For a moment there was silence.

Winters took over. "The jury clearly didn't think it was all your fault," he pointed out kindly.

"Yes but that doesn't make me feel any better. I keep telling myself I should have prevented it. We'd got in the habit of slowing down at that curve, to make sure we could see if the signal was red. But because we were late, I didn't slow down that night. And the 8.36 was slightly early. If just one of us had been on time, we couldn't have crashed into each other."

Winters could not think of a reply. There was another silence before Frank carried on.

"It would have been alright if Arthur, my engineer, had popped his head out as we passed the signal. There was no way I could see out the window that side, not when driving. Normally he would stick his head out and shout if the signal was red."

"So what happened that night?" Ambrose prompted gently.

Frank looked away, but only briefly. He seemed determined to tell the truth, however painful. "I told Arthur not to worry," he explained. "I mean he was already ill. I didn't want him to get worse. Looking out of a train doing over thirty miles an hour isn't good for you at the best of times."

He forced himself to carry on. "If only I hadn't said that. I shouldn't have worried about his health. I mean, Arthur died in the crash so I hardly helped him feel better did I?" The bitterness was audible in Frank's voice.

"But the jury clearly didn't believe you should go to jail?" Winters insisted.

"No, thank God," Frank replied, shaking his head. "The train company knew there was a problem. They were supposed to fit a warning system. Something to tell us drivers there was a red signal ahead. They didn't have the money, they said. I bet they wished they'd found the money now."

Ambrose looked down at the records Winters had copied for him. "So you learnt acting after the crash?" he asked.

Frank nodded slowly. "I had a bad time, when I came out of hospital and after the court case. I know the jury felt it wasn't my fault, but I just kept blaming myself. I'd spend every night awake, trying to work out how I could have done things differently. When I did fall

170

asleep," Frank paused, as if embarrassed, "I had nightmares. I kept reliving the crash. Seeing all those injured people lying there."

Ambrose lent forward slightly. "It's normal, you know," he replied kindly. "It's normal to feel guilty when you survive and those around you don't. It's normal to keep thinking about what happened." He patted Frank's shoulder gently. "At some point you realise there's nothing you can do to change the past. Worrying about it constantly doesn't actually help."

Winters glanced up quickly. Was it his imagination or was Ambrose actually talking of his own experiences?

"I know," Frank replied. "It's not as if I hadn't seen people die before. But it was different in the War. It wasn't my fault then. It was the Germans who were to blame. I couldn't cope with thinking that my actions had killed so many innocent people."

He hesitated before carrying on. "My doctor suggested I try an acting course and learnt something manual. I chose bookbinding. I think he hoped being busy would take my mind off things. It does help, a bit," Frank conceded.

Winters was suddenly alert. "Who was your doctor?" he asked.

"It wasn't Larry, if that's what you mean," Frank replied. "I only moved to Chalk Heath after the court case was over. And no, I didn't use Archie's firm when I changed my name." He pre-empted Winters' next question.

Ambrose rubbed at his chin – a habit he had whenever he was thinking hard. Frank Thomas could have a clear motive for attacking Miss Monroe, but only if she knew the truth.

"So no one in the Players knows your history?" he asked.

"No."

"Could Miss Monroe have known?" Ambrose persisted, staring at the suspect in front of him.

"Why should she?" Frank replied, looking puzzled.

Ambrose hoped he was on the right track. "She works as a judge's clerk," he pointed out. "She may have seen your court case. Perhaps she was blackmailing you ..."

"Marguerite? Of course not!" Frank sounded genuinely surprised at the suggestion.

171

"Are you sure?" Winters demanded. "It would have ruined everything if she'd told people who you really are. That sounds like a good reason to silence her."

For the first time Frank's calm was broken. "How dare you suggest I'd try to kill her!" he shouted, "or anyone else for that matter. It wouldn't even make sense. I've spent the past few years trying to build my life again. Nothing – and no one - would make me take someone's life deliberately."

Anger made his voice unsteady, but he was thinking clearly. "If Marguerite had tried to blackmail me, I would simply have moved away. I have no ties in Chalk Heath – or anywhere. I can work from home, wherever I am."

Ambrose could see the sense in what he was saying. "Could Miss Monroe have been blackmailing someone else?" he asked.

For a few seconds Frank Thomas reflected. "I doubt it," he replied more calmly. "She might think of doing so but she wouldn't have known how to frighten anyone enough. She did have something on her mind though. About two weeks ago, she came to me in a panic. She started talking about someone usurping her rights and a '*double cross*'. Then Larry appeared and she shut up. I have no idea what she meant."

Ambrose was intrigued. "Are you sure?" he questioned.

"I don't lie," Frank insisted. "People always find out if you do. Can I go now? I'm not feeling very well. Remembering what happened always has that effect on me."

Ambrose nodded. "Yes, of course," he said. "Thank you for being so open with us, Mr Thomas."

ooOoo

Ambrose and Winters sat quietly for several minutes. "Do you think he was telling the truth?" Winters asked at last.

"I'm sure he is," Ambrose answered sadly. "I know what it's like, the constant wondering, the permanent 'what if'? It can eat you up inside."

"I just keep thinking of all those co-incidences," Winters agreed. "One train running late, another early. A signal no one could see. An engineer who was feeling unwell and a driver who didn't want to make him feel any worse. Plus like you said last time, his whole manner suggested honesty. It's a pretty awful story."

"What matters now, though, is whether he had opportunity and motive for killing Marguerite. He may well have but I doubt it. I'm sure Frank would just have moved away, if anyone had found out."

"I wonder what Miss Monroe meant about 'usurping her rights'," Winters reflected. "At least Frank's version ties in with BJ's. Marguerite clearly had something on her mind. Pity neither of them got her to explain. We might have been able to work out whether she was actually blackmailing someone, and who."

"Perhaps Mr Moody can throw some light on the matter," Ambrose suggested. "If he's pushed hard enough."

CHAPTER TWENTY-EIGHT

Winters began with the usual formalities: "Time: 10.30am. Interview with Mr Douglas Moody. Present: DI Ambrose and DS Winters."

Ambrose settled back into his chair, as far from Mr Moody as he could. He just couldn't bring himself to get up close to the man who epitomised everything that he found so unattractive about his own son.

"Thank you for coming back this morning to talk to us, Mr Moody," Ambrose began. "This interview will take place under caution. You do not have to say anything but anything you do say may be given in evidence. Do you understand?"

"No. I don't ruddy understand," Douglas Moody retorted. "Why've you called me back like this? I told you everything last night."

Ambrose kept his voice low. "We've found a few things out since last night," he explained. "For a start, Mr Moody, we've found you've run up considerable debts. You have a weakness for gambling, I believe?"

"So? What I do in my own time is nothing to do with you. You've no right prying into my affairs."

"We do if it's relevant to our enquiries," Winters pointed out. "Do you, or do you not, owe £250 in gambling debts?"

"I might. I'm not sure of the figure. I can afford it."

"Can you?" Winters asked, incredulously. "That's almost enough to buy a house with!" he exclaimed.

Douglas Moody shrugged his shoulders. "I can earn that in a few months," he boasted. "I'm good. I'm known in the trade."

Ambrose smiled in disbelief. "Is that why you're working for the Chalk Heath Players?" he remarked.

"You don't think I'd do it for fun, do you?" Douglas Moody sneered. "I wouldn't spend time with a blasted bunch of amateurs otherwise. They haven't got a shred of talent amongst them."

"You told us last night that you didn't see Heather Broomhead leave the ladies' dressing room," Ambrose recalled. "But we now know that she did. Why did you lie to us, Mr Moody?"

"I didn't lie – just covered for her a bit. I didn't think it was important. Heather always goes out for her toilet break. I didn't mention it because I knew you'd only ask lots of questions. I was just helping a friend."

Ambrose was struggling not to shake Douglas Moody. "It would have saved a lot of time if you'd told us the truth last night," he told him firmly. "It also makes us suspicious of the rest of your story, Mr Moody. Were you really in the technical room the whole evening before Miss Monroe was attacked?"

"Yeah. 'Course I was. I was fixing that broken lighting, like I told you. I can show you if you want. I left everything in the technician's room at the theatre."

Winters looked up. "Don't worry," he replied. "I checked your workbench myself yesterday, after you'd gone home."

"Did you?" Douglas sounded startled. He glanced from one policeman to the other. Then he relaxed slightly. "So you'll have seen the right ruddy mess those cables were in then?" he grinned.

"I did indeed see the light and the cables, thank you." Winters glanced meaningfully in Ambrose's direction. He could see Douglas starting to shift in his chair. Douglas looked uncomfortable.

Ambrose nodded at his colleague then continued with the questioning. "Mr Moody, if you were in your room all the while," he asked, "why didn't Mrs Broomhead see you as she passed?"

"She must have seen me," Douglas Moody insisted. "Just wasn't looking. Or perhaps I was at the cupboard. I've got a kettle and stuff in there. I never left the room any rate."

Ambrose nodded. "Thank you Mr Moody," he said. "That will be all for the time being. I'd be grateful if you'd stay in the waiting area, however, until we've had chance to check what you've told us."

ooOoo

Winters waited until Douglas had left the interview room.

"So could you tell anything from Moody's work?" Ambrose asked him.

"Not really," he replied. "The light's there all right and a whole pile of burnt out electrical cable. There's just no way of knowing when that light broke. I mean Moody could have brought those damaged cables from home. He could easily have pretended that light wasn't working, even though it was fine. Then he'd have had the perfect excuse to go into his workshop."

Ambrose nodded.

"Still," Winters added. "If Moody did want to creep around that theatre, he'd have had to take all those keys and what have you from his pockets."

"Or he could just have taken his jacket off," Ambrose pointed out.

He lent forward, looking at the chair Douglas had just vacated. "Finally I think we have some light at the end of the tunnel!" Ambrose exclaimed.

Then he stopped himself suddenly. "Sorry that wasn't in the best of taste, was it?"

"Good job Frank Thomas isn't in the room," Winters agreed.

CHAPTER TWENTY-NINE

Winters almost felt sorry for Archie Framilode as he ushered the solicitor into the interview room. If Winters had read him correctly, and he was sure he had, then Archie would be horrified to be faced with his father's 'indiscretions'. Still, Winters knew only too well that if he did his job properly, he would be unlikely to win any popularity contests.

ooOoo

Once again, Winters started the interview. "Interview, beginning 11am, with Mr Archibald Framilode," he said clearly. "Present: DI Ambrose and DS Winters."

Then Ambrose greeted the director. "Thank you, Mr Framilode, for taking the time to answer a few further questions," he began. "This interview will take place under caution. You do not have to say anything but anything you do say may be given in evidence. Do you understand?"

"If there's anything I can do to help," Archie Framilode offered, "just let me know. I don't understand why it had to be under caution though. I'd have quite happily answered your questions voluntarily. I don't want people getting the wrong idea, you know." He was clearly uneasy at the official tone.

Winters smiled. "There's nothing to worry about, Mr Framilode," he assured him. "It's just a formality."

"Oh well," Archie agreed, "I suppose there's no reason to tell anyone I was interviewed again. What do you need to know?"

Ambrose took over again. "Well there is one thing," he started. "We're still trying to work out why anyone would want to harm Miss Monroe."

"I've been wondering exactly the same myself," Archie admitted. "I'm afraid I have absolutely no idea."

Ambrose continued quietly, "We saw that Miss Monroe used to work as a secretary at the Law Society. Did you come across her at all during that time?"

"Er-" Mr Framilode hesitated. "No, I didn't," he replied. "We didn't meet until she moved to Chalk Heath. That was after she left the Law Society."

"What about your father?" Winters asked. "Would he have met her at any time?"

Mr Framilode looked up in surprise. "My father?" he repeated. "What's he got to do with it? I think we can leave him out of this, don't you?"

"I'm not so sure that we can," Ambrose said. "Tell us why your father was struck off by the Law Society, please."

"How on earth did you find that out? It's totally irrelevant! It has absolutely nothing to do with Marguerite!"

"Are you sure, sir?" Winters persisted. "After all, she worked at the Law Society when your father was struck off the Solicitors' Roll. Wasn't that for embezzling client money, sir?"

Archie had gone red in the face. "He didn't embezzle anyone!" he almost shouted, leaping up from his chair. "How dare you suggest he did anything wrong?"

Ambrose was about to tell him to sit down again, when Archie did so of his own accord, with a thud.

"If he didn't do anything wrong, why was he struck off?" Ambrose demanded.

It was a moment before Archie replied. When he did, the solicitor seemed to have shrunk at least an inch in all directions. "It wasn't my father's fault," he insisted. "His partner wasn't pulling his weight. My father had to do everything by himself: all the client work, dealing with the staff, doing the accounts. He was so busy he made a couple of mistakes, that's all. A couple of times he mixed client money with office money. It wasn't deliberate and no one lost any money."

"It seems a little harsh to have struck him off for a couple of minor errors," Ambrose commented.

"You're quite right; it was totally uncalled for. The Law Society was being criticised for being too soft on solicitors, so they had to make an example of someone. Sadly my father was in the wrong place at the wrong time."

"The report we have says that your father mixed money on six separate occasions," Winters pointed out, "to the tune of £1,500. That was hardly a small error."

Archie's dignity was returning. "Young man, you have absolutely no idea how hard it is being a solicitor! It's fine for you to criticise, but you don't have the same pressures. You don't have to record every moment of your life; your time isn't for sale. You don't have hundreds of clients hounding you because they think theirs is the most important matter you're dealing with."

Ambrose smiled. "Being in the police isn't exactly a walk in the park," he countered.

"I take it you haven't told the rest of the Players about your father's unfortunate error?" Winters asked.

"Of course I haven't. It has absolutely nothing to do with them!"

"You see our predicament, then?" Ambrose continued. "We have Marguerite working at the Law Society when your father was struck off. We have you doing your level best to make sure no one knows about it. Are you telling us that Marguerite herself didn't know?"

Archie Framilode paused before answering, "Yes, of course she knew."

"So perhaps you felt she might let your little secret slip out sometime?" Winters persisted.

"Never! I wouldn't have needed to bump her off! Marguerite wouldn't have told anyone, not with what I knew about her."

"Really, sir?" Ambrose cut in. "So you knew that Marguerite wasn't on the stage? You knew that she was actually a seamstress at the Drury Lane theatre?"

"What? She was a *seamstress*?" Archie exploded. "You have got to be joking!"

Winters almost felt sorry for him. Clearly he'd had no idea. "Not at all, sir," he said as tactfully as he could. "Perhaps you'd like to see this report? It tells us all about Miss Monroe, or rather Miss Elizabeth (Betty) Fagg. Would I be right in presuming you helped Miss Monroe to change her name?"

Archie nodded slowly, as if struggling to take it all in. "Yes, I did. She came to me to change her name by deed poll. But she told me that she was on the stage in London. She claimed Marguerite Monroe was her stage name. If I'd known she was a *seamstress* I'd never have given her the leading lady parts." Archie's expression reflected his hurt. "It's not as if she's that good really," he admitted. "I mean she's ok as a singer, until she gets to the top notes that is, but she can't act or dance at all!"

"So how did you and Miss Monroe come to your 'understanding'?" Ambrose asked.

"Our understanding? What on earth do you mean?"

Winters explained. "Well, you wouldn't tell people her real name, and in return she'd keep quiet about your father's indiscretions."

Archie Framilode shook his head vigorously "It wasn't like that," he protested. He paused. "Well, not really. It's not as if I threatened to tell anyone about her name. It would be protected by client confidentiality."

"But you said you knew Miss Monroe would never talk about your father," Ambrose reminded him, "because you knew her real name."

There was a longer pause. "OK.............I'll tell you then," Archie agreed at last. "But it's not what you think, I promise. I would never have told anyone her real name anyway. It's just that one day, Marguerite took me to one side. She said it was a good job no one knew about my father. She suggested that people might not trust me either, if they knew. She told me it could have a huge effect on my practice."

"And what did you think she meant?" Ambrose asked.

"I really wasn't sure. If I didn't know better, I'd have said that Marguerite was thinking of blackmailing me."

Winters nodded. "Did she actually suggest that you pay her off?" he questioned.

"Not exactly, no. But she did want to know whether I would leave all my interest in the Players to her, if something happened to me."

"And did you agree?" Ambrose added.

"Well yes, I did. But only because I thought she'd be the best person to keep the Players going if I wasn't around. I mean, I thought she was an old pro. And I admit, I may have mentioned that I could tell everyone her real name, if I wanted to. Obviously, I had no intention of actually breaking the client confidentiality rules but Marguerite may not have known that."

Ambrose began to see the situation more clearly in his mind. "That's interesting," he said. "Thank you for telling us. And did you ever think about changing your mind? Perhaps leaving the Players to someone else?"

"No, no I didn't."

Winters took over the questioning. "What about your practice?" he asked. "Did you speak to Marguerite about leaving your firm to Alex?"

"No absolutely not." Archie shook his head emphatically. "I haven't discussed it with anyone. I mentioned it briefly to Alex one day at the office and then raised it again with him after a rehearsal recently."

"When was that?" Ambrose cut in.

Mr Framilode frowned. "I don't recall the actual date I'm afraid," he admitted. "It was about three weeks ago I believe. Do you think it's important?"

"It could well be very important, sir."

Winters saw where Ambrose was heading. "Do you know if anyone else may have overheard your conversation with Alex?" he asked.

"I have no idea. It's possible I suppose. I didn't think I needed to keep it secret. After all, it's entirely up to me whether Alex should be my successor."

"Quite," Ambrose agreed. "Is there anything else you wish to add?"

"Well, I'm not sure I will be leaving the Players to Marguerite now, even if she does survive. I can't believe she lied to me like that about her theatrical experience. I feel a total idiot."

Winters smiled. "I wouldn't feel bad if I were you, sir," he advised. "After all, how could you possibly have known the truth?"

"I suppose you're right," Archie admitted, but he looked crestfallen all the same. "And I may as well reprint all the programmes to show Julie as the lead. She's much more suited for the part and she's a better singer than Marguerite too. It'll cost me a fortune but perhaps Frank will be able to help towards the cost. He's always offering to contribute you know. Maybe this time I should take him up on it."

ooOoo

181

Winters turned to Ambrose as the door shut. "I'm beginning to wonder about Miss Monroe, sir," he said. He was still smiling at Archie's horrified reaction to learning the truth. "She doesn't seem to have been very honest with people."

"I agree," Ambrose replied. "She may not have been the innocent victim, at least not totally."

"That's what I mean. What she said to Archie Framilode sounds like a not very subtle attempt at blackmail doesn't it?"

"This isn't the first time we've had this suggestion. Marguerite as good as blackmailed Larry Lyndon so he'd drop his support for the understudy taking over. Mrs Worsley tipped us off with her little letter then Mr Lyndon himself confirmed it. And remember what BJ Godfrey told us about Marguerite 'having something' on someone? I'd initially thought that Frank Thomas was the obvious blackmail candidate but I can't see it actually working. After all, he seemed quite willing to move away if anyone found out about his past."

"I don't think anyone else has any dark hidden secrets," Winters replied.

"I certainly hope not," Ambrose agreed. "I think we have more than enough with two name changes, lies about Marguerite's previous profession, BJ and Olga's secret relationship, a dodgy solicitor and former train driver trying to forget killing twenty passengers. And there was me thinking this would be an easy job. What else are these people going to throw at us?"

CHAPTER THIRTY

A quiet tap on the door made both of them look up in surprise.

"Sorry to interrupt you, sir," PC Higgins addressed himself to Ambrose, "but Mr Black would very much like to speak to you, before he goes."

Ambrose glanced towards Winters but he shook his head. He knew nothing about the request. "You'd better show Mr Black in, then," Ambrose said.

"Er, well, sir," PC Higgins seemed momentarily not sure what to say. He rallied himself. "I'm afraid Mr Black was most insistent on seeing you alone, sir."

Ambrose looked astonished. He certainly didn't relish the idea of interviewing Michael Black on his own. It could undermine any evidence Michael might give him. Worse, it could be disastrous for their case if Michael confessed and they had no record.

"I'm afraid it's totally out of the question. I can't possibly see him without anyone else being present," Ambrose explained.

"He probably just wants more marriage advice," Winters laughed quietly. He was instantly serious again.

"Look, how about you see him on your own. If he does tell you anything really important, you can call me back in to act as witness. I won't go far. Once he's said whatever it is once, I'm sure he'll find it easier second time around."

Winters was probably right, Ambrose reflected. He watched as his colleague left the room, holding the door open for the WPC who'd been taking notes.

"Of course, if it's a confession you'll have to call me in pretty sharpish," Winters added over his shoulder, only half joking.

"Well, you never know, we may be in luck," Ambrose replied.

ooOoo

Michael Black looked nervous.

"I hope you don't mind … I think I ought to tell you something …. Can it be in private? 'Off the record' isn't it? At least that's what I think they call it," he spoke very quickly, barely pausing for breath between sentences.

"It depends on what you want to say," Ambrose replied, not unkindly.

"Well – it's … I'm sorry. It's difficult for me to know how to begin. It's just that I think you need to arrest me."

Ambrose started. He was about to call out for Winters to return, then changed his mind. There was something in Michael's manner. Ambrose didn't think he was about to hear a confession of murder.

"Why would I want to arrest you, Mr Black?" Ambrose prompted. "What have you done?"

"Nothing yet," came the reply.

Ambrose raised both eyebrows. Michael was clearly in a confused state and Ambrose was rapidly joining him there.

"Then what is it you *intend* to do?" Ambrose asked. "If you've not done anything wrong yet, then you must be about to do it soon."

"Yes I do intend to, believe me I do," Michael replied earnestly. "I'm not sure when, but I *hope* it will be soon."

Ambrose was beginning to wish Winters hadn't left the room. If anyone could help Michael get to the point, it was Winters. Ambrose sighed and tried again.

"Why don't we go back a step? Tell me what it is you hope to do."

Michael paused, then put his head in his hands. There was a soft muffled noise. With astonishment, Ambrose realised Michael was quietly crying.

"Look," Ambrose said kindly. "Whatever it is, I'm sure you'd be better telling me. I've no idea if I can help, but I won't arrest you unless I really have to."

Michael looked up. His eyes were red but he managed a slight smile. Looking at Ambrose's concerned face, Michael made up his mind.

"It's me and Alex," he started. "We haven't told anyone yet, and I don't want Kathy to find out before I can explain to her myself. I shall hurt her enough as it is."

"Are you saying that you and Mr Baker-Smythe are, well, more than just friends?" Ambrose queried.

"No, not exactly. At least not yet. We've only just admitted to ourselves … how much we mean to each other. It took me a long time to realise I love Alex, and then I didn't dare hope he would feel the same about me. But he does, and we both know it's what we want," Michael fairly blurted the words out. He paused for breath and carried on.

"We know it's illegal, but I just can't pretend any longer. It's just not fair on Kathy. And I don't care if Mother disapproves." He almost shouted those last words.

"So you're saying you haven't told your families yet?" Ambrose noted.

"Yes. That is, no we haven't told them," Michael sighed deeply. "I've always felt that I was different, I just didn't know why. I did try to tell Mother, you know, that maybe I wasn't the marrying type. But she didn't want to hear me. She was horrified. After all, I was her son and heir. I should have been producing grandchildren for her years ago. If she knew the real reason why I hadn't, she'd have been disgusted. "

"So why *did* you marry Kathy?" Ambrose asked gently.

"I know, I know. I should never have married her. I just thought, well *hoped*, that it would 'sort me out'. Somehow. I mean I'd known Kathy for years. She'd been coming to my mother for lessons since she was little, and we got on really well. I've always found it difficult to talk to women, but I could talk to Kathy - about music and teaching, and what she hoped to do. I can see now that what I felt was just friendship, or how an older brother cares for his little sister, but I convinced myself that I loved her. And I wanted to keep Mother happy. She was always nagging me about getting married and settling down, you see."

Michael passed a hand through his hair as he hesitated. Then he carried on. "I shouldn't have listened. I haven't made Kathy happy and she deserves better than me. Mother will find out soon anyway. I'm sure she's secretly suspected for years. And now I've finally met the only person I want to spend my life with and you're going to arrest me for being homosexual." Michael looked thoroughly miserable.

185

Ambrose scrutinised the man in front of him. "No I'm not going to arrest you," he said finally. He saw Michael look up in total surprise.

Ambrose carried on before Michael could say anything. "It's only against the law if you, well," he paused, searching for the right word. He finally decided and continued. "If you get physical. I'm not going to clutter up our cells with people who haven't done anything illegal but might do so in the future. Heavens, our cells would be completely full to bursting."

"Besides," he carried on. "Homosexuality has been around a very long time. It's mentioned in Greek literature and the Roman histories. Even Shakespeare was probably that way inclined. I've read that some of his sonnets may have been written to a male friend."

Michael was listening, rapt. "'Let me not to the marriage of true minds/Admit impediments...' he quoted, and managed to smile slightly. "Even the Bible has Saul and David, but nowadays, I could break into a house and steal everything, and people wouldn't think so badly of me, as if...." Unable to say any more, he broke off and turned away.

"I don't think for one minute it's something you chose," Ambrose continued. "It seems to have chosen you. And I'm sure sooner or later we'll stop criminalising it. But are you absolutely sure Kathy doesn't know already? Wives do have a habit of knowing our most private secrets," Ambrose smiled.

"Positive. No one knows about us. Alex and I have only been out together once so far. And then we weren't exactly alone," Michael replied. "We went to the final of the Jenners Park piano competition. There must have been well over a hundred people there."

"When was that?" Ambrose asked.

"About three weeks ago. It was being held at the Town Hall in Jenners Park. You know, the massive Victorian building at the end of the High Street. Everyone had to apply for tickets in advance so I ordered two absolutely ages ago. But then Kathy said she couldn't make it: she was teaching that night. I told Kathy I was going on my own but actually I asked Alex to join me. We arrived separately and we were very careful. No one would have had any idea we knew each other."

"Did you sit together?"

186

"Yes, but there was no one we knew in the audience," Michael insisted.

"What was the exact date, Mr Black?" queried Ambrose.

"The sixth of November. I think I've still got my ticket in my wallet. Yes. I kept it – for sentimental reasons." Michael passed the ticket to Ambrose. "You don't think it's important, do you?"

"It might be," Ambrose was non-committal. He popped the paper ticket in his pocket. "I'll return this to you shortly," he noted Michael's disappointment.

"Please don't say anything of this, if you can possibly help it," Michael beseeched Ambrose.

"But what about your wife? You can't just leave her without any explanation," Ambrose pointed out.

Michael signed deeply. "Yes I know I've got to tell Kathy. I can't be dishonest with her any longer and she deserves a chance at her own life. She's so young and beautiful. Without me making her miserable, she'll be fine." He truly meant it, Ambrose noted.

"But I can't ruin Alex's career," Michael carried on. "That was why he left the big City firm he was at – because his boss was starting to make unsubtle comments. In the legal profession, being different is a sure way to end your career. I think Alex is worried now that Archie won't hand over the business to him if he finds out. He might even fire him."

"Did Alex tell you himself about Mr Framilode's intention to retire?"

"No," Michael explained. "I heard Archie talking to Alex after a rehearsal a few weeks back."

Ambrose looked interested. "Could anyone else have overheard?" he asked.

"Marguerite and Olga were close by. They might have heard too. In any case, there's often gossip going round the group. I mean it's a small theatre, and people chat while they're waiting around. That's partly why I felt I had to talk to you myself. Please, Inspector, promise me you won't tell anyone about what I've just said - unless you have to. And if you do, *please* let me know first, so I can break it to my wife," Michael lent forward, appealing.

"I suggest you talk to her as soon as possible, Mr Black," Ambrose replied. "Not because I would gossip in the wings, but because some of the other Players might."

"Yes, I need to pluck up the courage I know. I'll tell Kathy tonight, if I can. Until then, you do promise not to say anything?"

Ambrose smiled. "I will do my utmost to keep your secret, Mr Black. Thank you for having the nerve to tell me."

As Michael left the room, Ambrose wondered just how much to tell his colleagues. Technically, he could indeed have arrested Michael, and possibly Alex too, for intending to commit a crime. He didn't want to put Winters or any of the others in an awkward position. The fewer people involved in his decision to turn a blind eye, the better.

On the other hand, Ambrose had a feeling what he'd just learnt was the key to the whole puzzle.

CHAPTER THIRTY-ONE

PC Higgins entered the interview room quietly. He handed a document to the now re-seated Winters, who smiled his thanks as he watched the constable leave.

"It's the forensics report, sir," Winters explained, passing it over to DI Ambrose, who opened the report.

"I knew as much. The black fibre definitely came from that roll of material Heather Broomhead was using to make the costumes," he noted.

"Which means almost anyone could have put that fibre on the fire extinguisher, sir. Heather herself, any member of the cast, not to mention Mr Moody with his pair of new trousers or Sara with her custom-made skirt," Winters groaned.

"Quite," Ambrose agreed. "It gets worse. That rope fibre isn't actually from a rope at all. The guys at the lab say it's from a piece of rough string. There's no way, apparently, the string would have been strong enough to carry the weight of the fire extinguisher."

"Which leaves us back where we were before doesn't it?" Winters replied. "Whoever used that extinguisher to hit Marguerite must have had a fair deal of upper body strength. That definitely seems to count out our older and frailer members of the cast. That's not including the difficulty some of them would have had climbing up to the lighting gantry, presuming that *is* where the assailant lay in wait for Marguerite."

"It certainly looks that way. It says there's no trace of blood on the lighting gantry but there are a few of those black fibres plus minute traces of red paint, similar to the type on the fire extinguisher. I think we can reasonably assume that someone was up there, with the extinguisher, waiting for Marguerite."

"Well," Winters mused. "We're looking for someone who had enough time to climb up to the lighting gantry and back down again, without being seen by anyone else. Plus they had to be able to pick up the fire extinguisher from its cradle and return it, again without being spotted. What with all the actors walking up and down the corridors, that was no easy feat."

"Absolutely," Ambrose agreed. "It would mean that our assailant would have to be missing for quite some time without anyone spotting them. I think that very much narrows down our field of suspects, doesn't it?"

"I've just had a thought, sir," Winters sat up straight in his chair. "Not that it helps us that much, but I bet I know what that string fibre is from."

"Go ahead," Ambrose stood and rubbed the small of his back.

"Do you remember I checked the safety record of the theatre? I was told that they'd just done their annual fire inspection. They would have had to mark each fire extinguisher to show whether it had been tested. I bet they put a label round the neck of each extinguisher after they'd tested it."

"Ah, you mean a label attached to the extinguisher by a piece of string?" Ambrose nodded.

"Exactly, sir."

"Well you're probably right, but as you say, it doesn't get us any closer to solving this. I just still can't work out who would want to bump off Marguerite. Despite her attempts, it doesn't seem that she was actually blackmailing anyone. She'd got what she wanted out of Archie after all." Ambrose sat down again wearily.

"You mean that he was going to leave the Chalk Heath Players to her in his will?"

"Quite. Although, hang on a minute, what if Marguerite overhead Archie's conversation with Alex. What if she thought he was going to leave the Players to Alex, rather than his practice?"

"That would explain her double cross statement to Frank Thomas, sir." Winters was looking through his notes again.

"It would indeed. But how on earth does that translate to a reason to bump off Marguerite? And how would the assailant have known she would run round to the wrong side of the stage? She must have been lured round there somehow. Perhaps it was for some kind of secret assignation between the curtains?" Ambrose sighed.

"I can't see that working, sir. After all, if it was another member of the cast, why not arrange to meet somewhere more private? They wouldn't have had long for their assignation either. Altogether most unsuitable, I would say."

"Yes, you're right. But how else do we explain Marguerite going to the wrong side of the stage to deliver her line? Not to mention she seems to have been the one who made sure the understudy wasn't there. Marguerite would have had to be complicit in the attack and I really can't see her going along with something that might kill her. It's a really odd way to commit suicide."

Winters raised an eyebrow. "Well, perhaps she had a life assurance policy that wouldn't pay out if she committed suicide. Maybe she paid someone to bump herself off?"

Ambrose shook his head then stopped abruptly. "You know, you might just have hit the nail on the head. But for the wrong reasons I'm afraid."

"Sir?" Winters was perplexed.

"What if Marguerite wasn't the actual target? What if someone made a horrible mistake?"

"What, you think young Julie was the intended victim?" Winters queried.

Without replying, Ambrose leapt to his feet. "I need you to check a few things for me. This is what I need," he scribbled a list for Winters and handed it over.

"Hmm, bank statements of all the suspects, no problem. Put a guard on Marguerite in the hospital, sure. Is that to make sure she isn't attacked again?" He looked up at Ambrose, who didn't reply.

Winters went back to the list. "OK, what's this? Is this Michael's mystery secret? Does he think his wife is having an affair with Alex?"

"I promised not to pass on the information Michael gave me unless I really have to, so there's no point trying to badger it out of me!" Ambrose replied.

Winters knew better than to argue. He went back to the sheet of paper.

"OK, so there were two seats booked in the name of Black at the Jenners Park Piano Competition on 6th November. You want me to check who else sat in that row, plus all the rows behind or near the Black seats. You want the names of *everyone* in those seats?" Winters was incredulous.

"Are you sure?" he continued. "That'll take absolutely ages, sir. What names would I be looking for? It'll be a lot quicker if I just look for Alex's name, if that's who we're checking up on."

"Just get me everything I've asked for," Ambrose replied firmly. "It wasn't a public concert so there should still be a record of who applied for tickets, all being well."

With a sigh, Winters went back to the list. "Speak to Frank Thomas' doctor. Fine, I'll have it all for you by this afternoon."

ooOoo

Winters had only had a few hours sleep the night before and it was starting to catch up with him. He was feeling irritable but he knew that he'd made good progress. He found Ambrose at his desk at around three. It looked suspiciously like the DI had only just woken up from a little snooze.

"Hello," Ambrose smiled brightly. "Did you get any sleep last night, by the way?"

"A bit sir," Winters replied. "Why, do I look rough?" he laughed.

"Not at all," Ambrose assured him. "It's just you've nearly done a double shift. I certainly didn't expect you to come in first thing this morning. And how was your wife? Did she understand?"

In surprise Winters looked at his superior. He seemed to have an uncanny knack of knowing his men's innermost worries. Winters had noticed it before.

"Not exactly," he replied guardedly.

"Oh?"

"I woke the baby when I came in."

Ambrose nodded in sympathy. "And that woke everyone, including your wife?" he suggested.

"That's about it."

"Oh dear!"

In embarrassment Winters laughed. "I ended up on the settee," he admitted.

192

He was about to pass Ambrose the file of material he had gathered when he felt his superior was still looking at him.

"What is it, sir?" he asked.

Pausing, Ambrose considered how to reply. Finally he decided that speaking directly was the best course – certainly the way Winters would most appreciate.

"I'm worried about you," Ambrose admitted.

"Me, sir?"

"Look, I know you want to do well – and you do. Very well. You could make top brass. You'll have my job in a few years without any doubt. But have a think about what you might lose along the way. You have young children and your Fran needs you." Ambrose sighed quietly then added, "don't push your family too hard."

"I don't mean to," Winters protested.

He was thoroughly annoyed. He didn't like having his personal life questioned.

"Besides, Fran knew what she was marrying. I was in the Military Police then," Winters said, slightly petulantly.

Shrugging his shoulders, Ambrose smiled at his colleague.

"All I'm saying is take a bit of time off as soon as this case is over," he said. "You don't need to keep working overtime. I don't expect it. And the money's not everything. There are things that matter more."

Resisting the temptation to retort that not everyone could afford to turn down extra money, Winters paused. He couldn't decide how to reply. Then he remembered the story Pauline Meadows had told them in the Copper Kettle. She had not said how long Ambrose's wife had been ill afterwards. He could well have nearly lost her. That would explain quite a bit, including his concern for Francesca now.

"I'll ring my mother and ask her to babysit on Saturday," Winters said finally. "That should help."

Ambrose nodded. "I'm told there's a good film on at the Odeon," he advised. Then it was back to business again. "Thanks for digging into this background stuff," he added. "What did you find?"

Winters passed Ambrose a small file. Ambrose ruffled through the pages, pausing every now and then.

"So, Frank Thomas Lucas made a rapid and full recovery after the crash, according to his doctor," he read out loud. "You know, I'm pleased to hear that, although I suspect Frank still has the occasional nightmare that he doesn't tell his doctor about. Ah, now this is interesting. Douglas Moody has been receiving large and mysterious payments over the last two weeks: £100 this week and the same last week."

"I saw that, sir," Winters confirmed. "But I'm not sure whether that's relevant. The payer was a Miss Liversedge and that doesn't match any of our suspects. It could be one of his gambling buddies, if he has any that is."

"Are you sure?" Ambrose continued his reading. "Ah, this is what I was looking for. The Black seats were five rows to the front of our mysterious Miss Liversedge. I wonder what would have happened if they'd seen each other. It would have been awkward, that's for sure, but maybe Marguerite wouldn't have been hospitalised."

Winters' brain was working too slowly, dulled by the lack of sleep. Then suddenly he sprang up, out of his chair.

"Oh my god," he cried. "What a terrible mistake."

"It's all quite ironic, don't you think?" Ambrose was smiling. "And what's better, we can check that we're right."

"How's that sir?" Winters was still rubbing his head.

"Marguerite Monroe has regained consciousness. I've just had a call from the hospital. I rather think we ought to speak to her. Let's see if she can explain herself."

"That's going to be an interesting conversation, sir," Winters smiled as he followed Ambrose out.

"Oh and we ought to arrest our two suspects." Ambrose pointed out.

"Don't you mean three?" Winters was confused again.

"Well I don't think Marguerite is going anywhere right now, but we ought to bring the other two into custody don't you think?"

CHAPTER THIRTY-TWO

Ambrose followed slowly as the nurse took them to Marguerite. He'd always hated hospitals, the feeling of being surrounded by death and disease. Being trapped in the basement of a maternity home most certainly hadn't helped either. He lowered himself quietly into the chair, jumping slightly when the nurse closed the curtain behind him.

He examined the woman in the bed in front of him, stared at the bandages around her head, the drip still connected to her hand. He couldn't help a small jolt of surprise. Marguerite looked so frail, so much older than he had expected. It was hard to imagine her dancing on stage, much less acting the part of young heroine. Still, she had almost died. She was not going to be looking her best. The hairstyle that had caused her such trouble had been shaved away before surgery.

Despite her appearance, Ambrose found he could not feel any sympathy for Marguerite. He reminded himself that he was about to interview a suspect for conspiracy to murder. Winters pulled up a chair beside him. Ambrose nodded to him as a WPC began getting out her pen and notepad quietly behind them to take shorthand. This interview was too important to rely on Winters' scribbled notes.

ooOoo

Winters opened the interview, as before. "Interview, beginning 5pm, with Miss Marguerite Monroe. Present: DI Ambrose and DS Winters. WPC Cottrell taking notes."

Ambrose started gently. "Good evening, Miss Monroe. I'm glad you're beginning to feel a little better. The doctor assures us you are well enough to answer questions, so long as we don't tire you too much." He paused. "We'll be as brief as possible. First of all, I need to explain to you that this interview will take place under caution. You do not have to say anything, but anything you do say may be given in evidence. Do you understand?"

Marguerite was glaring at him. "Yes. Well – no, I don't. Why am I a suspect? I was the one who was attacked." She spoke sullenly, in a low voice.

Winters lent forward slightly "If you are able, can you please speak up a bit?" he said. "We need to hear your replies clearly for our notes."

Marguerite cleared her throat, as if preparing for the stage. "Okay, I'll try," she raised her voice slightly.

"If you need a glass of water at any time, just tell me," Winters added.

Ambrose shuffled uncomfortably in his chair, glancing at the hospital equipment around him. "Who do you think hit you?" he queried.

"I don't know. I didn't see anyone. After all, I was hit from behind," Marguerite replied, petulantly.

"And you can't think of anyone who would want to harm you?" Ambrose insisted.

"No. Definitely not."

Ambrose smiled grimly. "That's what threw us to start with too," he explained.

Marguerite looked confused. "What do you mean?"

Winters continued. "We couldn't work out why anyone would want to kill you. We know you're not universally popular, and that people rather doubted your acting abilities, but no one seemed actually to hate you."

"That's nice." Marguerite's sarcasm dripped from her voice.

Ambrose went on. "We know you were blackmailing Archie, but he didn't seem actually to mind that much."

"Blackmail? That's ridiculous," Marguerite reddened. "Why would I blackmail Archie? He's not that wealthy!"

Winters nodded. "But he did agree to leave the Players to you in his will. Perhaps you thought you'd survive him? Or if he retired early, you'd persuade him to hand the Players over to you then?" Winters was watching Marguerite closely.

"And we know you were aware of his father's '*indiscretions*' from your time at the Law Society," Ambrose added.

"Of course, you were still Betty Fagg back then," Winters watched Marguerite wince.

There was a long pause. Finally, "I don't see what that has to do with anything," Marguerite sighed.

"Actually, I agree. It was only when we realised you weren't the intended victim that things started to make sense," Ambrose replied.

"It also explained why you'd run round the back of the stage," Winters added. "There was no way anyone could have forced you to do that against your will. And why you made sure the understudy wouldn't be standing in the wings that rehearsal."

Marguerite did not reply, but waved her hand towards the glass of water. Winters passed it to her carefully.

Ambrose carried on. "You know the irony is that you're still facing a criminal charge, even though you ended up here in hospital. After all, it's just luck that no one actually died. And it's really bad luck, from your point of view, that your 'true' target was unhurt."

Marguerite was drinking slowly. "I don't know what you mean," she kept her eyes steadfastly on the glass in front of her.

"And to think that Alex Baker-Smythe still has no idea he was your intended victim. But then, I guess you never for one moment thought that your new hair-do would get you injured in his place," Winters interjected.

"I take it Douglas Moody hadn't seen you before the rehearsal?" Ambrose took the glass from Marguerite's hand.

Marguerite seemed lost without her prop. "I have no idea whether he did or not. What's he got to do with it?" she stared at her now empty hands.

"Come now, Miss Monroe," Ambrose cajoled. "We know from your doctor that there's no sign of brain damage, luckily, and you're not suffering from amnesia. If you don't tell us your side of the story, we may well presume the worst. Perhaps the whole thing was your idea all along?"

"I'm sure that's how the jury will see it," Winters interjected.

"And we know one of your accomplices has been in touch with you since the attack," Ambrose added, although he was guessing. It seemed a reasonable assumption, however, from what WPC Meadows had observed.

"Before you answer, there's something else you might want to know," Winters caught Marguerite's eye.

She turned her head away hurriedly then suddenly became preoccupied with smoothing her bedclothes. "What's that?" she asked without looking up.

Winters explained. "You remember the conversation you overheard between Archie and Alex? I'm afraid you misunderstood, Miss Monroe. Archie was referring to his legal practice, not the Chalk Heath Players. He had decided to hand over his business to Alex. That was what he was discussing with him."

The silence was long, interrupted only by the gentle beeping of hospital equipment.

Ambrose sighed. "How can I put this gently? You agreed with Brenda to set Alex up. You arranged for the understudy Julie to be left out of the rehearsal so she wouldn't be standing in the wings. Brenda managed to release Douglas Moody so he could attack Alex. You must have known an innocent man was going to be injured or killed. And you did all this based on a misunderstanding."

"I never thought they were going to kill him," Marguerite said quickly.

"How can you expect a Jury to believe that?" Winters asked, incredulous. "Clobbering Alex over the head with a fire hydrant was guaranteed to injure him badly, at the very least, as you found out the hard way."

Marguerite shook her head, gingerly. "Brenda never said exactly what she was going to do to Alex. I thought they would just scare him somehow."

"Really? What did you think they'd do? Jump out at him wearing a ghost costume?" Winters sneered.

Ambrose was slightly more conciliatory. "Miss Monroe, surely you should have asked what Brenda had in mind?"

Marguerite paused. "Yes, I should have. You're right. I just presumed they'd break his arm or something: just enough to stop him being in the play."

Now Ambrose was confused. "How would that have helped you?"

"I thought that if his understudy took over, Archie would see how bad Alex really was. I thought Archie would then change his mind.

Are you sure Archie was talking about his legal practice, not the Players?" Marguerite looked pained.

Ambrose nodded. "I'm afraid so."

Marguerite seemed to rally slightly. "Even if he was, Archie wasn't being fair to us. The part should have gone to young Ken. It would have done, too, before Archie's 'blue-eyed boy' came along. Now poor Ken is just a servant, but he has miles more talent than Alex." She stopped, slightly breathless, and took to staring at her hands again.

"So you resented Alex's arrival?" Ambrose prompted.

"Archie promised me I would take over the Players next year," Marguerite answered. "He wants to retire and move to the seaside now his wife's passed away. He said I could carry things on for him. I had lots of ideas: getting a team of volunteers back stage, applying for funding ... that sort of thing. When I thought he was going back on his word, I was livid. Not so much with Archie, as with Alex – for coming in, a complete novice who couldn't even get his lines right, and then taking everything over. I wished he'd never joined us."

Winters continued. "So when did you first find out that Brenda also wanted Alex out of the way?"

"I knew for a while Brenda hated Alex. About a week ago she told me she had a plan, but she couldn't do it on her own. She said Alex was having an affair with Kathy. She thought that with Alex out of the way, Kathy would go back to her husband. Brenda was just trying to protect her son," Marguerite added hastily.

"Brenda may have been trying to protect her son," Ambrose replied, "but she didn't tell you the whole truth I'm afraid. I'm sure that doesn't matter though." He ignored the quizzical look from his colleague.

"Why was Douglas Moody involved?" Winters asked, already knowing the answer.

"Brenda paid him. Everyone knew that Doug was always strapped for cash, that he'd do anything for money. But I swear I didn't think he'd try to kill Alex. Neither did Brenda." Marguerite suddenly started rummaging in the drawer next to her bed. "Look, she sent me this note. "

"Ah, so that's the letter Brenda passed to the nurse," Ambrose noted out loud. Marguerite looked at him, slightly astonished, then held the note out. Her hand shook.

Winters took the note from Marguerite and read:

'*My Dearest Marguerite. How can I apologise enough? I had absolutely no idea that Doug would hit you instead of Alex. I just don't know how he got it all so wrong. And I never meant anyone to be so badly injured. Please believe me. Yours BL.*"

"Brenda Liversedge," Ambrose explained. "I'm surprised she still uses her maiden name after so many years."

"It's not just her maiden name; it's also her professional name," Marguerite replied. "She still uses it occasionally even though she's retired. I think she still has a bank account in that name."

"It seems that Doug mistook you for Alex and hit you over the head," Winters added.

"He got confused whilst he was hiding on the gantry above you," Ambrose agreed.

Marguerite indicated that she would like another drink. As Winters refilled the glass and passed it to her, Marguerite carried on. "I've been lying here thinking and thinking about how it could have happened. I suppose we're about the same build, and perhaps my new hairstyle made me look like him. Sara said so that very evening. I thought at the time she was just being bitchy, but maybe she was right. And you were correct, Inspector: Doug didn't see me before the rehearsal. I was a bit late and he was already in his room when I arrived. He wouldn't have known I'd had my hair cut."

Winters wanted details. "How did you ensure Doug had enough time to climb up the gantry?"

"Brenda saw to all that," Marguerite replied.

"Was it her idea to suggest you tried the rehearsal without the lighting cues?" Ambrose said. It was important to get everything in their notes.

Marguerite nodded gingerly. "Yes, but she was clever. She made Michael suggest it. Archie always listened to Michael, even when he'd have ignored the same suggestion from someone else."

"And you persuaded Archie to ask Julie to arrive later with the other servants?"

Another slight nod. "I told him she needed to prepare for her secretarial examination. I said Brenda and I would practise with her separately, so she didn't need to watch from the wings that evening."

It was time to wrap things up. "Well, thank you Miss Monroe," Ambrose frowned. "I hope the Judge accepts you didn't intend to kill or seriously injure Alex. The letter from Brenda definitely helps your case. We'll have to take that from you, of course, just to check it's not a forgery."

Marguerite sank back against the pillows. "I suppose I got what I deserved, in a way, but I swear I didn't mean for Alex to be badly hurt. And I don't understand how it all went wrong. Brenda was adamant that I had to come off Stage Left when Alex came off Stage Right. I couldn't work out what she meant, because Alex was coming off Stage Right anyway. But I ran round the back to Stage Left, to be out of the way, just like she'd asked."

"I'm afraid Mrs Black's inexperience at the theatre is to blame," Ambrose said gently.

"As Archie would say, 'the theatre is a very special place' and it has a lot of jargon," Winters added.

Her look of realisation said it all. "You mean Brenda got her stage directions the wrong way round?" Marguerite muttered.

Winters replied. "I'm afraid so. She actually meant you to come off *Audience* Left. She thought that you'd come off stage safely, and that somehow you'd ensure Alex went round the other side under Doug Moody."

"There was only one place where the lighting gantry was dark enough to let Mr Moody attack someone below him without being seen. We think he showed it to Brenda, but she got confused when she explained the plan to you," added Ambrose.

Marguerite sighed again. "What will become of the Players now?"

Ambrose smiled slightly. "The show will go on, as they say. I gather the talented Julie will be taking your part and Mr Black will be able to turn his own pages."

"Just one final question, Miss Monroe," Winters wasn't finished just yet. "Why did you lie about your theatre experience? It's no shame to be a wardrobe mistress – or to have a name you'd rather change. Lying about such things suggests you may be lying to us now."

Marguerite snorted. "You don't know what the theatre's like! People worship the stars and treat everyone else like dirt. I wanted to be somebody, so I changed my wretched name and talked myself up a bit. I didn't mean to lie to Archie when we first met. I just told him what I'd been telling everyone for years and the silly man believed me. I kept meaning to tell him the truth but he made so much of my 'experience' with the rest of the Players, I couldn't bear to. Of course I'm telling you the truth now. Please go now! My head hurts."

The three police officers quietly walked away.

EPILOGUE

The house had an air of being well cared for. It was a pleasant mid-terraced property. Its miniature front garden was crammed full of pretty flowers. Ambrose rang the bell on the pale pink door.

Kathy Black was surprised to see the detective on her doorstep. Hesitating slightly, she opened the door to let him in.

"I hope you don't mind me popping round," Ambrose explained. He was looking at the hallway, taking in the flowery wallpaper and the smell of baking bread. Everything felt homely and welcoming. "I was just wondering how you're getting on."

The question seemed to surprise Kathy. She looked intently at Ambrose.

"You've come round just to see how I'm doing?" she sounded surprised, but pleased.

"Well, you've had quite a hard time of it recently," Ambrose was starting to feel slightly foolish. "What with your husband and your mother-in-law, I mean."

"You mean my ex-mother-in-law," Kathy was smiling broadly. "Michael and I divorced, so I don't have anything to do with the old hag. He can decide whether he wants to visit her in prison. I rather doubt he will, to be honest. After all, she *was* convicted of trying to murder Alex."

"Quite. Do you know how your ex-husband is doing these days?"

"Yes. He and Alex seem to be getting along splendidly. They're working together on a musical. *Wedding Belle* went ever so well in the end. Julie was absolutely brilliant; she's a real star that's for sure. And it's given Michael and Alex the confidence to try writing something completely new they say. They're lodging together but of course we don't tell people the truth."

Kathy smiled at Ambrose. "It was so good of you not to pass on what Michael told you. It's rather ironic of course. Most people think Alex was the target to stop him having an affair with me. What people make of Michael moving in with Alex, I really don't know. Hopefully everyone just assumes they're now good friends," she added.

"Plus there was all the horrid business of Michael having to pretend he'd been unfaithful. You know, arranging compromising photographs in seedy hotels so we could get a divorce. Still that's one advantage of having friends who like acting. You can always find someone who's willing to play a part, for a price."

Kathy looked wistful, then carried on. "It's a shame we had to do all that just to bring our marriage to an end. Of course, I have to make it look like I'm still angry with him. Burst into tears or shout if we accidentally bump into each other in the street, that kind of thing. I'm sure you know; it's not like that at all really. Actually I had them both round for dinner the other day."

"That was very, er, understanding of you," Ambrose was surprised.

"I'll be honest; it was quite a relief to find out that my husband is, how shall I say it? How about, not my way inclined? I had taken it rather personally that he wasn't interested in, well *you know*. So now he's admitted he prefers men to women, I feel a whole load better!" Kathy was positively beaming.

"It's great to see you looking so happy," Ambrose smiled. "Does Archie know about Michael and Alex?"

"Well, he's never said anything but I'm sure he does. Or at the very least he must suspect. He dealt with our divorce and I'm sure he realised the photos were staged. And he must wonder why Michael and Alex are lodging together. Luckily it doesn't seem to matter. Archie says he's still going to leave his practice to Alex, in a couple of years' time," Kathy replied.

"That's great news. I don't suppose Archie is still planning to leave the Players to Marguerite is he?"

"God no!" Kathy laughed. "She's made herself scarce. No one has seen her since she got out of hospital. She was so lucky the judge decided she'd suffered enough already and didn't send her to prison. No, Archie said he's handing the Players over to Frank. Let's face it," Kathy smiled, "Frank is a far better actor and singer than Archie. It looks like Archie will continue bankrolling the Players for a few years, but this time jointly with Frank."

She paused, then suddenly cried out happily, "Oh and have you heard the news? The theatre is going to be rebuilt. Finally. And they're putting a new shopping parade on the land next door too. I saw the plans – it'll all be built of white concrete and glass. It'll look ever so modern. And we're doing *South Pacific* next season. I auditioned and got the part of the native girl, Liat. Julie will be the lead, Nellie Forbush, of course. I haven't read the libretto yet, but they say it's really progressive. You must come and see it."

"I'll try," Ambrose replied cautiously. "My job isn't great for my social life though."

"You don't need to tell me what it's like." Kathy was blushing slightly. "We're getting married next month so I'll be a policeman's wife soon enough!"

Confused, Ambrose looked past Kathy towards the kitchen. He could just see a male figure walking in from the garden, silhouetted against the light from outside.

"Greg has been mowing my lawn," Kathy explained. "I'd introduce you but he'll be covered in grass and, besides, you already know each other."

Ambrose raised one eyebrow as the kitchen door opened wider.

"Hello sir," PC Sutton smiled. Seeing Ambrose's quizzical look, he explained, "I took Kathy home after that night at the theatre, as you know, and well one thing led to another."

"So I see," said Ambrose, glancing at PC Sutton. He was indeed covered in grass.

Extract from

Poison Pen

PJ Quinn's
Forthcoming Novel

from

Stairwell Books

EXTRACT FROM 'POISON PEN'

Ambrose was certain this was the first time, and hopefully the last that he'd washed up wearing a dinner jacket. In fact, he was now in his dress shirt with his sleeves rolled up and the jacket hanging safely on the back of a chair in the kitchen.

Edith was standing behind him, drying up. Somehow she managed to look exactly the same as she had done earlier, but just a fraction smarter. She was still all in black, but at least it was a dress, and the red blanket had been replaced with a shawl of a very similar colour. When she stepped forwards, Ambrose noted that she was wearing shoes, rather than boots, but they were functional and flat.

"I hadn't realised," Edith was saying, "that when I signed up for cooking tomorrow, it meant we'd be washing up tonight."

"Quite," Ambrose replied, handing her yet another dessert dish to dry. It was only now, faced with the enormous amount of dirty crockery, that he realised just how many guests were staying at Chalk Heath Hall this week.

In fact, he calculated they'd probably have been there all evening if Margaret and Sheila hadn't taken pity on them. Promising to return the favour later in the week, when it was their turn to wash up, Ambrose was grateful for their help.

"To be honest," Sheila confided. "I'd rather be here helping than listen to that odious Jack Harper read extracts from his book!"

She was making short work of cleaning the cutlery, having almost pushed Ambrose to one side. Her blue satin trousers and matching jacket highlighted her trim figure.

"I do rather fear," Margaret agreed, "that he's nowhere near as funny as he thinks he is." She was clearly very experienced with a tea towel, despite her upbringing. Ambrose couldn't help but admire the beautiful grey silk dress she was wearing. As ever, she managed to look effortlessly stunning.

"Forgive me for asking," she said gently. "But I can't imagine you signing up for a week like this yourself. You'd think you were spoiling yourself; that you ought to be doing something more practical. Are you on official business?"

The woman's perception was unnerving, but Ambrose was well prepared. "It was a gift from my wife," he replied. "I've been telling her for years that I wanted to write, and with my job – well – I've never had the time. She gave me this week as a birthday present. I was really touched." He stacked plates carefully.

"She sounds like a very understanding lady – as well as generous," Margaret commented, smiling.

"She is," Ambrose agreed. He had told the truth, even if not all the truth. Mary had always encouraged his writing and was delighted when he had the chance of joining one of the Chalk Heath Hall's famous house parties, even if he did have an ulterior motive. And because the force wouldn't pay, she had bought him one of the Yates' gift vouchers. But at that moment he would far rather have been at home with his feet on the stool and a nice fire burning in the grate. The kitchen was cold; polite conversation over pots and pans with potential murder suspects was a strain.

The four of them made quick work of the remaining dishes. Sheila was just passing a cloth over the kitchen surfaces when Geraint appeared. He looked pale.

"Gosh, are you having a secret party? It's a good job the only man in here, with all these beautiful women, is a policeman!" he joked, but he didn't sound his usual cheery self. "I'd really appreciate a glass of milk, if there's one going."

Nearest to the fridge, Ambrose obliged, assessing Geraint as he did so. Before Ambrose could say anything, however, Margaret intervened.

"Are you feeling alright?" she asked, putting an elegantly manicured hand out to Geraint's arm. He seemed to wobble slightly. Edith stepped forwards with a chair.

"Just a bit queasy, nothing serious," Geraint managed a wan smile as he sat down. "I have a stomach problem and it flares up from time to time."

Ambrose wondered briefly if this was part of Geraint's act. After all, as Geraint had just commented, three of the best looking ladies were in the kitchen. But it seemed genuine. Ambrose felt certain that even Geraint wouldn't feign illness just to get attention. He was less sure about Phyllis Hey's injury, he realised.

"Perhaps you should go to bed?" Edith suggested.

210

To Ambrose's astonishment Geraint agreed. Then astonishment turned to alarm. Surely the young man couldn't have been poisoned already? While Ambrose was watching? They had all eaten the same meal, from the same tureens, so how could just one person have been poisoned?

"I'll take him up," Ambrose announced. Realising he was alarming the others, he lightened his tone. "It really wouldn't do for one of you ladies to be seen escorting a young artist to bed," he smiled.

Poison Pen is expected to be available in 2012 and will be followed by the third DI Ambrose tale, *Close Disharmony*, in 2013.